P9-DNO-460

YOU'RE
SO
DEAD

ALSO BY ASH PARSONS

Still Waters

Holding On to You (previously titled *The Falling Between Us*)

Girls Save the World in This One

YOU'RE SO DEAD

ASH PARSONS

PHILOMEL BOOKS

PHILOMEL BOOKS
An imprint of Penguin Random House LLC, New York

First published in the United States of America by Philomel Books,
an imprint of Penguin Random House LLC, 2021

Visit us online at penguinrandomhouse.com.

Library of Congress Cataloging-in-Publication Data is available.

Book manufactured in Canada

ISBN 9780593205129

1 3 5 7 9 10 8 6 4 2

Edited by Kelsey Murphy

Design by Monique Sterling

Text set in Berling

YOU'RE **SO** DEAD

On the island of Little Esau, the final day of Pyre Festival . . .

Plum Winter never expected it to end this way. "It" being both her life and Pyre Festival.

The festival was supposed to end with a celebrity-packed booze cruise.

As for her life's end, Plum didn't like to think about it, but when she did, she always imagined being a really old lady who died peacefully in her sleep.

But here she was at the end of it all, and there were absolutely no boats, booze, or beds.

Instead, Plum had to decide which of two extremely unattractive deaths she would rather have.

There was death by jumping off the cliff at her back, or death by stabby-stabby. *Stabbing,* that was actually the word, though her brain was slow in supplying it. Plum blamed the cliff at her back and the demented killer standing about twenty feet away.

Holding a very big, very sharp, very scary stabber.

Knife.

So, this was it. The end. Which way would she choose?

Maybe Plum could save someone, or several someones, on her way to her own death? If she could—well, that had to count for something, right? Maybe it would be enough to get her into the really good party in the afterlife. Get her through those exclusive pearly gates.

Plum could feel the wind sweeping up from the cliff at her back, almost like nature was trying to remind her of the sheer drop to the rocks and ocean far below.

In front of her, the killer slashed the knife in terrifying arcs.

This was where all her schemes had led her.

With no one to witness her last—some would say only—act of courage.

No one other than the killer . . . and the goats.

As if on cue, the black-and-white billy goat munching on the bush to Plum's right let out an annoyed-sounding bleat.

It sounded like a heckler in a comedy club, like the goat was yelling "Meh!"

No doubt the billy goat was annoyed at the humans trampling his favorite grazing patch.

"Yeah, buddy," Plum breathed, taking a tiny step back, feeling the wind from the cliff edge grabbing at her hair, snatching it up. "You and me both," she muttered.

There was nowhere else to go. She had to do something.

Maybe she could take the killer with her.

Plum took a deep breath and screamed.

The killer smiled, rushing at her with the knife outstretched.

So. This was how it was all going to end.

Plum Winter desperately hoped there would be a heaven for clueless kids who just wanted to have a good time.

1

They couldn't find it.

It wasn't going as well as she'd hoped: her big chance to break out of Normal Town, Ordinaryville. But damn it, Plum wasn't going to let a little thing like ride-share logistics stop her.

Besides, they'd already come so far. All the way to the island of Saint Vitus in the Caribbean. It was a whole other world from Huntington, Alabama.

If someone were to ask Plum, *What's it like in Huntington, Alabama?* she'd start by saying, *It's fine*. Her family had moved to Huntington when Plum was in the seventh grade and her dad left the army. Next she'd say that Huntington *wasn't like the rest of Alabama*. It was reflexive, saying that, because while she knew Alabama had so many beautiful regions—it also had a lot of shortcomings. A lot.

But Huntington was different, mainly because of the university, which added a lot of diversity to the town, with faculty from all over, international students, and so on.

Was it still boring? Especially if you'd been there since seventh grade, were a senior in high school, and had an itching desire to have an adventure, to chase something, to become someone, to *go places?*

Yes. Yes, it was.

So Plum and her two best friends were here, on Saint Vitus. Just a little more time and distance to go, and they'd *arrive*. Both metaphorically and literally. They'd get to a private island, a luxurious villa resort, attending the most amazing event ever put on in the history of music and art and new media. Pyre Festival was so exclusive that it even promised not only that the performers would be famous, but that *all* the attendees would be celebrities and influencers as well. There would be hundreds of stars, and they would be with them.

Not that Plum and her two best friends were celebrities. Or influencers.

But Plum's sister was.

"It says it's right here." Marlowe Blake, Plum's best friend, stopped and lowered her cat's-eye sunglasses. Her blue-green eyes glanced out to the street. She was white, like Plum, but where Plum tanned easily Marlowe burned, so the minute they'd stepped outside the airport Marlowe had put on a floppy sun hat. She looked impossibly elegant even as she craned her neck to peer around the people lingering at the curb.

Some of the elegance was just inherent to Marlowe. The rest

of it was because she dressed like she was a movie star from a bygone age. Her mother, Elizabeth, was a theater professor at the university, and she had gotten Marlowe sewing lessons the minute she had shown an interest.

Plum remembered the day she'd met Marlowe. The memory ran in her head like a flickering movie reel in one of those old-fashioned film archives. It had been the first day of their freshman year of high school. Plum and her other best friend, Sofia Torres, were sitting on the brick bench in the courtyard at break, and Marlowe had walked out of the double doors, dressed in a gorgeous navy suit-dress, perfectly elegant, deliberately retro. Making matters worse for Plum's instant crush, Marlowe was built like a movie star from yesteryear, too. She was completely curvy in a way that made Plum think of words like *lush* and *plush* and other *-ush* words, probably.

"You're staring." Sofia had hissed the warning. But Marlowe had already spotted them and headed over to the bench.

"Hi, I'm new," Marlowe had said. "Can I hang out with you?"

She'd smiled a little, whether at the rhyme or in friendliness Plum hadn't known, but it was a swerve-y bit of crooked perfection that made Plum's heart skip a beat. Or several.

So confident. So *real*. So ready to put it out there.

Can I hang out with you?

Today, standing outside the Saint Vitus airport, in addition to the floppy hat, Marlowe was wearing an eggshell-white linen suit with wide-leg trousers and a black camisole under her double-breasted coat.

"Shouldn't there be a sign for attendees?" Marlowe asked. She pulled a hand down her sideswept sheet of wavy blonde hair.

"Did we pass it?" Sofia asked. She looked anxious but also adorable, as always. Sofia was Puerto Rican and short—at least, she seemed short to Plum—with a small face and a cute, pointy chin. Sofia paused to adjust the shoulder straps of both her favorite olive-green romper and the pink-sequined tank top peeking out underneath. The warm beige skin of her arms had a golden tone in the island's bright sunlight.

Sofia was a worrier. Her family was incredibly close and involved in Sofia's life in a way that Plum's family wasn't involved in hers. On one hand, that could sometimes make things harder for Sofia, Plum thought. But on the other hand Plum often wished her own family was more like that—both that her family was larger and that her parents were more . . . well . . . *observant*. That'd be the nicer word to use.

Attentive. That would be the one she really felt.

It wasn't Plum's parents' fault that they really loved their jobs. And each other. And going out to stuff. And they loved Plum, she knew it.

They just liked being alone more than Plum did.

Her parents were just two only children who had an only child who wasn't actually an only child, because of her older half sister.

Meanwhile Sofia had two sisters: a younger sister, Mia, in tenth grade, and an older sister, Krystal, a sophomore in college in Atlanta. Sofia's parents always wanted to know everything about each of their children. They seriously wanted to know where Sofia was at all times. They wanted her and her friends to hang out at their house instead of anywhere else. Sofia's mom, Linda, was white, with piercing brown eyes and long brown hair shot through with gray. She was honestly a bit intimidating. She was a research librarian at the university, and she'd stop whatever she was doing to greet Plum whenever she'd arrive. She was nice but also intense. When Plum talked to her, she always felt like she was getting subtly interrogated.

Hector, Sofia's dad, was second-generation Puerto Rican, and he loved everyone, especially if you loved one of his daughters. Plum was his favorite of all of Sofia's friends, a fact that absolutely delighted Plum. Sofia and her sisters would lovingly tease Plum about being tall and skinny (too tall and too skinny, in Plum's opinion. She'd heard all the jokes about ironing boards and stick insects and being bony, and she agreed with them, sadly). But when Sofia's family called her "flaca" she'd feel the affection in it. It wasn't a criticism but instead a term of endearment. A normal and good part of who she was.

Hector was a geologist at the university, but his second passion was feeding people. He loved cooking dishes that his mother had taught him. Whenever Sofia had friends over,

Hector would always carry down plates stacked with tostones or empanadillas.

The year before Sofia moved to Huntington had been the loneliest year in Plum's life. And that was saying something, because as a former army brat, Plum had moved around, been uprooted from friends, been lonely, and started over again and again.

But seventh grade in Huntington had been the worst. There was no familiar army base, no old friends or acquaintances who showed up halfway through the year (as had happened with previous deployments), no connections.

The whole entire year, Plum hadn't made a single friend.

Well, not a true friend. Not the lifelong kind. It was a feeling Plum thought everyone knew, even if no one ever talked about it. She'd had temporary friends, the kind who look at you like, *You'll do*. Who "let" you spend time with them, but who don't really like who you are, in the end.

Thank God Sofia had arrived a few months into eighth grade. When Plum got sent to the principal's office and made a true friend all in one day.

But that wasn't how they'd ended up here on Saint Vitus—for the spring break to end all spring breaks.

2

The hot wind of Saint Vitus was scented with the fumes of idling cars. Sofia grabbed Plum's suitcase handle to stop her.

"It doesn't make sense that it would be this far down here. We must have passed it."

Sofia let go of Plum's suitcase and lifted her thick dark hair up onto her head, puffing out a breath.

"No," Marlowe said. "This *is* it." She gestured at the bench and the crowd of travelers staring at their phones.

The single lane the airport had devoted to ride-share cars was clearly not enough.

Plum frowned, glancing down at her own phone, trying not to drag the wheels of her bag into her heels. Again. *Thank God for Doc Martens, amen.*

Plum always dressed for comfort and movement first and style second. Or rather third. But even Plum had stepped up her fashion game for the fest, wearing her favorite black skinny jeans and oversized white V-neck men's undershirt with a black tuxedo jacket over the top.

Well, the jacket was now draped over her suitcase handle. Unlike Marlowe, Plum felt the heat.

Plum still couldn't believe they were doing this. Just thinking about it set her heart racing in a combination of excitement and apprehension.

Back when Plum had told her the plan, Sofia had frowned. "It's technically fraud, isn't it?" she'd asked.

Marlowe had chimed in, "Mail tampering's a federal offense."

But it wasn't mail fraud. Or identity tampering. Or whatever. It was courage! It was boldness! It was reaching for the life you wanted and for who you wanted to be!

By being the person you were impatient to become.

Plum felt dazzled by her own audacity, as if inside her all these years there was a secret mirrored disco ball, just waiting for one bright act of courage to scatter speckles of light all through her.

And anyway? It was totally something her older half sister, Peach, would do. Absolutely. Except for the part where Plum was pretending to be Peach.

Peach was famous, an Instagram and TikTok star. To Plum, it seemed like Peach had *always* been famous. The glow of personal charisma was a force that practically lifted off Peach's seemingly poreless, golden tan skin, like heat shimmers lifting off hot pavement, so palpable that even as a child Plum imagined she could see it twining into the air.

Peach was ten years older than Plum and had never been anything as ordinary as a high school senior with a severe case of senioritis and a spring break with nothing to do.

Objectively, Plum recognized that since she'd been only in second grade when Peach was a senior in high school, she probably wasn't accurately remembering how Peach had actually been.

Peach had dropped out of college and started her own company when her social media started paying so well. She was a true influencer, bestowing an effortless patina of cool with a single post or click of a heart-shaped button. Peach's life was the very definition of *aspirational.* The fancy parties, attending Coachella as a VIP, endorsement deals, modeling gigs, private boats and planes, everything special flowing to Peach like water flowing downhill.

So much so that Peach was now moving to LA from NYC to pursue acting. Peach asked that her mail be forwarded to her dad's house during the move and while she renovated her new place.

Some kind of secretarial service was supposed to come and sort through the drifts of catalogs and samples and invitations that had gathered in laundry baskets on their dining room table.

Meanwhile, for Plum, spring break loomed and there was nothing to do. Plum's mom said they would have a "staycation"—but it was fairly obvious that meant Plum would spend her days alone (as usual) while her dad went to work at the local hospital where he was a radiologist and her mother went to work at the day care she managed.

Plum's spring break then would have included nothing but scrolling her phone, cooking ramen, and bingeing some shows. They were all things that Plum actually enjoyed, but it didn't feel like enough. Not when there was a whole world out there and yearning pulling at her insides like the moon pulls the ocean, to just go, to be a part of something, to dare.

To act as she wished. To be bold.

Then, as if Plum had somehow summoned it, the invitation had arrived.

3

Standing on the crowded sidewalk in front of the small Saint Vitus airport, Plum could feel the invitation in her mini backpack, as if the paper were actually physically heavy with the promise of adventure.

She'd memorized every word.

YOU ARE INVITED TO SET THE NIGHT ON FIRE! the front read. The background was black, the letters a gorgeous swirl of reds, oranges, and blues, like the words were made out of writhing flames.

Even though the envelope had been addressed to "P. Winter," Plum knew instantly that it wasn't for her.

Of course not.

Plum had taken it from the delivery guy. She'd signed for it, the envelope suddenly a piece of kindling in her hand, ready to ignite. Because she knew instantly, on that day, the Friday two weeks before spring break was to begin, that this was her chance.

To have an Adventure.

To be Somebody.

Her mom and dad, not to mention her teachers and her friends, would absolutely hurk into their hands to hear her say that last one.

Plum Winter, you are somebody! Somebody special!

They'd tell her that she was all the normal things she was. Listing them as if the qualities were somehow extraordinary.

Nice, generous, kindhearted, funny, loyal, and depending on who they were, they'd maybe continue with *cute, amazing, the best friend anyone ever had. Shut up about Instagram, already, goddamn it. No one has it all!*

Okay, so it was Marlowe who would say that last part. Unfailingly. Like the skipping section of one of those records she loved to play. Crackly 1920s or 1930s songs, the singer's voice like that of a beautiful ghost that had been trapped in a hallway (which incidentally had perfect reverb).

Marlowe was like that, though. Not like a beautiful ghost, but like a good friend, obviously. The best friend. And also heart-stoppingly beautiful. And conveniently blind to Plum's faults. Or at least, if not blind, she was accepting of how desperately Plum wanted to be . . . wanted to become . . . something. Marlowe noticed how restless she was sometimes, like there was a green, growy thing inside her heart, hungry for nourishment.

Like a secret ability, waiting to awake. To be seen.

What Plum wanted more than anything was to be

extraordinary. She wanted to be the kid who discovers they're a wizard, if wizards were real. Or that there's a vampire in love with them, if vampires were real. Or that they somehow have magical powers, like the ability to control the elements or harness the power of an amulet or move things with their mind or literally *anything.*

If any of those things were real.

She wanted to be the kind of person famous people would be drawn to. She'd imagine meeting her favorite musicians, actors, artists, and each and every one of them would think, *She's so cool. We should hang out.*

Meanwhile Marlowe was immune to all of this sort of thing. Even on a small scale, at their school, the whole social media game, keeping up, the constant hunger to post, to have anyone click love or like. To see what everyone else was up to.

Honestly, it was sometimes annoying how resolutely disconnected Marlowe could be. On one hand, Plum admired it, because it was like Marlowe was cultivating something inside herself, protecting it. But other times it felt . . . pretentious. Especially joined with her retro style, it was as if Marlowe was too cool for anyone else.

Which, if she was being completely honest, Plum had to admit that a) Marlowe never said anything like this, b) Plum did actually think that Marlowe was cooler than everyone else, and c) Plum only truly felt this particular annoyance when she was lonely.

It seemed like Marlowe never felt lonely. And wasn't that part of what this yearning to be somebody was all about? Not just to have adventure, or excitement, or all those other valid things, but to be someone who would never, could never, be lonely.

Not that Plum felt that deep level of lonely often. Usually, there was just yearning tugging at her. A thrum of anticipation, excitement, and impatience.

Sofia was somehow both too anxious and too grounded to feel the pull of yearning the way Plum did. Her family was part of it, because she wasn't alone all the time. Not like Plum, who could admit that she was lonely sometimes, a lot of times, especially last year when Sofia and Marlowe both had boyfriends.

If Sofia ever heard Plum's negative self-talk, she would also say affirming things, give a rushed but heartfelt speech about authenticity, vulnerability, being real. Which Sofia actually was, online and off. Like she had a spiritual compass in her head, guiding her.

Neither Sofia nor Marlowe *really* understood.

How could they? They didn't have a famous relative, much less memories of that famous relative cuddling them and telling them stories. Shining love on them like the sun.

To Plum, Peach was perfect. When Plum was growing up, Peach would dart into her life regularly but then flit away again, her time split between two houses, theirs and her mom's.

Until the day she disappeared. Well, went to college. To Plum, it felt like the same thing. Peach's visits home became shorter. She didn't ever have time to talk on the phone. And then she stopped coming home completely.

Plum's mom and dad looked resigned whenever Plum would complain about it. They'd squeeze Plum's shoulder, or give her head a peck, and say, "Oh, honey, I know how you feel. But try not to hold it against her. This kind of thing is totally normal for a young person finding their way in the world. They lose touch. Time doesn't feel the same to them."

Every time she heard that, Plum's heart would fill with hot iron nails. And she would make a fierce promise.

I will never do that. I will never be that way.

So, no, there was no way her two best friends could understand.

The weird loneliness of having a famous older sister.

Which was compounded by watching her, on Instagram or TikTok, just like anyone else could.

When the Pyre Festival envelope arrived, the thought slid into Plum's mind like a spill of black oil onto water.

She would never miss just one invitation.

Inside the card, the background changed to flame orange, bright like an adrenaline dump.

PYRE FESTIVAL: A LUXURY MUSIC AND ART FESTIVAL LIKE NO OTHER. EXCLUSIVELY FOR ARTISTS, MUSICIANS, INFLUENCERS, AND NEW MEDIA. APRIL 18–20, LITTLE ESAU, SAINT VITUS.

A festival. A new social media app, Pyre Signs, which apparently the whole thing was promoting (Plum had immediately downloaded it). The app didn't seem that revolutionary. It had a cool theme, though, with flames and black backgrounds. Other than that, it felt like a combination of already existing apps. Users could post text only, or text and pictures, or short videos, all in the same feed. Still, Plum reasoned that if she was going to Pyre Festival, she should definitely have the app.

The invitation also came with a verification code that unlocked an account with links to confirm a voucher for an airline ticket (first class!) and other transportation information. Once on the island, P. Winter was promised luxury accommodations in the large resort—a converted villa from the 1920s.

Before she could think about it, Plum had begun hatching a plan.

And now, with her two best friends, she was there!

Well, almost there.

"If we miss the boat, we're going to be in so much trouble," Sofia moaned.

A fissure of doubt spread through Plum. What if they did miss the boat? Literally! What if they got stranded on Saint Vitus? With not enough money to stay two nights, much less buy food.

What if they'd made a terrible, terrible mistake in coming?

4

Plum took a deep breath. Then she took another.

"We're not going to miss the boat," she said. Plum stuck her lower lip out and puffed, blowing her brown-red fringe off her forehead.

"We'll be fine," Marlowe said, backing her up. "And if we missed it, we'd just get a hotel."

"We don't have enough money for that!" Sofia said.

"We'd use the credit card." Plum glanced at Marlowe's phone. How far away was the driver, anyway?

"I told you that's for emergencies only!" Sofia actually stamped her foot.

"Well, it would be an emergency, though?" Plum mumbled.

"I should never have let you two talk me into this." Sofia crossed her arms over her stomach. "I always go along. Why? Why do I do that?"

A tiny needle of guilt poked Plum in the guts. She glanced at Marlowe.

"We're going to be fine." Marlowe put an arm around their petite friend. "We're going to have a great time."

"So help me, Marlowe," Sofia warned. She was truly exasperated.

"I'm sorry, I know you're feeling stressed," Plum began, then she adopted Marlowe's supportive tone. "But I'm sure the boat is going to wait for us. As far as they're concerned, we're the big fish! *Peach Winter*."

"I'm going to get into so much trouble," Sofia moaned, pushing her hands into her long, wavy hair.

"No, *we* are not," Marlowe said. "We've thought of everything."

"Like you'd even get grounded," Sofia mumbled. "If we get caught."

Marlowe shook her head. "No, it'd be worse than that. I'd get *Disappointed Looks* until I provided a grandchild. I don't even know if I want kids! And in the interim, I'd be flayed with deep sighs, articles emailed to me about various dangers and tragic ends that could have been me. Worst of all, I'd lose my parents' trust."

Were Marlowe's eyes actually glittering with tears at the thought? She took a deep breath. "But we're not going to get caught. It's like a rite of passage, and we're going to pass it. We've thought of everything. We're going to stick together. We *are* going to have *a good time*."

Plum had to hand it to her: even though Marlowe hadn't

really been enthusiastic about the plan initially, she was completely on board now.

It was risky. It was exhilarating.

It was also—probably—completely safe. As long as they took care of each other.

Their parents all thought they were at the beach. That was the story: they'd found an affordable Airbnb in Vero Beach, Florida, and said they wanted to go together for one big spring break. They hadn't mentioned the festival, or the Caribbean island, or any of that, because it would have been an automatic no. At least from Sofia's parents.

The secret plan had been to skip Vero Beach and instead stop in Orlando to catch their flight to Saint Vitus. It was only three days and two nights, so they'd leave Marlowe's car at airport parking.

Of course, when trying to convince their parents, the friends had simply talked about spending time together, that it would be a magical, last-minute, senior-year, spring break opportunity. Before they graduated and separated and went out into the wide world.

They hadn't spared their parents the "halcyon filter," as Marlowe put it.

All Plum's parents had needed to hear was that Sofia and Marlowe were going, and they said okay. And Marlowe's parents simply agreed with whatever she wanted anyway.

Maybe it was a part of that trust thing.

Sofia's parents nearly ruined the whole adventure. Fortunately, Sofia's older sister, Krystal, had agreed to lie for them. Krystal and her college roommate Emma would actually be staying at the "cover" Airbnb Plum had found in Vero Beach, so they'd be there if anything happened. All Krystal had asked for in return was that the girls give her their festival swag bags.

Truthfully, Krystal was more pumped up about Sofia's "once-in-a-lifetime chance" to attend something like this than her little sister was. But it was reassuring to all of them, Sofia most of all, that at least *someone* knew their true plan and would be waiting to hear that they'd arrived safely.

Even with all these precautions, Sofia was still a mess of nerves. Hopefully she would be able to get over this hump. They were supposed to have a good time.

It *hadn't* felt great to lie, but they were almost out the door to college, independent, or whatever was next. They were supposed to be free.

Plum dreamed that "what's next" for her could be running off to a big city and "making it," or working her way across a different continent like Australians all seemed to, or even just going to visit Peach in her new LA digs and getting discovered. Or going to college, starting an amazing band, anything along the lines of green, growy things awakening.

Anyway, as far as Pyre Festival was concerned, it was only three days and two nights. They were all about to leave their nests, anyway. Wasn't it time to prove they could make it on their own?

"The universe wants us to have this," Plum said. "You said that. Remember, Sofia? When we traded the voucher for the first class ticket and got three in coach?"

Marlowe turned her crooked smile from Sofia to Plum, nodding her head at the memory.

Plum's stomach did a flippy thing, which happened sometimes but not in a really long time, at least not with Marlowe.

But just look at her.

Plum had to stop herself looking too much sometimes.

"What?" Marlowe asked Plum. Marlowe lowered her sunglasses again, peering over the frames at her friend.

"Nothing," Plum said, feeling a matching crooked smile pull across her mouth. "Just, do you even sweat?"

Marlowe snorted. "Trust me, I'm sweating."

Plum was *not* in love with her best friend. Plum was smarter than that and wasn't going to eat her heart out, just because she kind of maybe probably could like her best friend romantically, if she let herself, but she wasn't going to let herself, because her best friend definitely would not reciprocate the potential emotion. Because Marlowe didn't like girls that way.

And neither did Sofia for that matter, and that had never been a problem for Plum, either. Mostly.

Sofia and Marlowe knew Plum was bisexual, and that for

her that meant she was attracted to the person, not their gender. But to Plum it was sort of a moot point, because at least in Huntington, she didn't date.

Which was fine, and certainly for many people their preferred way of life. But Plum couldn't help but feel a certain romantic longing, and not just when she looked at Marlowe.

It wasn't as if Plum hadn't had a few flings here and there. (Okay, two. It was just two flings. The first a boy and the second a girl, both summer romances at performing-arts camp exactly one year apart from each other.)

Meanwhile Marlowe had had a steady boyfriend last year, the Danish exchange student, Lars, as broody and intense as Hamlet himself and just as gorgeous as Marlowe. He'd returned to Denmark, so they'd broken up rather than try long-distance.

Sofia was still dating and crazy in love with her boyfriend, Louis. They'd been together since tenth grade.

Plum forced her eyes off Marlowe, again, and looked out for their ride. Everything was going to be fine. Better than fine. It was going to be perfect. It was going to be #*LivingTheDream!* And #*Goals!* And #*LivingMyBestLife*!

It was going to change her life. Plum was certain.

5

Their car finally arrived, and in no time Plum and her friends were tugging their bags down a dock with a small boat waiting at the end.

"Well, that's not exactly what I expected." Marlowe quirked an eyebrow at Plum while handling the pier planks with her usual grace.

One of Plum's suitcase wheels got caught in a gap between the boards.

"Yeah, it's smaller than I would have thought?" Plum yanked at her suitcase handle, freeing the trapped wheel.

The boat bobbed at the end of the dock. It looked like a charter fishing boat. White hull and chrome fittings, with a navy-blue canopy shielding the few other passengers already waiting on the padded U-shaped bench.

"Hi," Sofia chirped as they drew up to the boat. "Hello!"

"Hi!" a young woman's friendly voice replied.

The boat's captain, a middle-aged Black man, stood on the dock to help them board.

"Hello, is this the Pyre Festival boat?" Sofia asked him.

"Yes, it's a charter boat," the captain answered. "Going to Little Esau, yes."

"Okay," Sofia said, but her voice was still uncertain.

"It's okay," Marlowe reassured their friend. "I'll go first."

As she waited to board, Plum darted her eyes over to the other Pyre Festival VIPs waiting in the boat. She held her breath. Would she recognize anyone?

Apparently not.

There were only three others on the boat: two young women who were probably in their late teens or early twenties—one was white, the other was maybe Latina—and a white teen boy, who smiled at Marlowe and her friends with open welcome.

He was . . . well, wow. He was super cute, actually.

Plum usually noticed girls more than boys, but he was absolutely her type, with curving dimples and sun-streaked blond hair and a tan.

"Hey there," the boy said, jumping up to help the captain stow the bags behind a nylon cargo net. His perfectly floofed hair fell over one eye in a rakish veil.

Plum stepped onto the boat, trying to act like standing on boats was something she did all the time.

Sofia came last. She looked a bit anxious to leave solid ground.

"Hi!" the white girl said, glancing up from her phone with an apologetic *I have to get back to this* smile. She looked back down. She was pretty, with freckled skin and long, chemically bright red hair. She wore a scarf skirt and a white lace tank top. Her ears, neck, and arms glittered and chimed lightly with every movement, her large jewelry mesmerizing.

"Hola," the other girl said, smiling affably and moving over so the three new arrivals could sit together. She was gorgeous, with long brunette hair pulled into a high ponytail that trailed down her back.

"I'm Cici." She stuck out a manicured hand. Her nails were pink and sparkly. "Cici Bello."

The name didn't ring any bells in Plum's mind, despite sounding so much like music that she wanted to say it again, wanted to hear her say it again.

Cici cocked a perfectly shaped eyebrow at Plum's pause in replying.

"I'm Pl . . . um . . . I mean, uh . . . I'm Pea . . ." Plum stammered.

Should she give her real name? They weren't at the festival yet. What if the pretty redhead still on her phone worked for Pyre Festival? Or what if Cici did?

Marlowe saved her, smoothly cutting over the moment of Plum's indecision.

"I'm Marlowe Blake." Marlowe stuck out her hand.

"Nice to meet you!" Cici replied, smiling at Marlowe warmly.

Plum noticed the interested light in Cici's eyes as they quickly swept down, taking in Marlowe's impeccably stylish suit.

"Oh my God, I love your outfit!" Cici said.

"Thanks!" Marlowe said.

"Marlowe is so talented! She makes so many of her own clothes! And others she finds online or at vintage shops. She's got such an eye." Sofia stuck her hand out in the middle of the cascade of words. "I'm Sofia Torres."

"¿Habla español?" Cici asked.

Sofia smiled. "¡Sí! ¿Eres una blogger de moda?" Sofia glanced over at Marlowe and Plum, switching to English as they all sat down. "I asked if Cici was a fashion blogger," Sofia explained.

"No, makeup. I do tutorials and stuff." Cici smiled. It explained a lot, because her makeup was flawless.

How had she not sweat any of it off?

"Well, that makes sense," Plum joked, leaning forward. "You don't look hot at all."

Cici laughed uncertainly, glancing at Sofia. "Thanks? I think?"

"Oh, crap." Plum slapped her hand to her forehead. "I meant hot as in sweaty. You don't look sweaty."

"She's obsessed with sweat," Marlowe told Cici, keeping a completely straight face.

Plum glanced daggers as Marlowe.

"No, I mean, you totally look hot," Plum plowed on. "As in good-looking." Plum held up a thumbs-up.

"Anywaaaaaaaay," Sofia drawled, cutting into Plum's unremitting awkwardness. "Cici—is that a nickname? I like it!"

Cici laughed and fluffed her hair. "Yes, it's short for Cielo. I like how Cici is more casual, but also that no one mispronounces it."

Sofia gave a little chuckle of recognition, then asked, "Where did you travel from?"

The boat rocked as the captain climbed back out onto the dock and began unwinding the first of two mooring ropes.

"Miami," Cici answered. "My entire family lives there. Cousins, the whole deal. Big Cuban American family. How about you? Where'd you travel from?"

"Huntington, Alabama," Sofia answered. "My dad's a geologist at the university, and my mom's a librarian. I'm Puerto Rican on my dad's side."

The girls continued to chat as the captain jumped back onboard, the last rope that had held them to the dock looped in his hand. He spun the helm, pointing the small vessel out to the open ocean.

Plum's fears of whatever would happen if she was discovered receded with every moment they pulled farther from land.

The disco ball of excited light scattered through her again.

Pyre Festival! Set the night on fire! It was starting! Well, near enough, and as the dock and the cliffs of Saint Vitus grew smaller behind them, Plum felt safe.

She couldn't wait to see the villa in person. She had no doubt the festival would be life-changing. When she got back, she knew all the other kids at school would die of jealousy.

They'd just die.

6

"I'm Plum Winter," Plum said, at last following her friends' lead and sticking out a hand first to Cici, then to the pale redhead with the flowing scarf skirt.

"Nice to meet you!" Cici said, giving a glowing smile to Plum.

"I'm almost done, I swear, I'm sorry," the redhead said. Instead of shaking Plum's hand, she winced another apology, glancing up and back down to the phone in her hand so quickly that if Plum hadn't been looking right at her, she would have missed the hazel flash of her eyes.

"I'm Jude," the cute boy said. He shook everyone's hands. "Jude Romeo," he said, smiling in what looked like mild embarrassment at his perfect last name.

"Oh my God, that's adorable." Sofia gave Jude a look like she'd just found a puppy.

"It's silly," Jude said. "Too much." He gave his head a little shake. The sun-streaked blond forelock fell across his eyes.

"Did you say *Winter?*" Jude asked, turning back to Plum.

"Yes, Plum Winter."

Plum was looking forward to what was coming next. As much as she missed her older sister, and as much as she often felt like an outsider looking in on Peach's Instagram-perfect life . . .

She really did love the rush when people realized Peach was *her sister*.

Jude shook his forelock aside so he could look at her better.

"Hey! You're Peach Winter's sister!" he said. "I've seen her share your picture!"

Peach would sometimes do flashback posts to "*when life was easier, quieter, but we still had the whole world . . ." or she'd post a huggy animation with the caption "Happy Sister Day!" And even on Plum's last birthday, instead of calling or sending a text, Peach posted a picture of the two of them: "Happy birthday to my kid sister!"*

It wasn't as nice as talking to her, but hundreds of thousands of strangers had clicked love.

"Yes," Plum replied.

"Is Peach coming?" Cici asked eagerly, leaning forward to look around Sofia at Plum.

The boat started to pitch more dramatically as they left the shelter of the large bay and motored out into the open ocean.

"Whoa," Marlowe murmured, falling onto Plum slightly. Plum helped her friend steady herself.

"I think so?" Plum stalled. Perhaps it would be best to act

like Peach had *sent* her to the festival and that there was a chance Peach would come later. "I mean, she wanted us to come and, uh, meet her here."

Sofia gave Plum a little look, indecipherable if you hadn't known her since middle school. But Plum could read it as easily as if it were the smoke trails of a skywriter.

STOP LYING.

But it wasn't Sofia who had urged her friends to come. Who promised that they'd get into the festival, have the whole adventure with famous people, and that it would happen no problem, easy-peasy rice and cheesy.

Plum looked away from Sofia.

"Yes," she lied. "She's coming later on. You know how it is. Busy-busy!"

The last two words were a singsong that made Plum wince. So fake.

Jude Romeo didn't seem to notice. In fact, he looked so transported with delight that Plum almost felt bad the moment the lie left her lips

"That's so cool!" Jude's smile was lottery-winner wide. "Maybe I can get a selfie with her!"

He said it with the same tone of *Maybe we'll be friends!*

"Yeah!" Plum's smile back felt like a mask.

The boat fell down the trough of another wave.

"Oh," Marlowe groaned. A new tightness pulled her forehead into a frown.

"Look at the horizon in front of us," Plum told her. "It's supposed to help."

Plum never got motion sickness, but Marlowe sure did. When they went to the playground in the nearby state park to hang out at night, Marlowe wouldn't even sit on the merry-go-round.

The boat reared up the top of another wave, the highest one yet. Marlowe sat ramrod straight, her knuckles gripped white around the railing behind them.

"I'm Shelley Moon!" the redhead across from Sofia said, finally looking up from her phone. "Sorry, I had to finish setting up some posts." Shelley held up her phone, almost like it was a star pupil. "I have some private clients I do readings for, and I don't want to have to worry about that once we get to the island."

"It's no problem," Plum said.

"You do tarot readings?" Sofia asked.

"Yes, and, like, color channeling and auras. I mainly do horoscopes." Shelley tipped her chin down, like she was both shy and proud of this specialty.

Sofia let out a little squeal of delight. It morphed into a squawk as the small boat skidded alarmingly down another wave.

Marlowe moaned, closing her eyes.

Jude looked sympathetic. He turned toward the captain at the helm. "Is it far to the island?"

The captain yelled something back, but the wind whipped his words away. The captain reached for something under his feet.

His hand came up, holding the lip of a wide blue bucket.

"Dear baby Jesus," Marlowe chanted in dismay.

7

Jude took the bucket, glancing at it skeptically.

Marlowe gestured for it, so the boy handed it over.

"I do horoscope poetry." Shelley was still talking, unfazed by the pitch and yaw of their small craft.

"Oh! Are you one of the Astro Poets?" Sofia asked.

A look of supreme frustration flitted across Shelley's face. "No, I'm Shelley Moon. Of Shelley's Moons. I do horoscope poetry."

As if that somehow distinguished her from the other account. Which also did horoscope poetry. And which was well known.

There was a brief, intensely awkward silence.

"I mean, yeah," Sofia started, pressured words rushing into the painful gap.

"I do poems with structure. You know. Classical stuff. Like quatrains. Rhyming couplets. Sestinas."

"Yeah, I can see how that's different." Sofia quickly appeased her, eyes cutting to Plum for help.

"Me too," Plum agreed.

"*They* do free verse."

"Completely different," Sofia said.

"Sonnets, for God's sake," Shelley continued. "On winter solstice every year, I do a sonnet for every star sign. That's twelve sonnets!"

"That's a lot," Jude agreed.

"No one else does that!"

"Amazing," Cici said. "I'm going to follow you right now, if I don't already." Cici swiped her phone screen and glanced down. The boat tilted upward like a rearing horse. "When we get to the island," she said, letting out a breath. "Wooooo." Despite the sea spray, her makeup was still flawless. Plum would definitely have to follow Cici's channel to learn a few things.

"What do you do?" Sofia turned to Jude Romeo.

"I'm a streamer." Jude shook his forelock out of his bright blue eyes. "Mostly hangouts with my fans. Or I talk about what's important to me, especially positivity—anything is possible!"

"Videos?" Plum asked. "On YouTube?"

"Nah," Jude said as the boat skidded into another trough. "YouWow."

Plum had never heard of it. She nodded.

"It's a better place for me, my manager says. He's a great guy, King Michael, that's what we call him, 'cause he's a kingmaker. He made Tommy McGee and Billy Paul and the Holsy twins." Jude pitched forward. He righted himself and leaned back.

The names were all new to Plum. She nodded again.

"Anyway, it's a good place to grow my platform." Jude Romeo smiled a completely adorable and devastating smile.

Plum realized the others on the boat had fallen silent.

Plum turned to look at Marlowe. Her best friend was still holding the bucket as she watched the horizon. Her lips were pressed tight in a grim grip.

Plum turned the other way, to Sofia, who held her head in her hands. Just past Sofia, Cici had a definite greenish cast to her previously glowing, light olive-brown skin.

"Um." Plum turned back to Jude. "I think we might need another bucket."

"Oh no." Cici urgently gestured.

At least her hair was already pulled back in that high ponytail.

Marlowe handed the bucket over. Cici was immediately sick into it.

Jude Romeo made a sympathetic face, and when Cici leaned back, he took the bucket and dumped it overboard.

"Thank you," Cici breathed.

Next to Plum, Marlowe's slender hand extended.

Plum handed the bucket to Marlowe, who immediately leaned over and made the most miserable noises into it. Plum pulled Marlowe's hair back and held it out of the way.

When Marlowe sat up, Jude took the bucket and emptied it again.

The boat pitched and slid, up and down, a sickening seesaw.

Or actually sea-saw, Plum thought. She breathed a prayer of thanks for her inner ear, which was somehow fine with all of this.

Because when Jude Romeo had emptied the bucket again, two pairs of hands had gestured for it urgently. Shelley Moon, the horoscope poet, and Sofia.

Plum snagged the bucket for her best friend. Because that's what best friends do.

She held Sofia's dark hair back as she hurled her lunch into the bucket.

Across the aisle from her, Jude held Shelley's bright red hair as she leaned over the railing.

Plum met Jude's gaze, across the aisle, as their charges each yakked copiously. Jude's blue eyes lit up with suppressed mirth.

Plum couldn't help but snort back. The laugh caught in her throat.

Her poor friends.

These poor other passengers.

"I never get seasick," she explained to Jude.

"King told me to take a motion sickness pill," Jude explained back. "He said, 'Burst capillaries around the eyes do not an influencer make.' "

Plum couldn't help it. She laughed, an actual all-out laugh, erupting from her chest like a seal's bark.

"Really, Plum?" Marlowe breathed. She was looking . . . greener.

"I'm sorry," Plum said. She rubbed her friend's back.

"Just give it to me. Again."

8

The cliff had arisen out of the ocean, first a pointy speck, then a pointy dot, then a pointy bump. The entire time they approached, Plum offered Marlowe and Sofia encouragement, along the lines of "We're almost there" and "Oh, look, I can see palm trees now" and "I see the dock!"

"I will never own a blue bucket for the rest of my life," Marlowe proclaimed shakily. The harbor waters were suddenly smooth, like landing on a runway.

At least compared with the open ocean.

The dock was fairly short. A speaker somewhere blasted music—bass-heavy club hits. A small white canopy stood at the end of the dock. Beyond it, a large white-and-blue-striped tent was set up on the rocky beach.

But it was completely abandoned. Where were all the people?

While the others were gratefully disembarking from the

boat, and while Jude Romeo was helping the captain lift the suitcases out of the cargo area . . .

Plum couldn't help it; she took a picture—and a short video—of the blue bucket, and the boat, with the ocean behind them. She posted the photo on both the Pyre Signs app and Instagram. She typed a caption: `That wasn't quite the triumphant entry we expected. #PyreFest` She added a big puke emoji and a laughing GIF.

She added the same text to the video and put it on TikTok, with an emotional ballad playing over it.

Should she have posted their puke bucket?

Probably not.

Was it something Peach would post?

Definitely not.

But was it still funny, hilariously so, and true?

Absolutely yes.

Plum laughed as the first few likes started coming in.

"Welcome." A British man's voice, burnished smooth like a fine mahogany, carried over the music.

Plum put her phone in her back pocket and squinted at the tent.

The man's voice continued. "To Pyre Festival."

"Yeah!" Jude cheered. His voice was different than before. A new demeanor suddenly took over his whole posture: he slouched, swooped one hand at his inner leg, and scrubbed his floppy hair with the other.

"Yeah, oh my God." His accent was different, too. Like a famous rapper or DJ being interviewed. A performance of himself as someone else.

"Pyre Festival! Ohmygoooood." Jude shook his head in a humble, amazed, can-you-believe-it move that looked as fake as his voice sounded. "Pyre Festival!" He did a little whoop-whoop move, punching the air in time with two quick jumps. "Can you believe it? Whoa." The boy leaned from side to side, his hands coming together, then opening out, then coming back together again.

"Pyre Festival, the place to *be*!" Jude cycled back to the whoop-whoop move.

Did he think someone was filming? The change was startling.

"Pyre Festival, by the creators of Pyre Signs," the British voice continued. But the person's voice was almost completely flat, especially compared with Jude's.

"Where is he?" Sofia murmured the question so only Plum could hear it.

Plum shook her head. "I can't see him from here. Let's go find him."

"First let me text Krystal." Sofia rapidly tapped on her phone, letting her older sister know that they'd arrived on Little Esau safely.

"Ready," Sofia said. "Let's go to the festival!"

Marlowe still held Plum's arm. She nodded emphatically. "The sooner I get to dry land, the better."

They headed toward the beach and the tent.

9

"Where is everyone else?" Plum asked. The dock was completely empty except for their small group.

Marlowe and Sofia both looked decidedly relieved when their feet hit the rocky beach.

Together they walked to the small white canopy. It felt almost like a valet stand. Or a small sunshade for their baggage while they waited for the bellhop. But there weren't any valets, and no bellhops, either.

"I bet everyone's up at the villa already!" Jude said. "Man, I can't *wait* to see who's all here!"

"I'm here," Cici announced. She walked under the tent and put her bag down. Her aura was powerful, Plum decided. She had "it"—not quite as much as Peach, but maybe that was a talent that could be grown?

"Yeah, you're here!" Jude affirmed. "Light it up!" Jude swooped his hand at his crotch again, still speaking in that different voice. "Ha, ha, ha."

The wide-eyed boy actually said "ha" like a punctuation, instead of an actual laugh.

Plum felt a combined rush of embarrassment and protectiveness for him. God love him, he was so . . . awkward.

"Where's the guy who was talking to us?" Shelley the astrologer asked.

"Maybe he's up at the villa? Talking to us through a mic or something?" Sofia pointed at a single large speaker on a tripod stand that stood under the large blue-and-white tent.

As if prompted by her point, the British man's voice returned, coming directly from the speaker. "The villa is up the path to your left."

The group turned as one. A winding trail carved up to the top of a cliff.

"The others are there," the voice continued. "But before you join them, your hosts, the creators of Pyre Festival and Pyre Signs, *it's lit, set the night on fire, melt your face off*, have set out this repast for you to enjoy. Under the blue-striped tent."

"Sweet!" Jude Romeo yelped, in his regular voice. The lanky boy rushed ahead to the food.

"Can you hear us?" Sofia called to the disembodied voice.

"The creators of Pyre Signs, Pyre Festival, your hosts, welcome you," the flat British voice came back.

"Who are you?" Sofia called again. She'd pulled her thick, wavy hair into a messy bun. Her cheeks looked flushed, but that was an improvement from her previous seasick pallor.

"I'm Wadsworth, a virtual assistant, or butler, if you will," the voice proclaimed.

Under the tent, Jude had already removed the mesh covers off several dishes and had piled a plate high and was unceremoniously shoving food into his mouth.

"Hold up." Cici followed Sofia's lead, speaking into the air. "You're not a person?" She cocked a perfectly sculpted eyebrow skeptically.

"Correct," the voice answered. "I am Wadsworth, a virtual assistant, or butler, if you will. Invented by the creators of Pyre Signs and Pyre Festival. *Light it up, set the night on fire, melt your face off.*"

"Huh," Shelley said, brushing her red hair back over her shoulder. "I wasn't expecting a virtual assistant."

Sofia shrugged. "I guess it makes sense since they're a tech start-up."

It seemed strange to have all this food sitting here unattended, though. Even though it appeared to have been recently set out, with fresh ice still under the platter of shrimp, and mesh covers to keep birds and insects away.

But where were the hands that had prepared it? Why wasn't even one attendant here?

The rest of their small group followed Jude to the blue-striped tent.

"Is there an actual human in charge we could meet?" Cici asked the virtual butler.

"Everyone is up at Mabuz Villa already. Famed for its gun-running history and the exploits of movie stars of yesteryear, construction on Mabuz Villa began in 1918 when railroad baron Edward Mabuz won the island in a card game."

It was reading the Wikipedia page about the villa, Plum realized. She'd read it herself before convincing her friends to come with her to Pyre Festival.

As "Wadsworth" droned on, they clustered around the table under the tent.

In addition to the bright pink shrimp on ice, there were various tropical fruits, platters heaped with skewers of grilled meats, pastries, cookies, and chocolate bowls filled with some kind of pudding or icing, topped with raspberries.

"Do you want anything?" Plum asked her friends.

Marlowe closed her eyes, shaking her head. One hand rested protectively over her stomach.

"Nooooooo, I don't think soooooooo," Sofia groaned.

Plum looked around to the other passengers. Shelley Moon had an ice cube from the shrimp platter and was rubbing it on her wrists—pushing her jangling bangles out of the way. Cici Bello was tight-lipped, looking away from the food as if the sights and smells alone might cause her to be sick. Again. Some more. Though her makeup was still on point.

"Maybe just some water?" Plum asked the air.

Wadsworth stopped reading the Wikipedia page.

"Certainly," the smooth British voice said. "A champagne

cocktail service is laid out in the villa's conservatory."

"That sounds lovely, but we just need some water?" Plum asked.

"A range of beverages are available at the champagne service." Wadsworth's automated voice was both smooth and firm, as if the right tone could act as an iron, pressing out complications like they were wrinkles.

"You're kidding," Cici said, her voice sharp. "There's no water here?"

"If the young miss will simply proceed to the villa," Wadsworth's voice repeated.

"I don't want to go to the villa, I want to rinse my mouth out."

"I regret that—"

"There's nothing to drink?" Shelley asked, sounding on the verge of tears.

"What kind of event planner puts out a spread like this and forgets the beverages?" Marlowe asked Plum in a low voice.

"The founders of Pyre Festival are at the top of their fields," Wadsworth said. It clearly had heard Marlowe's whisper. "Never in the history of music and art festivals has there been an event such as Pyre Festival."

But the voice was flat. Like it was reading a list of side effects in a prescription drug commercial. "*Pyre Festival, melt your face off. Pyre Festival, set the night on fire. Pyre Festival, burn, baby, burn. Pyre Festival, the fest, the fest, the fest is on fire, we don't need no water, let the—*"

"Forget it!" Cici shouted, cutting off the chant. She stalked off toward the path, pausing to pick up her small suitcase and huge, boxy makeup case.

"If miss would like to leave her things, they will be sent up to the villa later." Wadsworth's disembodied voice was somehow creepily aware of their movements.

Plum looked into each corner of the tent. Was there a camera? She couldn't see anything.

"Sure," Cici snapped over her shoulder. "Like I'm going to trust whoever didn't think of having anything to drink at the buffet to carry my bag up a cliff. I have hundreds of dollars' worth of beauty products in here. I'm not gonna let someone steal them or leave them out here to melt."

Cici started up the path, tugging one bag behind her.

"I regret that miss feels thusly." Wadsworth's voice echoed out of the large speaker. "I assure you that your bags will all be sent up to the villa."

"I think Cici has the right idea," Marlowe said to Plum and Sofia. "Um, about not leaving the bags here."

"I agree," Sofia said. "I'd feel better keeping my bag with me."

The roar of a motor sounded loud behind them.

Reflexively, they all turned toward the noise.

The captain was casting off. He held up a hand in farewell, moved to the helm, and spun it, turning the boat back out toward the open ocean and Saint Vitus.

Plum couldn't explain why, but watching that little boat

move away from them gave her a creeping feeling of dread. As if by leaving, the captain had stranded them here on Little Esau, where they would live until the day they died.

That was ridiculous, of course. Everything was going to be fine.

10

The path wound up the cliffside in a series of switchbacks that were wider than they had looked from the beach. The ragged procession had to stop every now and then to rest. Jude Romeo ended up carrying Cici's suitcase and boxy makeup case along with his own backpack.

Finally, they made it to the top, where a windswept field was the first thing Plum saw.

The entire island of Little Esau was tiny and completely elevated from the ocean that surrounded it. Knee-high grass swept in from the cliff's edge, then met a row of stunted palm trees. Persistent vines and bushes clumped in the tall grass, right up to the edge of the land.

Past the stunted palm trees was a weedy-looking lawn, mowed low, and beyond that, a wide terrace. Then, rising from the center of an otherwise empty promontory, was the famous villa.

The villa?

More like a ruin.

A ruined villa.

Or at least a villa that had definitely seen better days. Many, many better days.

It had two stories and at least two wings, with a round central point, almost like the hub of a wheel.

"That can't be it." Cici said what Plum was thinking.

There wasn't any other structure in sight.

"No way." Shelley Moon shook her head so hard her red hair whipped like the blowing grass at their feet.

The villa was the parched and faded color of sun-ruined paint and crumbling terra-cotta, all scorched wood and bleached stucco, pressed into the crumbling mortar of the first floor.

"There has to be another villa," Cici insisted. As if saying the words could make another villa, more luxe, or even just more maintained, appear.

"This isn't the one from the website," Shelley agreed.

Shelley was right. Well, she was partially right. The Pyre Festival website had gone into some detail about the historic Mabuz Villa, mostly the same information as the Wikipedia page, but going on to explain it had been a luxury yachting stop for bootleggers, robber barons, and celebrities of the age.

But this most definitely wasn't the spotless and preserved villa from the website.

Though if she squinted, Plum could sort of see it. Maybe

it had been photo-manipulated, cleaned up, a digital coat of paint slapped on a moldering and rotting skeleton.

"Where's the hot tub?" Cici gestured expansively, an irritated sweep of her arm. "There's supposed to be a hot tub right there!"

"Maybe we got the wrong island?" Shelley's voice went up, as if it was easy to just arrive at the wrong island in an entire ocean.

"This is the place," Sofia said. Her voice was quiet but firm. "The butler thingy said so, at the pier. Pyre Festival . . ."

"Set the night on fire," Marlowe finished, a wry note of amusement under her words.

Plum shot a glance to her two besties and was relieved to see sparks of amusement in their eyes.

Good old Sofia. Ready to take a risk in spite of her worries. Instead of getting upset, she was just ready to roll with whatever, go with the flow. Got to love that about her, and Plum did.

Good old Marlowe. Always up for an adventure. Always ready to find the humor, even if dark, in any hardship or disappointment. Got to love that about her, and Plum totally did. Like a friend . . . like a friend would.

"I'm sure it's better inside," Sofia said, in a gently bracing voice. She touched Cici's arm. "Let's go check it out."

Cici nodded, a quick, grateful assent.

"It looks so rad!" Jude Romeo said as they clattered over

the weed-choked cobbled sidewalk. "Like a Venice version of something you'd see in one of those old movies. *The Sea Captain's Wife and the Ghost* or something."

"*The Ghost and Mrs. Muir*?" Marlowe darted a surprised glance at Jude.

"Yeah!" he agreed. "Or like that one where the lady moves into the haunted house on the cliffs? You know? *Rebecca*?"

"You like old movies?" Marlowe asked, her voice brightening to find another fan.

"No, I mean, yeah!" Jude revised his answer when he saw Marlowe's face. "I mean, I watch a bunch with my grandma every summer when I go visit. She loves them. Some are pretty good, too, even though they're old."

Marlowe looked both affronted and gratified. "Many of them are good," she began.

Just then a scream sliced the air, making Plum jump.

Cici let out a yelp. At the same moment, Shelley jumped, and Sofia pressed in closer to both Plum and Marlowe.

The scream climbed higher, echoing off the front of the villa. It sounded like someone was being tortured.

11

Plum whirled to find the source of the scream. As she did, the sound changed, turning into a whoop of celebration.

A white man stepped out from behind one of the stunted palm trees onto the path behind them. He looked like he was in his late twenties or early thirties. It was hard to tell, with his spiked bleached platinum hair and mirrored aviator sunglasses. He was big and tall, burly like an ex-linebacker.

The man held out his phone, filming them. He was still screaming and whooping.

"AW, YEAH!" he yelled, tilting his phone from side to side. "KILLING IT, DUDES!"

The spiky-haired man messed with his phone, zooming in and out, as he continued screaming, like he'd seen a rock star or had just won the lottery. His voice sounded ragged from the shrieks that climbed ever higher as he kept yelling.

"Oh my God, you're killing it, duuuuudes!"

There was something familiar about it. Even though Plum

knew she'd never seen him before, even though she'd never stood on this path before, in front of the ruined villa on Little Esau.

Their small group, which had crossed the choppy ocean together, had been denied water, and then hiked up the dusty, twisting path in blazing heat, stood there, mouths agape, shell-shocked at the man's continued shrieks at them.

They were not killing it, Plum thought. They had never been further from killing it. Shelley's lacy tank top was slightly stained with her own stomach bile. Jude's formerly lofty hair had deflated, looking sticky with sweat and languishing product. Plum didn't want to think about what she herself looked like, and even still-somehow-spotless Marlowe looked wan.

There had never in the history of triumphs been a less triumphant group making a less triumphant entry.

And that's when it clicked.

"Oh, God," Plum said, as Cici looked like she was about to scream right back in the face of the man filming them. "The *Killing it* dude." Plum flapped a weary hand at the man. She shook her head. This tier of internet entertainer was not exactly who she'd imagined attending Pyre Festival.

And it was less than auspicious that he was the first "influencer" she actually recognized.

He was more of an internet prankster than a celebrity, Plum thought. And to make matters worse, he had only one gimmick. One bit he was completely committed to.

"Oh yeah!" Jude nodded, a bright smile suddenly spreading across his face. Jude, at least, seemed excited to recognize somebody. Either that or his relentless positivity caused his showy enthusiasm.

Abruptly the man stopped filming and lowered his phone.

"Thanks, that was great," he said, voice no longer raw, like a switch had been flipped.

"Y'all just standing there like a bunch of dummies," the *Killing it* dude continued. "Priceless."

"Don't use that word!" Marlowe said, her eyes flashing in anger.

"What, *priceless*?" the *Killing it* dude asked. But his smirk told the story, that he knew exactly what word he'd used that was offensive.

"You do *not* have my permission to post that!" Shelley Moon's eyes flashed.

"Don't need it, we're in a public place," the man answered with blithe unconcern. He was messing with his phone, tapping away.

"I don't give my consent! Everyone hear me?" Shelley said. "Let the record show."

"Can't have an expectation of privacy in a public place." The *Killing it* dude was still smirking.

"But this is a private island," Plum said. "Surely we can have an expectation of privacy on a private island?"

"Internet's patchy out here." The man sighed. Then he

grinned. "But it's going up on TikTok when I get back to the villa."

Shelley let out a shriek of anger and stomped her foot. "You *will* be hearing from my lawyer!" It was the most lively she'd looked since getting off the boat.

"Okay, whatever," the man answered. His unconcern spoke volumes about the many—no doubt many, *many*—times he'd been in this situation before. "I'm Sammy," he said. "Sammy Ponder, but my friends call me Dude."

"That makes sense." Jude smiled in clear understanding. "Because you're the *Killing it, dude* dude."

Dude grinned and held out a fist.

Jude bumped it.

"You got it, dude!" Dude said.

"Dude!" Jude said happily, holding out his own fist for Dude to one-potato bump him back. Dude didn't seem to notice, turning to the others.

"Don't be sore," he said to Shelley. "It's just the internet. It's how it is, you know."

Shelley glared at him.

Jude dropped his fist, looking around like he hoped no one had noticed that he'd been left hanging.

"Let me carry that, huh?" Dude asked, pointing at Shelley's suitcase.

"Here." Cici took her bags from Jude and shoved them at

Dude. Then she stalked forward like the cobblestone path was a runway and she was an angry model. “I need a drink.”

She walked away, her high ponytail swinging emphatically with each step.

For good measure, and because she had been scared at first and that had been unpleasant, and because she no doubt looked foolish in the video, staring at the screaming jerk like she'd been poleaxed, Plum also shoved her bag, Marlowe's bag, and Sofia's bag at Dude.

“Sure, sure,” he said. He picked up all the bags, placing several under each arm. He looked like an old-timey bellhop as he chased after Cici and Jude, now on the terrace ahead.

As a group, they walked up the crumbling steps of the villa. The main door hung open, almost looking like it was broken. As if someone had nearly torn it off its hinges, trying to get in.

Or get out.

They filed inside.

12

The atrium was dim. Long, sun-damaged curtains blocked the many windows, shielding the already-ruined antiques.

The late-afternoon sunshine slanted in through the cracks and tears in the curtains and through the open back doors of the villa on the opposite wall in front of them.

Wait, was that the back door or the front door? It was difficult to tell, because the design of the villa was perfectly symmetrical. Each side of the building matched the other, a balance that was completely disorienting.

The atrium was the central circle of the building, with two long wings coming off each side. The wing to Plum's left had a long hallway faced with closed doors. To the right of Plum was a large curved wall with a closed door, then another that was partially open.

"God, I'm glad you guys came," Dude was saying as he gently placed all their bags by the door they'd just walked through. He pushed his mirrored sunglasses up onto his head.

"Sure, you gotta keep posting that sweet, sweet content." Cici's voice was a scalpel.

"I mean, yeah, that's how that goes," Dude said. "But also, like, I mean there's hardly anyone else here. I'm just glad more people arrived."

"Wait." Shelley held up a finger. "What do you mean there's no one else here?"

"Just what he said." A woman's sardonic voice cut in from the partially open door.

The group turned and moved into the adjoining room.

It was a combination greenhouse and sitting room. There was a large glass dome in the two-story ceiling. A blaze of light shone through its cracked colored glass. The room was rounded, with a sunken middle section and an ornate fountain set in the center. But instead of splashing water, the thigh-high ledges contained soil and dead plants. A large pedestal towered in the middle of the fountain-planter. It was topped with a huge ball made of wrought iron, openwork bands.

A spear bisected the metal ball, almost like an overlarge arrow through a heart, its sharp tip pointed at the tinted glass dome.

A large bamboo-and-wire birdcage stood on one wall between two mildewed armchairs. Faded and moldering sofas, settees, and fainting couches were interspersed around the raised edges of the room. Marble statues of clothing-challenged maidens holding jugs or garlands of flowers dotted the entire space. On the opposite side of the derelict fountain was an antique iron liquor cart stocked with at least a few decanters full of amber or clear liquid, as well as a set of crystal tumblers. Around the room, huge pots of sunburned palms and other desiccated ferns and spiky blades of vegetation gave the entire room the feeling not of a greenhouse but of a funeral parlor for dead plants.

A young white woman, probably in her early twenties, sat immediately inside the doorway. Her pose was stiff, ready to pounce.

There was something shriveled and brittle about her, despite her youth. She wasn't unpretty, or at least, she might actually *be* pretty, if it weren't for a certain meanness in her face, a curve at the corner of her mouth like a sneer waiting to come out.

The young woman held out a hand at the dilapidated room.

"This is it," she said. "Welcome to—"

"Welcome to Pyre Festival, set the night on fire," Wadsworth's voice interrupted. The voice was emanating from another single speaker on a tripod stand, exactly like the one that stood on the beach. "Melt your face off, it's lit, the festival is—"

"Shut up, robot!" the young woman snapped.

The British voice abruptly stopped.

"This is the conservatory, and that's the champagne reception." She pointed to a card table in the corner of the room.

Mini bottles with twist-off caps were set out on the table. A punch bowl filled with melting ice sat beside them. There were no cups, no glasses. A few generic cans of soda with names like *Soda Cola* and *Dr. Sage* stood on the floor under the card table.

Plum didn't care. She rushed forward, snatched up a can, and popped the top.

Next to her, her two best friends popped open cans of their own.

Marlowe started chugging a *Hillside Dew.*

It was a relief to drink, but the soda didn't taste right, even for generic. It tasted . . . old. Like when Plum used to go to her grandmother's house and would drink the Diet Cokes her grandmother had bought on sale nine months before. Saving them just for Plum, not realizing they actually did have a best-by date.

"I'm Jude Romeo." Jude stepped forward, holding out his hand.

"Sure you are, kid," the woman sighed.

Jude looked confused instead of hurt, and Plum felt that surge of protectiveness again.

"I'm Plum Winter," Plum said.

"Sofia Torres," Sofia chimed in.

"Marlowe Blake," Marlowe followed.

When the woman didn't respond—like they didn't matter, like manners didn't matter—Plum felt a bolt of anger shoot through her.

"Who are you?" Plum asked.

"I'm Wadsworth, a virtual assistant, or butler, if you will."

"Not you! She's talking to me!" the woman snapped to the air.

Wadsworth went silent again.

The woman ignored Plum's question. She stood, fluffing her hair as she did. Her yellow hair didn't fluff well. It was thatch, bleached and ironed nearly to the point of breakage.

"I'm leaving," she announced. "It was a mistake to think this event could somehow be salvaged. I only stayed this long because I thought it would be fun to skewer whatever ignorant rubes showed up."

"Including yourself in that number, huh?" Marlowe drawled.

Sofia snorted.

"Not as much as you people," the woman said. "I'm here as an activist and influencer. What are you here as?" She shot a derisive look to Jude. "Huh, boy toy? You're a streamer, right? Here to do a meet and greet?"

Jude seemed constitutionally unable to recognize mockery. He dropped into his fake accent again. "Oh man, I love my fans. I would love to go on tour. Ohmygoooood, can you imagine?" He scrubbed his head, the limp hair throwing off sweat droplets like a sprinkler.

"Jesus, never mind," the young woman muttered.

"I know you," Dude said. "I knew who you were the second I saw you. Bet the *Killing it* video I posted of you has already gone viral."

Anger lanced through the woman's eyes. "I told you not to post that."

"I didn't listen, duh."

There was a moment of venomous silence from the woman, matched by supreme unconcern from Dude. He smirked and took his mirrored sunglasses off his head and began twirling them in one hand.

"So," Shelley finally began, "who is she, anyway?"

13

"This here is Brittlyn Alexander," Dude said, pretending like he was holding a trumpet and doing a little flourish. "You might have even seen the picture that made her go viral. She's amassed quite the ammosexual troll army. Ain't that right, Brit-Brit? And to think, it all started with a photo of you in a bikini holding an assault rifle."

"I was exercising my Second Amendment rights," Brittlyn said. "I'm an activist."

Oh. Plum felt deflated. A gun-rights activist. Not the other, cool kind.

"Great, a gun nut," Marlowe whispered.

"Gross," Sofia agreed.

Dude and Brittlyn were still arguing.

"Sure, exercising your *rights* at the site of one of the worst gun massacres in the history of our country. Just chilling in a stars-and-stripes bikini, open-mouth kissing your gun muzzle, as one does."

Dude might look like a gone-to-seed linebacker with bad hair, but the man could sure take a swipe, Plum decided.

"So what? We all start somewhere, right, Dude?" Brittlyn said, then smiled. "Well, some of us build to bigger things. Others just keep doing the same old shtick."

Point to Slytherin.

"I have more followers than you," Dude said. "Read it and weep, lady." He held out his phone.

"But how many did you buy?" Brittlyn asked. She stalked forward. "I have a book deal. I'm getting paid to tell my story."

"Oh, that'll be good. What kind of 'hero's journey' can you have?" Dude made air quotes with his fingers. "'How I overcame anorexia to become a bigoted tool'?"

"Hey," Sofia said softly, "let's not make fun of eating disorders."

"Yeah," Plum agreed, backing up her best friend. "Not cool."

"See?" Brittlyn scoffed, curving that mocking smile at Sofia. "This is what's wrong with the world today. What's wrong with their whole generation." As if she were decades older, instead of just a few years. "You're all soft," Brittlyn continued, waving a hand at the group. "Everything is about protecting feelings, not about the truth! You're all a bunch of *delicate flowers*."

She emphasized the last two words. They sounded like they were an insult she'd used many times before.

"*Delicate flowers*, grown in a hothouse similar to this conservatory, have long been associated with vast quantities of wealth. Especially the orchid, Mr. Mabuz's favorite flower, previously exorbitantly expensive before modern propagation methods—"

"Shut up, Wadsworth!" Brittlyn shouted.

The virtual butler was silenced once more.

"Delicate flowers as in precious. As in too soft. You're all too special to survive."

Even though Plum wasn't quite sure exactly what she was going to say, she could feel the words jumping to the tip of her tongue. Cold fury stroked her throat, and she felt the quick-fire instinct to stand up for her people. To stand up for *feelings* and *gentleness*! And for *flowers*!

Another voice beat her to it.

"God, Brittlyn, shut yer yap." The man's Yorkshire accent was so broad it would have been almost comedic, if it also weren't so tough-sounding.

They all turned to the French doors that led out onto the scraggly lawn.

An impossibly buff white man, a military-looking guy with a close-shaved head, stood in the doorway.

Brittlyn made a face at him, as if her mouth had been stitched closed in disgust.

"Hello?" Sofia said, her voice lifting at the end like a question rather than a greeting.

The new arrival nodded a greeting, but he didn't smile. "Hello," he said.

Sofia introduced herself, Marlowe, and Plum.

Cici spoke next. "And I'm Cici Bello, makeup tutorials and

product reviews, and this is Jude Romeo, streamer." She gestured to Jude. "And Shelley Moon, astrologer."

"And poet," Shelley added, bringing the palms of her hands together and giving a small bow.

The man with the Yorkshire accent didn't stick out his hand or reply. Instead he was preoccupied with repositioning a black pillow tucked under his arm, a fuzzy thing pressed tight under the broad flare of his improbable biceps.

It was a stuffed animal, Plum decided. The texture was strange, more like a fluffy marabou feather boa.

No, it wasn't a stuffed animal. Why was he carrying a black feather duster under his arm?

"This is some festival, eh?" the man asked. His smile was rueful.

"Well, how did the search go?" Brittlyn's voice was drenched in sarcasm.

"Great, princess, just great," the man sliced back. "There's nothing else on this island, just a moldy caretaker's cottage and a few FEMA tents on the beach. How's that for posh?"

"I don't understand," Sofia said. "Where is everyone?"

"Don't you get it, ducks?" the burly newcomer asked. With his free hand, he gestured around to the eight other people standing in the conservatory.

"We are everyone."

14

"That doesn't make any sense," Sofia persisted. She pulled her hair out of the loose bun, fluffing it now that they were inside. "This is supposed to be a festival?" she continued. "With, like . . ."

She didn't finish the sentence, and Plum knew immediately why.

Sofia had been about to say something that Plum was already thinking.

That it was supposed to be a festival *with famous people*.

The new man didn't seem to mind that Sofia's voice trailed off midstatement. "Just telling you what I know." It was difficult to decide if the note in his voice was the slight hum of aggression or conviction.

"I didn't catch your name, dude," Dude said, his voice lowering. He stopped twirling his sunglasses.

"Didn't throw it, mate," the man said.

"Jesus, not a pissing contest already," Brittlyn said.

The man ignored Brittlyn and turned to Plum. He stuck out a hand.

"Sean Bentham." Fine sunbaked wrinkles in the corners of his eyes appeared with his smile. "On Insta I go by . . ."

"Chick Magnet!" Sofia squeaked. She actually gave a little jump, clapping her hands in delight.

Sofia turned to Plum. "He travels the world with his hen!"

Plum shook her head, a fond smile on her lips. Leave it to Sofia to know an obscure Instagram animal account. But it was nice that her friend, at least, was having a fan encounter with an influencer.

"Is . . . is that . . . ?" Sofia trailed off, pointing at the feather duster.

"Yeah," Sean said. "Here she is. Henrietta."

His thick accent made it sound like *'enry'et-ah*.

He pulled the feather duster out from under his arm.

A fluffy black chicken tilted first one eye, then the other at them. The chicken was some kind of fancy breed, a soft plume of loose feathers standing out from her head and almost covering her eyes.

Plum thought she looked like a sheepdog, or a Muppet.

"Oh my god," Sofia cooed. "She's beautiful! Can I hold her?"

"Be my guest." Sean unceremoniously dumped *'enry'et-ah* into Sofia's arms.

There was a squawk, flapping, a mild flurry of loose feathers, and Sofia cooing, "Good girl. Who's a good girl?"

The hen nestled into the crook of Sofia's right arm.

Plum might have been projecting because she loved her friend so much, but honestly it looked like the hen was gazing up at Sofia with both relief and adoration.

"Chick Magnet, huh?" Brittlyn said, more derision than question. "What's that involve, I wonder."

"Listen, princess." Sean stabbed a finger in her direction. "I have more followers than you, and I've never posted a bikini shot in a graveyard."

Plum wondered if at some point during the festival everyone would line up in order of followers or something. Just to have it over with and establish a pecking order. Clearly, followers meant clout, but it was weird to hear them referred to when they were all at a nearly deserted festival.

"You may have more on Instagram, but that's one platform—across all social platforms, I demolish your numbers! And regarding the bikini shot—it wasn't a graveyard, and you should talk. You only went viral because you were shirtless in that picture."

"Shirtless 'cause I was swimming," Sean said. "Then the chicken fell off the dock, and the lady I was chatting up freaked out. So, I saved her." He glanced around. "The chicken, not the lady. I saved the chicken."

His eyes landed on the chicken, now drowsing, giving little murmuring clucks in Sofia's arms.

"I didn't even know she took the picture." There was a note

in his voice like he would take it back or change something.

Plum realized she did know who he was. Or at least, she'd seen the picture. It had been almost everywhere, this burly soccer hooligan, or military-looking tough guy, super buff to boot, with a few artful tattoos, standing on a beach, holding a bedraggled chicken. In the photo that went viral, he was even smiling, that attractive, sun-worked crinkle around his eyes, as he stared down at the hen he'd saved.

And while she'd seen the picture and therefore technically she guessed this guy was somewhat famous, still, this wasn't the type of influencer or celebrity Plum had expected at Pyre Festival.

She'd imagined someone like . . . well, like her sister. A celebrity who gave off that ineffable aura of "someone"—who was courted by brands, who effortlessly was the center of their own carefully curated universe.

Someone that Peach would be impressed with later, when Plum would inevitably tell her, "Oh yeah, Pyre Festival? I was there. David Guetta's DJ set was the best."

Instead she was here with a cute but clueless streamer, an admittedly gorgeous makeup-tutorial YouTuber, a horoscope poet (but not one she'd heard of), the *Killing it* dude, a gun nut looking for notoriety, and a man who traveled with his chicken.

It was far from inspiring.

Plum sighed.

They were still arguing.

"Okay, can we stop all this?" Marlowe asked. "Or you can keep going. Just someone point us in the direction of our room?" Even though she looked mostly unrumpled, there was a slight stain on her jacket, a reminder of how very sick she'd been on the boat ride over.

"There are thirteen bedroom suites in Mabuz Villa," Wadsworth's smooth voice interjected.

"Thirteen, noooo," Sofia whispered to Marlowe and Plum.

The website had listed over forty rooms in the resort, with thirteen being in the original villa and the rest in newer buildings on the grounds.

"Bedrooms are on the second floor. Every room in Mabuz Villa is available for your use," Wadsworth continued. "Other guests will be housed in our luxurious, bespoke yurts."

Sean shook his head. "FEMA tents."

"According to my resources, the founders of Pyre Festival and Pyre Signs have procured bespoke yurts that were featured on Goop. Other guests will be staying in yachts, which will be anchored in the island's bay."

"Got news for you, Wadsworth: there's no yachts and there's FEMA tents on the beach," Brittlyn announced to the air.

"The Glurt, or Glamour Yurt, a new company founded by yoga star Stephanie Leeks," Wadsworth droned. "Canvas made from organic, naturally-released-from-the-stalk cotton and hemp. Struts from noninvasive bamboo, no artificial dyes, crystal enhanced to—"

"I swear, if you don't shut up, I'm going to take a claw hammer to every speaker I can find," Brittlyn said.

The virtual butler silenced so suddenly, Plum could almost imagine the AI producing a gulp of fear. But who knew how many speakers there were? Wadsworth seemed to be everywhere.

Sean turned back to Plum and her friends. He raised a broad hand, indicating the rest of the villa. "Take your pick. I don't intend on staying overnight."

"Finally, you're making sense." Brittlyn shrugged at the trio. "Go ahead. I won't be staying, either."

"Do you want to go back?" Plum murmured to Marlowe and Sofia. "Or should we stick it out? Go find a room?"

"I can't face that boat ride again," Marlowe said. "Not anytime soon, at least."

"It's okay," Sofia said. "I'm good to stay. It doesn't matter if it's . . . you know . . . not quite what we thought . . ."

"Well, how about we take our bags up?" Plum said. She nodded at Sofia, indicating the snoozing fluffball. Sofia gently handed Henrietta back to Sean. Sean looked like he had been given a bag of dog poop.

The three girls walked out of the conservatory and back into the atrium. They grabbed their bags and started ascending the staircase.

"Let's share a room," Sofia suggested, her face gleeful. "That will be fun, at least."

"Yes, and it didn't sound like there are that many rooms anyway," Plum agreed.

Marlowe shot an amused look over her shoulder at Plum. "Can you imagine Peach *here*?" she said in a low, mirth-filled voice.

Behind Plum, Sofia snickered. "She would die," Sofia said.

As if in punctuation, an earsplitting shriek pierced the air.

15

Marlowe dropped her suitcase in shock. It thumped over, then slid down the stairs behind them.

The screaming continued.

Sean crashed through the door from the conservatory, skidding on the marble tiles as he rushed into the atrium.

"You all right?" he called up to them, even though it was transparently obvious none of them were the source of the screams.

"It's not us!" Marlowe said.

At the same moment, Plum blurted, "It's outside!"

The four of them rushed outside together, through the main doors, back out past the terrace edge, and onto the cobbled path.

No one was there.

The shrieks were moving, as if the screamer was being carried forcibly away from the house.

Sean lowered his head like a bull and charged after the screams.

Plum's heart jumped into her throat and stayed there, pounding terror into her veins as the girls followed.

They reached the row of stunted palm trees.

"This way!" Sean said. He lunged forward, the particular lunge of someone who's done a lot of lunges.

The scream cut off abruptly, then sounded again, still in front of them but now off to the side, both toward the cliff edge and into the spiky and waxy bushes that bordered it.

"We're coming!" Sofia yelled. "Where are you?"

The scream paused, only for the barest of moments. It started again, with renewed vigor, then stopped again.

"They're being killed!" Marlowe cried. Plum, her friends, and Sean stood in the windswept grass, waiting for the intermittent scream to come again.

"They're getting weaker, maybe?" Plum suggested.

"Oh no, oh no," Marlowe chanted, hugging herself.

"Why do you think that?" Sean asked Plum. His frown drew his scalp forward.

"The screaming was constant when we came out here," Plum explained.

"Maybe they heard us. She heard us—it's a woman, right?" Sofia asked.

The scream *was* very high, but before Plum could answer, the scream came again.

It was uncanny, a high shriek that sounded nearly like words, or a single word. Plum could almost make it out.

“That way!” Marlowe pointed exactly as the scream cut off again.

They crashed forward into thorn-spiked branches.

“Impossible,” Sean muttered. “There’s nothing here, it’s too low. We’d see something.”

As if to underscore his words, at that precise moment, the dense wall of green bushes in front of them shivered violently.

16

A large black-and-white goat popped out of the front of the thicket. The goat had green stains on its beard and a flat, almost disdainful look in its eyes.

The goat was intimidatingly large. It looked like it weighed close to two hundred pounds and had wickedly sharp, curved horns.

The goat screamed.

Marlowe—the least outdoorsy person Plum had ever met, who, on their junior-year ag-expo field trip, had actually started hyperventilating when a college kid tried to get her to feed a carrot to a horse—operated on pure instinct. She screamed back.

It was an impressive scream, like something Janet Leigh in *Psycho* might have let loose in the shower. It was louder than the goat's scream.

The goat, Plum decided, no longer looked disdainful.

"Better stop, Marlowe." Plum shushed her friend. Marlowe gave a little gasp and nodded, clutching at Plum's shoulders.

Yes, there was a scary goat right there, and, yes, Plum sort of hoped the goat would never move if it meant Marlowe would keep grabbing on to her like that.

The billy goat gave a rear and landed hard, stamping his black-and-white-stockinged hooves on the ground.

Sofia made a soothing noise. She tugged gently on her friends. "We should move back a ways. We don't want to make it think we're challenging it."

"It's a goat," Sean said. He stuck a hand out at the animal and laughed. "It's a bloody goat."

Marlowe huddled closer and slightly behind Plum, still holding Plum's shoulders tightly. "I don't like goats," Marlowe whispered.

"Oh, but he's so cute," Sofia cooed.

They quietly eased another step away from the huge goat.

"A screaming goat." Sean shook his head in disgust as he followed them. "Bloody figures, don't it?"

"He's just trying to eat grass and leaves and stuff!" Sofia rose to the goat's defense. "It's not his fault he scared us."

Sean gestured back toward the house. "I'm getting a scotch," he said. "If they have it."

Plum glanced over her shoulder in Sean's direction and let out a yelp of surprise. A stranger stood on the path right behind them.

"Saints and biscuits, what are you about?" Sean growled. "Sneaking up on people?"

The young man held out his hand. He was about their age, Black, and cute, with square, black-framed glasses, short buzzed hair, and long eyebrows that pulled up in an expression of happy surprise or eagerness.

"I'm sorry. I didn't mean to startle anyone," he said. "I just arrived, so I was following Wadsworth's directions."

"Well, if the computer hasn't told you yet," Sean said, "the festival is a complete wash. I'm leaving."

"What? Why?" the young man asked.

"There's no one here!" Sean said angrily. He turned and marched back to the villa for his bags. The young man shrugged and followed, and Plum and her friends went along, too. What else could they do?

Sean yanked the sagging villa's door open and strode into the atrium. "And as far as I can tell, no one else *is* coming. Pyre Festival is complete rubbish. So you hear me, Wadsworth! I'm leaving!" He shouted the last words into the air of the villa.

"Oh no," Wadsworth replied, the unruffled voice falling from a small speaker set into the curving staircase. "No, you won't be leaving, sir. None of you will."

17

"What do you mean none of us will be leaving?" Sean's voice was spiked with tension.

"This is Mr. Jalen Jones," Wadsworth said. "Who seems to be the last guest to arrive."

"There was another guy on the boat with me, some gamer," Jalen called up to the speaker. He turned a dimpled smile to Sofia. "Why do y'all want to leave?"

The conservatory door banged open as Jude came out, a wide smile of welcome on his face.

"Wadsworth, did you hear my question?" Sean spoke with the slightly raised voice of someone addressing a toddler.

"If you would be patient, sir." Wadsworth put the tiniest sliver of insulting emphasis on the last word, so subtle you could almost pretend you didn't hear it.

Was that a programming trick? To have the virtual butler insult them based on their own tone of voice?

"I merely meant," Wadsworth continued, "that no one would

be leaving, as the last boat has just left. There won't be another until tomorrow morning."

Sean let out a stream of curses.

"Wait," Sofia called. "Do you mean nobody else is coming to Pyre Festival?"

"Not today, no, miss," Wadsworth said.

"Did I come at a bad time or something?" Jalen asked. "What happened, the toilets all back up or something?"

"No," Plum explained, "it's just that it's not much of a festival."

"Oh my God, can you believe it!" Jude whooped, missing the previous sentence and clearly hearing only the last word. He pumped his arm in the air and shouted, "Pyre Festival!"

The rest of them stood, staring at Jude. No one joined his cheer.

Jude let his arm slowly drop. "Um, set the night. Like. On fire."

Wadsworth's voice fell from the stairs. "Melt your face off."

18

"What's your name again?" Sean asked the new arrival.

"Jalen Jones." He stuck out a hand. "I'm a podcaster."

"Sean Bentham." He shook the offered hand. "I'm a traveler."

Funny how he kept neglecting to mention the chicken.

"Hey, where is your hen?" Sofia asked.

"With the ladies in the conservatory," Sean answered. "I told them to wait there when I heard the scream."

"The goats," Wadsworth's voice explained. "They do make quite a racket."

"Goats? Plural?" Sofia clapped her hands in delight.

"Yes, there's a herd of about ten on the island," Wadsworth informed them.

"What kind of podcast do you do?" Plum asked Jalen. The young man put down his duffel bag on the checkered marble floor.

"True crime!" He rubbed his hands together. "I just started

it! It's called *Bloody Grounds.* Our biggest sponsor is a coffee company, so it works on two levels."

Okay, so it was *definitely* an eager expression.

"Uh, nice," Marlowe murmured.

"Well, hopefully people will remember the name." Jalen adjusted his glasses, his happy expression undaunted.

"This seems a strange thing to be invited to, don't you think?" Plum commented. "I mean, why would a true-crime podcaster be invited to Pyre Festival?" She quickly held out a mollifying hand. "Not trying to insult you or anything. I know those shows are super popular."

"I get it." Jalen smiled at her. "Seemed strange to me, too, but the background of this island and this villa are kind of intense, murder-suicide-y, so I thought maybe that was why. And at the least, I could come and do an episode on that history."

"Oh, scary!" Marlowe said. "I love that—and cool to cover the history! I love the 1920s. Especially fashion-wise." She put a hand to her flared linen pants, tenting them out slightly.

As if she needed to indicate that she was a fan of retro looks, Plum thought, with her gorgeous Veronica Lake hair and *His Girl Friday at the Tropics* pantsuit.

Plum had to stifle a sigh. It was unfair that someone could be so beautiful.

Sean crossed the atrium, thrusting open the double doors again. "It was a goat," he announced to the three girls waiting inside the conservatory.

"Wonderful." Brittlyn gritted out the sarcasm. "All this and screaming goats, too."

"And we can't leave," Sean continued. He glanced at the freestanding speaker in the conservatory and addressed it, scowling. "Want to explain it to them, Wadsworth?"

"Certainly, sir." Wadsworth droned on.

"Should we go back upstairs?" Sofia whispered to Plum and Marlowe. "Pick our room and unpack?"

"Yes," Plum replied.

While Wadsworth kept conversing with the others in the conservatory, the virtual butler's voice also emerged from the atrium's small stairwell speaker. "For the best room—" he began.

Plum gave a small, startled jump. Even though the butler's voice was disembodied, she'd somehow started to personify him. Or rather *it*. It was jarring to hear the AI in two different rooms.

Wadsworth continued. "I recommend the room at the top of the stairs on the right. It affords an excellent view of the beach."

Marlowe let out a little cheer at the mention of the beach.

"And, of course, should you wish to go down to the beach, you will also see a path from the top of the cliff," Wadsworth said.

"Let's do it!" Sofia balled up her fists, bouncing on her toes. "Beach! Beach! Beach!"

"Dinner will be served in the great hall at eight. Do enjoy your swim and the villa."

Marlowe led the way up the curving stairwell. They were halfway up when a door slammed on the ground floor.

A hyperaggressive male voice yelled, "WHAT THE HELL IS WRONG WITH THE WI-FI?"

19

A white man in his twenties strode into the atrium. He wore loose, glossy track pants, a torn white T-shirt, and Converse high-tops printed with a galaxy-swirl pattern.

"Hey! Wad! What the hell?" He crossed his arms high on his chest and waited.

"Sir?" The virtual butler's voice was almost a parody of a stuffy British man.

Sean opened the door to the conservatory and stuck his head out to see who the new arrival was.

The new guy tossed his jagged brown bangs out of his eyes. He was kind of cute in a puckish way, with a jutting chin and arching eyebrows, making him look sly, or as if he was on the verge of getting into mischief. "Why can't I get online?" he asked.

"My tests inform me that the Pyre Signs app is working perfectly, sir."

"Who are you, then?" Sean's question sounded more like a command. The new guy ignored him.

"I can't stream *War: Innate and Powerful* on Pyre Signs, Wad."

"Pyre Signs is the official app of Pyre Festival. The creators of Pyre Signs invite all guests to use Pyre Signs. Share with your followers!"

"Dude." The guy shook his head. "The website said there'd be T1-line-level connection. It's *War* day. I gotta stream for at least three hours to feed my fans."

"There is high-speed Wi-Fi throughout the island," Wadsworth explained. "Perhaps the problem is your device."

"Anyone else having problems connecting?" The boy turned and glanced up at Plum and her friends. A sharky yet still cute smile stretched his narrow face. "How about you?" he asked the girls standing on the stairs. His glance lingered on Sofia.

"I sent a text," Sofia replied. "From the dock."

"Text? Jesus." The boy shook his head.

Sofia laughed. "It was to my sister."

"Oh, is she as cute as you?" He cocked an eyebrow.

Sofia laughed again and touched her hair.

"Oi." Sean stepped into the atrium. "Who the hell are you?"

"A pissed-off gamer, who the hell are you?"

Sean stepped forward, looming over the new arrival.

The new guy held his hands up. "Chill, dude. Whatever. I just got here with that podcaster. Didn't mean to ruffle your feathers." There was a taunting glint in his eyes.

The gamer turned to the stairs again. "I'm Warix. Who are you, cute thing?"

Although he was looking at Sofia, and even though Sofia didn't seem to mind the attention, Plum felt herself bristle.

Cute *thing*?

"Sofia Torres, and these are my friends Plum and Marlowe." Sofia touched her hair again, giving it a little fluff.

"Nice to meet you, ladies," the gamer said.

"You too!" Sofia replied brightly.

"Hmmm," Marlowe murmured, and darted a look at Plum.

Plum shot a glance at her friend, confirming that they were definitely on the same page regarding "Warix."

"You play *War IAP*?" Sofia asked.

"Yeah, I'm one of their top streamers," Warix answered, not at all modestly. "Wanna watch me play later?"

The words popped out before Plum thought about it. "Sofia's a gamer, too."

Not precisely true, but Plum had seen Sofia completely smoke Louis a few times in *Brawler*. And it grated at her, because it felt like it was unconscious: this regular assumption that a girl would watch, instead of joining in the game herself.

"Only a little," Sofia explained quickly, giving Plum a mystified glance. "And, yeah, maybe!"

"Let's find our room," Marlowe interjected. "Finally, please." She smiled.

Warix stopped at the door to the conservatory.

"Catch you later, Sofia," he called up, with that sharky smile again.

"Later!" Sofia called back, even as Marlowe grabbed her elbow, tugging her upstairs.

Brittlyn's harsh voice floated up the stairs as Warix walked into the conservatory. "Oh, God, not another one."

20

"You shouldn't encourage him," Plum told Sofia as they dragged their bags down the upstairs hallway.

"Stop judging me." Sofia's voice was friendly yet held an unmistakable note of *back off.*

"I'm just saying," Plum muttered.

Plum didn't have to watch him play to know that he'd be one of those guys who yelled insults at his friends and enemies alike. That he'd probably be the type to deliberately wreck someone's painstakingly built base or shoot an ally just because he thought it was funny.

Total edgelord vibe.

Sofia turned and raised an eyebrow.

"Sorry," Plum muttered. "Sorry. I love you. I just think, maybe he's a jerk? What about Louis?"

"It's not your job to worry about Louis. Or to say that I did anything wrong." Sofia propped her hands on her hips and stared at Plum. Hard.

Sometimes it was like Sofia—happy, sometimes anxious, generous, loving Sofia—was ready to rebel about anything. The dutiful daughter, the best friend, the good girl . . . it was as if she was frustrated about something, but she'd never talk about it.

Maybe she felt the same green, growy feeling inside that Plum did. The same restlessness.

But now it was spilling out of her friend, directly onto Plum.

Plum couldn't stand it when anyone was angry with her. Not that she had to make everyone happy, but she couldn't take it when people were mad at her. It felt like something burrowing under her skin, digging into her heart, trying to make her cry.

And if it was someone she really loved? Like her parents? Or Marlowe and Sofia?

Forget it.

"I'm sorry," Plum said. "I care about you."

"I'm fine," Sofia said. Then she smiled at Plum a little. "It's okay. Just . . . stop trying to tell me what to do."

"Good luck with that," Marlowe drawled, but she leaned into Plum's shoulder, a gentle bump of affection.

"I know I do that!" Plum cried. "I don't like it either!"

Sofia looked up at Plum and gave her a cockeyed smile. "Then stop."

Marlowe leaned over the opposite way and dipped her knees slightly to give Sofia's shoulder the same affectionate bump. "I've got it!" Marlowe pointed a finger at Plum. "She'll stop telling you what to do when you"—she pointed a finger at Sofia—"stop being such an incorrigible flirt."

Sofia shook her head, but she was laughing. "Seriously, stop flirt-shaming me!" She crossed her arms. "Louis likes it when I flirt."

"Sure," Marlowe said. "When you're flirting with *him*."

Sofia made a grunt of frustration. "Like *you're* perfect." But then Sofia leaned against Plum's shoulder. "Isn't she, Plum? Just perfect."

Plum felt a warm bubble of happiness rise in her heart at the shoulder lean. Forgiven.

"Yeah. What she said." Plum crossed her arms and leaned right back into Sofia. Well, a little. She was almost a foot taller, after all.

"You two." Marlowe shook her head.

"You love us," Sofia replied. She kissed the air.

Marlowe laughed. "Always."

"Me too," Plum said.

"Forever," Sofia agreed. "Now, let's check out the rooms."

21

It didn't take long to ascertain that, yes, the room the virtual butler had said was the best was in fact the best.

They'd peeked into the others, just to be certain.

But it wasn't much of a competition. Each of the thirteen rooms upstairs at Mabuz Villa had French doors that opened onto narrow Juliet balconies. Or they would open onto the balconies, if they hadn't been painted shut. The girls tried each set of doors just in case *one* of the balconies was actually accessible. No luck.

But what did you do on a Juliet balcony anyway? Other than deliver soliloquies to the moon.

The entire upstairs was free from Wadsworth's speakers. Which was fine, since Plum couldn't imagine wanting to talk to the virtual butler in the bathroom or in bed. It was already weird enough having the AI in the entire downstairs and at random locations on the island.

The bedrooms each had a heavy-looking antique double

bed, complete with faded, threadbare coverlets and flattened pillows. And they all shared a similar unpleasant odor of mold or mildew.

Each bedroom also had a private bathroom. Although the bathrooms' proportions were weird, and some fixtures were clearly new while others were antiques. They'd probably needed a lot of renovations back in the day to make the villa a working hotel.

"That's strange," Plum said, returning from the last bathroom.

"What?" Sofia asked, turning back from the doors to the Juliet balcony.

"None of the bathrooms have any towels."

Marlowe flipped the threadbare maroon coverlet on the bed down. "No sheets, either."

"Maybe we're supposed to get them from somewhere," Sofia suggested.

They walked back out into the hall and all the way down to the first room with the small view of the beach. Which, Plum had to admit, was nice.

They pulled their suitcases into their room.

"What do you think about the other influencers?" Sofia asked. "Other than Warix, which . . . noted."

Marlowe shrugged. "They're fine. Hardly famous, though." She held up a hand. "Not that I really care."

"Yeah, but it's strange. Pyre is supposed to be packed with celebrities," Plum agreed.

"Maybe more will come tomorrow," Sofia suggested with a cute *who knows?* expression.

"I like Jude," Plum said. "I think he's sweet."

"Yeah," Sofia agreed. "A bit . . . um . . . clueless, though."

"Maybe that's part of his appeal on YouWow," Plum said. "The whole sweet, harmless, adorable guy appeal."

"I mean, I'm not saying I won't be checking out his channel later," Sofia said with a wink. "Brittlyn's horrible," she continued. "Clearly a troll out to stir up awful people. Sean's okay maybe? I don't know, he seems a bit aggressive." Sofia shook her head. Her small face took on a fierce scowl. "I don't think he even likes Henrietta!"

The ultimate wrongdoing in Sofia's eyes. "And Dude's annoying," Marlowe said. "To say the least."

"What a thing to be famous for." Sofia shook her head again. "'Killing it!' Making people look bad. Just doing the same thing over and over. Doesn't it get old?"

"He sure looked like he was enjoying himself," Marlowe pointed out.

Plum sighed. "Yeah, but then he seemed surprised we were mad."

"Jalen seems nice," Sofia said.

"Yes." Marlowe nodded. She lifted her suitcase onto the bed. "Though I don't really like true-crime stuff."

"It's popular, though." Plum shrugged. "I wonder if he's done other podcasts before. Since he said *Bloody Grounds* was new?"

Sofia just lugged her bag to the corner of the room and sat on the bed. Plum joined her, choosing to sit and watch Marlowe unpack rather than take any of her own stuff out.

Marlowe rolled her eyes at her friends sitting when they could have been unpacking. "What about Cici and Shelley? What do you think of them?"

"Shelley's fine," Plum said, thinking about the horoscope poet and her constantly jangling jewelry.

"I can't wait to check out her stuff," Sofia said earnestly. "When they get the internet figured out, I'm going to follow her."

"You should ask her to do a reading for you," Marlowe suggested.

Sofia was a true believer in astrology. Plum thought it was interesting, but she also hated the way it tried to box her into labels. Like those online personality tests where the results never felt quite right, even when she'd just finished taking them.

"I like Cici, she's so smooth. Like, confident. And I don't know . . ." Plum trailed off.

"Who has a crush now?" Sofia teased.

"No, but I'm just saying," Plum stammered. "Her look, her makeup, like, she clearly has expertise and she knows it. She's got that aura."

"I know what you mean." Marlowe lifted a skirt and jacket out of the suitcase. She draped them across the bed. "It's effortless for her. Like, innate. Some people are like that."

"Exactly," Plum said. "Just like Peach."

"You guys, just because it looks easy doesn't mean it isn't also work," Sofia said. "I think Instagrammers and stuff, even Peach—they're like ducks floating on the water."

The image of peaceful ducks floating along the surface of a tranquil lake appeared in Plum's mind. She nodded.

Sofia continued. "Sure, on the surface, they're serene. No effort at all. Otherworldly, even." Sofia went to the mirror and adjusted her tank top straps. "But under the water, they're paddling like hell."

Marlowe snorted.

"What?" Sofia turned around, smiling. "It's true."

"It's perfect," Marlowe said.

Plum thought about Peach. It was hard to reconcile Sofia's belief that she was paddling like hell. Not that Plum didn't think Peach worked at what she did! Of course she did. Just . . . wasn't it possible she both paddled and glided?

"I don't know about you guys, but I want to go check out that beach," Marlowe said.

"Let's go, let's go!" Sofia chanted, clapping her hands and pointing at the slight fingernail of beach that they could see.

"Okay, but I didn't pack a towel," Plum said. "I assumed this place would actually have stuff."

"Me too, but who cares? *Beach.*" Sofia tugged on Plum's arm.

"We can use our cover-ups to dry off, plus wind and sun," Marlowe suggested.

They changed into their swimsuits and went back downstairs.

As always, Plum tried not to feel like a stick bug standing next to Marlowe's curves. She also tried not to stare too long.

"Have fun!" Warix called from the patio. Two empty bags of chips and a diet cola sat on the ground next to his galaxy-printed shoes. He pointed a fancy camera in their direction.

"Hold up." Plum held out a hand, feeling the smallest bit like maybe Peach felt when she attended events packed with photographers. Of course, Peach always smiled for the cameras.

Sofia had already thrown one arm in the air, posing expansively.

Plum sighed.

"Why not?" Marlowe encouraged. "He can send it to us later."

They huddled close together, smiling. Plum had to duck her head under the serving-plate-wide brim of Marlowe's hat.

Sofia kept one arm high in the air.

"Say 'Pyre!' " Warix said.

"Pyre!" they chorused.

"Gotcha!" Warix smiled that sharky grin.

"Bye!" Sofia called, waving.

"Bye!" he replied, smiling somehow with more teeth.

"I have a boyfriend, by the way," Sofia said, and shot a look at Plum.

"Sad to hear it," Warix replied.

"Oh, for Pete's sake." Marlowe pushed fat black sunglasses

up her nose. She gave the gamer a glare. “She’s still in high school.”

“My bad!” Warix’s voice was as buoyant as his smile. “I went to high school, too.” His voice floated down the path after the girls. “Fairly recently.”

Sofia snorted a laugh. “He *is* kind of cute,” she said as they walked toward the beach.

“So, it’s finally happened.” Marlowe’s voice was dry.

“What?” Sofia asked.

“Seven-year itch,” Marlowe said. “You know, that you’ve been dating Louis too long.”

Sofia gasped and placed the fingers of one hand on her chest. “It’s not that *at all,*” she insisted in wounded tones. “It’s just that I have eyes, you know.”

Marlowe laughed. “If you say so.”

“They’re right here.” Sofia pointed at her eyes, an irritated jab.

“Oh, never mind.”

A strong breeze grabbed at them as they made their way down the cliff path toward the sliver of beach below.

Marlowe had to grab at her wide hat to keep it from blowing away.

“Anyway, it’s true, isn’t it?” Sofia insisted.

Even with the wind blowing and while still holding on to her hat, Marlowe managed to lower her sunglasses, specifically to roll her eyes.

"Okay, I give. Warix is kind of cute. Don't you think so, Plum?"

Marlowe turned that mischievous smile at Plum.

Two feelings burned in Plum's veins. The first: annoyance, because Marlowe knew she liked girls more than boys and, more than that, that Plum was lonely (they couldn't all date foreign exchange students).

But under that was a pain, slick and sharp as an astringent in a wound, because Marlowe thought Warix—well, anyone—was cute.

And, yes, Plum was not in love with her very best friend.

And, yes, it was normal for friends to talk about who they liked or didn't like.

And, yes, it still felt like a cotton ball stroked on a fresh wound.

Except it was the same old wound, wasn't it?

The one she promised herself she didn't actually have. Really.

All she had to do was . . . maybe find someone else to crush on. That might help.

"He's okay, I guess," Plum said, just to get it over with. To move the cotton ball of slight pain and annoyance away. "He's not really my type."

On the path in front of her, Marlowe turned back again, this time lowering her sunglasses to get a better look at Plum. She had a strange expression on her face, though it was hard to make it out, what with the wind whipping Marlowe's hair away and the glamorous but almost completely unsuitable sun hat and the hand hovering there by her cheek, holding the sunglasses.

"Maybe we—" Marlowe started, but then she stumbled, a comical little "Oop!" coming out of her mouth. Sofia turned to catch her, and Plum lunged forward to grab her, and at the exact same moment Marlowe caught herself and stood upright, so the three of them ended up pinballing into each other like the Three Stooges, or another old-timey vaudeville comedy trio that only Marlowe would know. The collision caused them to drop Sofia's cover-up, Marlowe's hat, and Plum's phone, and by the time they'd stopped laughing and picked their things back up, the moment was over. Plum didn't have the heart to chase the cotton-ball moment to ask Marlowe what she had been going to say.

Although she did wonder what "maybe we" could do.

22

The beach was not much, as far as beaches go.

That was actually an understatement. It was narrow, and instead of sand, it was completely covered in rocks. The surf was rough, pounding the shore.

“I guess this is a beach?” Sofia said.

“Is it?” Marlowe asked.

“It’s not sand, though. Don’t beaches have to be sandy?” Sofia asked. She bent and touched the mass of rocks under their feet.

“I guess not,” Marlowe said.

“Don’t usually find those on beaches, either.” Plum pointed to the billowing white FEMA tent. It looked like a squat beehive, a honeycomb network of struts holding it in place even as the strong ocean winds caused it to shiver, as if it were scared of their inevitable disappointment.

They tried going into the water, only to have the rough surf churn up a cloud of small rocks around their feet.

"I can feel the protective layer on my soles being scrubbed off," Plum said.

"It's better than a pedicure!" Sofia suggested, trying to put on a brave face for the whole excursion.

That had been before a bloated puffer fish with damp and rotting spikes had floated by, looking like a dead, fishy beach ball. After that, they all got out of the water quickly.

And after taking some selfies to post later—#PyreFest—they decided to return to the villa.

"The sun's going down, at least," Plum panted, as they climbed back up the path.

"That's pretty," Sofia huffed behind her.

Marlowe lifted her cell phone and snapped another picture as the sun lowered.

"Sorry about this, guys." Plum stopped, blowing a hair out of her eyes. "I guess it's not much of a festival, huh?"

"It's fine, but it is weird there's not more people," Marlowe said.

"Yes, it is really weird," Sofia agreed. "But maybe more people will come tomorrow? Like, you know, being fashionably late and stuff."

"Maybe," Plum agreed.

"I'm more interested in why we haven't actually met a real person from Pyre," Sofia continued.

"They left when they realized they couldn't pull it off," Marlowe said. "They didn't want to be here to face the music."

"Or the lack of it," Plum joked darkly.

"It's a lot of trouble to go to," Sofia said, "for something to turn out so half-assed. It's almost deliberate. I keep expecting someone to jump out, like it was all an elaborate prank."

The thought made goose bumps rise on Plum's arms. Not because she actually thought it was a prank, but at the idea of a deliberate staging of the "festival"—almost as if it had all been planned for some other purpose.

But what?

Plum wasn't sure what exactly was bothering her, but she thought if she could just put her finger on it, she could feel better, reassure herself. Before she could chase the idea, it was gone, evaporating with Marlowe's smile.

"Anyway, we're here now, and I'm sure we'll have fun, even if it's not quite what we thought," Marlowe said. She turned and pointed toward the horizon. The sun abruptly disappeared beneath the ocean, a flash of aquamarine light skipping across the water, a split-second flash of beauty.

"Besides," Marlowe said, "we're not quite what they thought they were getting, either."

The First Night of Pyre Festival

The Island of Little Esau

The First Two Will Die

1

Plum, Sofia, and Marlowe quickly changed out of their swimsuits, then went back downstairs to get to dinner on time.

Everyone but Sean and his pet chicken were already waiting in the conservatory. The three pairs of French doors looked out on the night.

"Hi!" Jalen said as they entered.

Warix was sprawled on an antique sofa with an open laptop resting on his satin track pants. Plum wondered how he kept the laptop from sliding right off. He glared at the screen and didn't stop typing or say hello.

"Hey, hey, the gang's all here," Brittlyn drawled, lifting a heavy crystal highball glass she'd no doubt taken from the antique liquor cart. She winced as she took a sip of the liquid within, so it was either really good or really bad; it was hard to tell with both liquor and Brittlyn's face, Plum decided.

"Well, almost everyone," Shelley said. She was standing behind a long library table that stretched behind one of the high-backed sofas.

"Yeah, where's Sean?" Cici agreed. Her makeup was as perfect as it had looked on the boat. A newly applied, shimmering pink gloss on her lips matched her fingernails.

"Shelley, did you see him?" Jude asked. He had clearly taken the opportunity to get cleaned up. His hair no longer languished from product and sweat. Jude carefully tossed a reinvigorated shock of sun-streaked hair over one eye.

"Wow," Sofia murmured. "That's like . . . movie-level hair."

Jude smiled brightly.

"I'm sure Sean won't miss a meal," Brittlyn said. She winced as she took another sip.

"Just like you wouldn't miss a cocktail, princess?" Sean strode into the lounge, somehow giving the impression, despite the chicken under his arm, that he was part of a security detail for an important politician or a celebrity.

Sean crossed to the ornate bamboo-and-wire birdcage. He pulled open the large-parrot-sized door and shoved a squawking Henrietta inside. "That's better!" Sean crowed.

"Anyone else have any luck with the internet?" Dude plucked his mirrored sunglasses off his head and started twirling them again, a fast gesture of tension.

There was a chorus of nos.

"I could only post on Pyre Signs," Jude said.

"Pretty sure the app is data-strangling everyone else," Warix said, still not looking up from his laptop. "I'm trying to find a work-around."

Plum thought it made a sort of sense, for all other social media apps to be slowed down or stopped altogether. Especially since they were at a festival designed to specifically promote a new social media app.

"Wadsworth? Where do we go for dinner?" Cici asked the air. The makeup YouTuber was wearing a sparkly pink baby-doll dress and shoes with such high heels they'd give Plum altitude sickness. She looked like one of those fashion plate dolls, or a celebrity standing stock-still while their photo was being taken.

"He did say dinner at eight, right?" Marlowe smoothed her wavy sheet of blonde hair over one shoulder. Like Cici and Jude, Marlowe had taken the opportunity to get cleaned up.

Cici turned to Marlowe. "Oh my God! I love your outfit!"

Unlike both Plum and Sofia, who had changed back into their outfits from before the beach, Marlowe had changed into all new clothes. She now wore a long pin-striped pencil skirt and a crisp white blouse. "Thank you!" Marlowe answered.

The virtual butler's voice came over the speaker. "Ladies and gentlemen. If you will open your Pyre Signs app, then open the menu to 'food,' you will be able to make your selection for dinner."

Plum and everyone else started messing with their phones, trying to follow the virtual butler's directions.

"The door along the back wall leads to the dining room," Wadsworth continued. "The food you select will be waiting for you in the kitchen beyond."

"Whoa!" Jude made a comically large amazed expression—his

eyebrows receding under his hair and his mouth hanging open. "That's amazing! Will it be, like, 3D printed or something?"

"The creators of Pyre Signs invite you to experience the next evolution of food," the virtual butler said.

"Something's wrong with my app," Dude said. "There's no choices listed. Just franks and beans."

"Same here," Jalen said.

Plum's own app showed the same thing. The only food available under the menu list was franks and beans.

"Oh man, beanie weenies!" Jude's smile was wide. "How do I order more than one?"

"Simply tap the plus button twice, sir," Wadsworth said.

"Is there anything else other than franks and beans?" Sofia asked.

"One of the first canned foods, shelf-stable baked beans have been a convenience food and pantry staple since the Civil War," Wadsworth droned.

"I'm guessing that's a no," Sofia drawled.

"Great." Brittlyn laughed roughly. "There's a 3D food printer, but only the *beanie weenie* cartridge is loaded."

"That's not the only thing that's loaded," Sean muttered.

Brittlyn held up her cocktail glass to him mockingly.

"Your food is waiting for you in the kitchen, sir, when you're ready," Wadsworth said.

Jude smiled happily. "Everyone else order theirs?"

"Yeah," Plum sighed. She was hungry, after all. But it was yet another unsettling development. No staff in the kitchen. And no variety of food.

"I'll pass, thanks," Sofia said. "I'm vegetarian."

Plum nodded, relieved that Sofia always planned ahead and carried a stash of meal-replacement bars in her suitcase. Although how crappy was it that there were no vegetarian options?

That doubt pulled into Plum's mind again, the unsettling feeling that everything was so bad that it was almost deliberate. It went beyond mere incompetence. Something was off. This wasn't just a failure to organize or plan.

Plum shuddered. The darkness pressed against the windows. It was as if they, all lit up and inside, were onstage, visible to something or someone waiting in the darkness beyond the glass.

The thought felt like an invisible spider crawling across her skin.

Ridiculous.

Plum gave herself a little shake, breaking the spell.

Nothing was dangerous here. Disappointing, yes. Dangerous, no.

Then why couldn't she completely get rid of that vague feeling of unease?

2

The dining room was surprisingly dark and stifling. There were only two narrow windows. They seemed more like archer slits in a fortress than windows.

Since the sun had set, the only light came from the crystal chandelier and the candelabras on both the table and the heavy serving furniture set in intervals around the room.

"Please continue through the door at the back right to access the butler's pantry, and through that, the kitchen."

Wadsworth's voice was becoming ubiquitous. Like the voice of a god. Plum barely registered yet another speaker, this time set on an ornate wooden sideboard.

Jude led the way, following the virtual butler's directions. Plum and her friends trailed the boy into a large, walk-through closet. Mostly empty shelves covered the walls. Two shelves nearest the conservatory held more cans of generic soda and a sleeve of plastic cups.

"This pantry would usually hold all the china," Marlowe

told Plum and Sofia. "Instead of, um, Solo cups and sodas."

"Well, I guess they got rid of most of the valuable stuff ages ago." Sofia shrugged.

They kept walking, through the butler's pantry and down several steps into a small kitchen.

It looked a little like a photograph of a narrow kitchen in an old English cottage. There was a wood-fired wrought iron stove, as well as a more modern walk-in refrigerator and smaller gas-powered stove top. The room was partially subterranean on three sides. One exterior wall was mostly set into the earth, the window above them level with the ground outside. A scrubby bush sent a green-filtered light into the room. Standing beneath the window was a baker's rack crammed with pots and pans. To the left of the window, the wall continued until it met the wall perpendicular to it. The back wall of the kitchen had clearly been excavated out of the surrounding dirt, or it had been landscaped away, because a door led out to a derelict kitchen garden.

In the kitchen, hanging along the wall above a massive butcher block was a row of bells on coiled springs. Marlowe pointed. "Oh! I wonder if those still work? They'd be connected to a button or cord in the bedrooms."

"Where's the food, dude?" Dude asked. He craned his neck around. "I don't see anything that looks like a food printer?"

Wadsworth's voice, smooth and refined, fell from a speaker hung in the corner. "The creators of Pyre Festival, and the app

Pyre Signs, invite you to experience the next innovation in mobile food preparation."

"Okay, but where is it?" Dude crouched down to peer under the butcher block.

Jude stood there smiling, no doubt happily dreaming of his beanie weenies. If he were a dog, he'd be a golden retriever with a super-waggy tail, Plum thought. Maybe that was his entire appeal on his streaming channel. Maybe all he had to do was turn on the camera and start talking about "canned foods I have loved" and his viewers just ate it up.

Warix strolled into the kitchen, apparently having given up on the Wi-Fi. "I don't even smell food. Do you?" Warix asked.

Sean stomped past Dude and started opening cabinets. "I don't believe this." The man stood back. Row after row of canned franks and beans stood inside the cabinet.

Jalen moved to another cabinet and opened it. He pulled out a large saucepan and a can opener.

A *click-click-click* sounded from the gas stove as Sofia turned one of the burner's knobs. A blue spurt of flame ignited.

"Pyre Signs: the nexus of entertainment, art, and media," Wadsworth's voice recited. "Pyre Festival: the apex of art and influence. The summit. The pinnacle. The future is now." The AI butler's voice took on that prescription-commercial drone.

Warix started laughing harshly, curling and twisting into himself, as if it was so funny, if he didn't contort his body, he'd fall to pieces. It was a performative laugh more than a real one. The laugh of a bully on the playground.

"What's so funny?" Sean demanded.

Warix gestured at the stove and the shelves full of canned franks and beans.

"Don't you get it?" Warix asked, that sharky smile taking on a mean twist of *game recognizes game*. "This is all deliberate. We're being trolled."

3

With no other options, they heated up ten cans of franks and beans.

Warix found a fancy cheesecake in the walk-in fridge. It had edible flowers on each precut slice.

They dished out their own bowls of franks and beans and grabbed slices of cheesecake before filing back into the formal dining room.

"Please take a seat," Wadsworth instructed from the speaker on the sideboard.

Plum found places for herself, Sofia, and Marlowe in the center of the vast dining room table.

Jude sat on her left. "Wow, this is fancy," he said, smiling as he pulled out his heavy chair.

"Except for the franks and beans and having to serve ourselves." Shelley sat on the other side of Sofia, stirring her beans in slow circles. Her bright red lipstick accentuated her frown of disgust.

"Yeah, but the room does feel like something from an old-timey movie," Plum agreed.

Brittlyn had already claimed a seat at the head of the table. She poured herself a glass of wine from a crystal decanter she'd brought from the liquor cart.

Jalen sat at the opposite side of the table, with Warix and Dude on either side of Sean, who'd claimed the foot of the table, across from Brittlyn.

"Hey." Sofia leaned forward in her chair, calling down the table to Sean.

"What?" Sean frowned, as if knowing already that he wouldn't like whatever Sofia had to say.

"You have to get some food and water for Henrietta."

Sean rolled his eyes. "Later," he said, his accent making it sound like *lay'ah*.

Sofia leaned out farther over the table, as if she would reach through Sean's refusal with sheer intensity. "No, now. When was the last time she had anything to drink? You've been carrying her around since we got here."

"She'll be fine," Sean grumbled.

Sofia fumed, anger rising from her in a nearly palpable heat.

"Guess that bird's days are numbered," Brittlyn said, her tone mild and amused. "How in the world will you ever explain to your followers what happened to Henrietta?" She picked up her wine, taking a self-satisfied sip, her eyes mockingly wide over the glass rim. "There goes your fame. Goodbye, meal ticket."

Speaking of meals, Plum took a bite of her franks and beans. It was as advertised.

Sean shrugged and rested his forearms on the table, almost in defiance of the fancy table setting. "Well, here's a little trade secret." He leaned forward conspiratorially. His shoulder muscles flared somehow wider. "There's always another chicken."

Sofia gave an audible gasp.

Brittlyn laughed.

Plum didn't get it at first, but then the implication rolled through her brain: *'enry'et-ah* wasn't the first *'enry'et-ah*.

"How many?" Sofia's voice was small.

"Five, maybe six." Sean shrugged. "They're all black silkie hens. That's the name of the stupid breed."

Marlowe turned wide eyes to Plum, then an expression of sympathy to Sofia. Sofia looked like her dog had just died, or something equally tragic.

How long had she followed Chick Magnet?

"Why are you telling us?" Cici asked. "Aren't you taking a risk?"

"Yeah," Dude said. "How do you know we won't rat you out?" The mirrored sunglasses nestled in his spiked, bleached hair glimmered in the dim light from the chandelier.

Sean shrugged. "It's getting where I don't care anymore. Not really. I hate those damn birds."

"But what about your followers?" Jude asked. His tone was reverent on the word *followers*.

"What about your sponsored posts?" Brittlyn asked more pointedly.

"Who would believe you, anyway?" Sean said. "When I have a chicken and no one can say she's not the same hen. It's my word against yours."

"It'd be a flame war," Dude murmured. "Those are always fun."

"They are if you're doing the flaming," Warix said, his mouth full of beans.

Sofia shoved her chair back. "I'm going to take care of that poor creature."

"You shouldn't take on responsibility for a pet if you aren't committed to taking care of it," Shelley scolded him.

"Wouldn't call a chicken a pet, luv," Sean rejoined.

Sofia stalked out of the room.

4

Jude was checking his hair in the reflection of his cup. He glanced over at Cici sitting across from him.

"It tastes better than it looks," Jude reassured her. "I ate this all the time as a kid."

"Oh, okay," Cici said. She picked up her spoon and took a tiny bite.

"I wonder what happened to all that fancy food at the beach?" Jalen asked wistfully.

Marlowe's stomach audibly grumbled at the mention.

"Unfortunately, the meats sat out in the sun too long," Wadsworth reported, answering a question but not the bigger one. Who had provided the fancy food on the beach? And why didn't they have more of that food now, instead of franks and beans?

Warix snorted that ugly laugh again. "Someone's a professional troll. Gotta hand it to them."

"Stop saying that!" Shelley said. "It's like you're trying to scare us." She pushed her red hair back forcefully, her jaw clenched.

Warix took another bite of beans and talked around it. "Well, it's true. So what you gonna do? Stars got any advice?"

Shelley opened her mouth to retort, then closed it, looking away.

Plum felt bad for the astrologist. No doubt it wasn't the first time Shelley had been mocked for her beliefs. Why did men, specifically at the moment Warix, feel the need to belittle her?

It's not like Shelley's account was any less important to her followers than his account was to his followers. It wasn't like playing video games was somehow more noble than writing poems about stars and what they might mean.

They ate, or more accurately some of them ate, and others didn't or just nibbled. Brittlyn wasn't eating at all, more focused on the rapidly emptying wine decanter at her elbow. Sean ate like a man deployed in the field, head down, spoon rapidly scooping food into his mouth.

Sofia returned with one of her meal-replacement bars.

Marlowe and Plum ate their bowls of franks and beans. Food was food, and it had been a long time since lunch.

Jude ate his meal with transparent enjoyment, his happy expression falling only slightly when he scraped the bottom of his plastic bowl.

"This is the weirdest festival I've ever been to." Jalen pulled his slice of cheesecake to the center of his placemat. "Tell the truth: How many of you are planning to leave first thing tomorrow?"

Marlowe leaned over to Plum, murmuring softly, "What do you say? We probably should go with the others. It's getting weirder and weirder."

Plum had to suppress a shiver, at Marlowe's breath or her nearness; the effect was the same. Her heart flip-flopped. She could feel herself blushing and gave a completely fake cough to cover for her blush. "Definitely, we should go," she said.

Plum turned and met Sofia's eyes. Plum asked her friend's opinion about leaving with a quirk of her own eyebrows.

Sofia gave a small, decisive nod of agreement.

Plum inclined her head back. It sucked that the whole endeavor had been so disappointing, but there was no point sticking around hoping for it to get better.

Around the table everyone nodded or murmured their assent that, yes, they would all be leaving the next day.

"Ugh, what a waste," Cici groaned. "I was going to do some great posts from the fest. I thought I'd be able to do some beach and festival makeovers, or that I'd meet body artists here, maybe even make some connections for styling." Cici heaved a sigh at all the possibilities that weren't going to happen.

"That buffet at the beach was a whole other level, though." Warix let the beans fall from his spoon, plopping unappetizing chunks into his bowl.

"It's almost like . . ." Plum began, then shook her head.

"Like what?" Jude asked.

"Almost like the buffet was to make sure we stayed."

There was an uncomfortable silence as they pondered that possibility.

5

Brittlyn was the first to break the unease. "More likely that's the last thing they actually had money for." She poured herself the last of the wine.

Silence reigned for a moment after that.

"This looks nice, at least." Cici followed Jalen's lead, pulling her own plate of cheesecake over. She took a big bite.

"Mmm," she assessed.

They all began eating the dessert, even Sofia and Brittlyn.

"Is it okay if I take a moment to share something with you?" Shelley put down her fork and pushed back her chair. She stood, pulling a slender sheaf of papers from her skirt pocket.

"This afternoon, after the goats, and after realizing how . . . different . . . Pyre Festival was going to be from my previous understanding . . ." Shelley looked around the room, and her normal cadence of voice shifted, becoming more soothing and insubstantial. Like a new age singer in one of those harmonious synthesizer songs, or the voice on a mediation or yoga app.

"Here we go," Warix murmured somewhat darkly. He shoved his chair back and propped both his galaxy Converses on the table.

Shelley didn't seem to hear him. She continued. "I decided to redo my horoscope, and I redid all of them, really, so if you want to tell me your signs, I'm happy to share."

"Ooooh!" Sofia said in appreciation.

Marlowe gave Plum a *why not?* shrug.

"Yes, all the stars align with—" Shelley began.

"Oh, for Pete's sake," Brittlyn interrupted with a laugh. She paused, her fork holding an edible purple flower hovering near her lips.

"I find the star signs to be wildly helpful," Shelley sniffed. "For example, you seem like a fire sign. Are you?"

"What does that even mean?" Brittlyn scoffed. Then she shrugged. "I'm a Sagittarius."

Shelley nodded. "Exactly, here's your poem: 'Like a comet so very bright, yet this day might dim your night.' "

" 'Dim your night'?" Brittlyn scoffed. "What the hell does that mean?"

"Sounds bad," Jude said.

Warix elbowed Jalen. "Sounds *real* bad!" Warix mocked.

"No, not necessarily." Shelley's airy voice hardened somewhat. "The star signs aren't predictors of the future, they're more guidelines, a map—"

"Okay, star child." Brittlyn nodded, an exaggerated *yeah,*

sure expression on her face. "A guide. It gets dark at night. Groundbreaking."

Plum wasn't surprised that Brittlyn, whose entire persona seemed rooted in internalized misogyny and "I'm a tough broad" aggressiveness, would be as bad as the gamer in ridiculing Shelley's "soft" work.

"Go on," Plum encouraged Shelley. "I think it's interesting."

"Me too," Sofia agreed.

Marlowe, who didn't go in for much of that stuff, smiled and gave Shelley an encouraging nod.

"It's not like we have any other entertainment," Warix said.

Brittlyn rolled her eyes to the ceiling. She put the fork holding the flower into her mouth and chewed with enthusiasm.

Even though Plum knew the flowers were edible, she couldn't bring herself to eat hers. It was so pretty.

Brittlyn bit down, grinding her teeth on the flower in her mouth.

"Do me next," Dude volunteered. "I'm a Scorpio."

"Okay." Shelley smiled, turning to Dude. "Your star-sign guide is, 'There once was a Scorpio's web—'"

"Scorpions don't have webs," Warix said.

"'Who alone will tread,'" Shelley continued, forcing the not-quite-rhyming words to sort of sound right. "'Into the dark, then be gone. The Scorpio goes on and on.'"

"Great! I'm like the Energizer Bunny!" Dude laughed. He hung the sunglasses he'd been twirling on the collar of his shirt.

"You don't have to take this seriously," Shelley sniffed. "But if you did, it might help you."

"Go on, Shelley. What's mine?" Jude asked encouragingly.

Shelley turned to Jude with a brighter expression. "Thank you, Jude," she said primly. "When you're open to the cosmic confluence, you can best align your intentions with your path."

"This is a bunch of nonsense," Brittlyn muttered darkly. She cleared her throat.

Plum glanced at Brittlyn. She was flushed, no doubt from drinking all that wine. Sweat popped on Brittlyn's face.

"Jude, you're a Pisces, of course. That's obvious to anyone."

"It's true!" Jude glanced around, his wide blue eyes delighted that Shelley was so skilled.

"Didn't he tell her that on the path up from the boat?" Marlowe murmured to Plum.

Plum nodded, and they tried to stifle their smiles.

"Your weekend horoscope is, 'Little fishy, swim away, there's a better place to go. Little fishy, avoid the small, fishy-fishy, heed the call.' "

Brittlyn gave a laugh that was hoarse. Almost a cough.

Shelley ignored her.

"That's cool!" Jude chirruped. "What does it mean?"

Shelley smiled indulgently. "It's a guide. You carry that in mindfulness, and when the moment arrives, you'll know what to do. You'll be on the lookout for it."

"Thanks, Shelley!" Jude said. "I'll remember."

At the end of the table, Brittlyn coughed another laugh.

"Brittlyn, I am sick of your crap." Shelley whirled to face the mocking woman.

Brittlyn was bright scarlet. She coughed and thumped at her chest.

"What's wrong?" Jude asked her, leaning toward the head of the table.

Brittlyn couldn't reply. Purple juice foamed at her mouth, bubbles spitting as she coughed and clawed at her throat, her eyes bugging out.

"She's choking!" Dude yelled.

But that wasn't right; if she were choking, she wouldn't be able to make those horrid noises, which sounded like a combination of coughing and heaving.

Brittlyn fought to her feet.

"Pound her back!" Warix said.

Jalen jumped out of his chair and rushed to her. He clasped his hands around Brittlyn's middle, putting her in the classic Heimlich position.

Brittlyn coughed worse, juice and flecks of food dribbling out her mouth.

Sofia sat, eyes wide, her hands hovering in front of her face. Marlowe grabbed Plum's arm. Plum reached for her water with the other, thinking that maybe if Brittlyn could drink something, it might help.

But Brittlyn's face was so deeply red it was almost purple.

She fought out of Jalen's grip and grabbed for her wineglass.

Before she could pick it up, she vomited, a stream of mostly liquid and purple flower petals.

Brittlyn dropped the glass, which clattered on the table.

She fell over, eyes rolling back. The dead weight of her lifeless body slumped first in the chair, then slid to the floor.

6

There was a moment of shocked silence as the group stared at the dead woman, collapsed on the floor, in a pool of her own vomit.

"What happened to her?" Sofia gasped, her voice trembling.

"She's dead," Dude replied. He shook his head.

"No way," Jude whispered.

Jalen knelt carefully next to Brittlyn and rolled her onto her back, away from the purple-tinged puddle of bile and wine.

"Is she still breathing?" Cici stood to the side, her hands clutched together near her mouth. Her brown eyes were wide.

Jalen placed two fingers against Brittlyn's neck, checking for a pulse. "No."

"We should do CPR!" Jude said.

"Gross." Warix shook his head, taking a step back from Brittlyn's body.

Jude looked away from Brittlyn, wide eyes sweeping around the group. "Does anyone know CPR?"

Plum wanted to say no. She didn't feel confident, she wasn't sure, and what was the compression number? Ten compressions, then two breaths? More? Less?

"I'm certified," Marlowe said. "But I don't remember it. Is it thirty compressions?"

"I don't remember, either," Sofia replied.

"It's a lot," Plum agreed. The girls all moved together as a unit. Sofia kneeled and adjusted Brittlyn's head.

Plum grabbed a napkin and a water from the table.

Marlowe knelt across from Sofia, adjusting Brittlyn's arms, moving them so they could perform the chest compressions. Whatever number they decided to do.

Plum wet the napkin, swiped it across Brittlyn's mouth, and then looked to Marlowe.

"Do you know how many chest compressions it is?" Marlowe asked, turning to Sean.

Of course. The thought thrummed through Plum like relief. The jacked man no doubt had some kind of tactical training or other special-ops training. He just oozed a prowling, ex-military vibe.

Sean shook his head. "They changed them. I think it's on the higher end?"

Plum's heart sank. She realized she didn't really want to know the correct number of chest compressions; she had simply wanted someone else to take over. But no one was stepping forward.

"Wadsworth?" Plum called to the air. "Can you look it up?"

The virtual butler stayed silent.

"Oh, *now* you've got nothing to say!" Warix shouted at the speaker.

"Does she have one of those food-allergy bracelets?" Cici asked. "I don't even think CPR will help?"

"We've got to try!" Sofia said. She stiffened her arms and nested her fingers over each other. She started pressing down on Brittlyn's chest.

"One, two, three, four," Marlowe began counting.

Plum waited while her two best friends counted up and up.

"Twenty, twenty-one, twenty-two," Marlowe continued.

Plum pinched Brittlyn's nose and leaned forward, waiting for Marlowe and Sofia to come to the moment they'd stop, and then she'd give the two big breaths.

"Wait!" Shelley's voice cracked out like a slap.

They all froze in place, startled.

"What if she was poisoned?"

7

Plum froze, her mouth mere inches from Brittlyn's. If there was poison, could a residue still be on Brittlyn's mouth?

Would it be enough to kill Plum?

"What?" Jude yelped the question.

"I'm just saying." Shelley waved a helpless hand around the group. "We don't know what just happened!"

Marlowe and Sofia stopped their compressions.

"Thirty," Marlowe said.

Seconds pulled away in the air, the moment feeling interminable.

Plum wanted to help; she wanted to do the right thing. But she also didn't want to be poisoned.

"Is there a first aid kit?" Sean yelled the question at Wadsworth's speaker, silent on the sideboard. "It might have one of those mouth guards."

The virtual butler remained mute.

"There's no time!" Sean gritted out, looking as if he was on the verge of a painful decision.

"Oh, for Pete's sake. Move." Dude crouched next to Plum.

Plum moved aside.

Dude pinched Brittlyn's nose, adjusted her neck, and took a deep breath.

He gently placed his mouth over hers and blew out.

Dude lifted slightly, took another deep breath, and then blew it into the woman's mouth.

"Wow, Dude," Jude breathed, in a tone of profound respect. "Killing it."

8

The CPR didn't work. It had been too late, or CPR wasn't enough to fix whatever had choked or poisoned Brittlyn Alexander.

Time slowed to a crawl. But after several minutes passed, the group admitted defeat and stopped. Jalen picked up an unused cloth napkin and covered Brittlyn's face.

"Oh, God," Shelley sobbed. Her bangles chimed as she stumbled back out of the dining room, into the conservatory.

Cici followed Shelley in shocked silence. Marlowe tugged Plum and Sofia after the other girls. The others followed them. The door to the dining room swung heavily closed behind Dude, who was the last to leave.

Brittlyn's body was on the other side of the closed door.

Plum couldn't believe Brittlyn was dead. That a person who had been talking and eating mere moments before was now deceased, lying on the floor.

Dude crossed to one set of French doors and threw them

open onto the island night. He stood just outside the conservatory in the open air, taking deep breaths.

Shelley perched on a settee, crying. Cici moved over to comfort her while skillfully dabbing a tissue under her own dark eyelashes to prevent smudges.

Warix plopped back on the sofa he'd been sitting on earlier. Sean crossed straight to the liquor cart and poured himself another large scotch.

Jude looked mystified as he moved into the room like a frightened puppy, skirting along the edge.

Plum and her friends retreated unconsciously, from both the scene they'd just witnessed and from the others. Plum felt like she was moving underwater, or that she was somehow in slow motion. They stopped in the atrium at the bottom of the arcing staircase.

"That was horrible." Marlowe's voice was shaky.

Sofia clutched Marlowe's hand and nodded wordlessly.

Through the still-open door into the conservatory, the girls saw Jalen hold his phone up to his mouth, almost like a tape recorder. He shook his head, then started talking. His voice was deeply serious.

"Listeners, I'm standing in the desiccated remains of the Mabuz Villa conservatory. There's . . . well, there's no gentle way to put this. There's just been an untimely death. I suspect it might actually be murder, and I witnessed it."

Behind his black glasses, his brown eyes were bright. He

almost seemed lit from within. Even though his voice sounded dire, as he described Brittlyn's death, it was disconcerting to watch him—his voice so at odds with his demeanor.

Surely he wasn't *happy* to get to report on an untimely death. Or even a murder?

Marlowe glanced at Plum, her eyes wide with disbelief. Sofia shook her head slightly.

"We don't know if it was a murder. I don't suppose we could know that," the podcaster continued. "I'm not a coroner. I'm just a true-crime podcast host."

There was now an underlying current of amusement in his tone. Jalen frowned. "Fix that. Edit that out. Try again." He schooled his expression into gravity. "We can't know for certain until there's an investigation. But it's a murder. It has to be—who chokes on cheesecake? And there was no allergy bracelet."

"He's . . ." Marlowe's voice was faint with disbelief. "He's recording for his podcast? *Now?*"

"Looks that way." Sofia was frowning in disgust.

"We came here for Pyre Festival," Jalen reported into his phone. "We found untimely death, perhaps even murder. Ladies and gentlemen, this is a *Bloody Ground*." Jalen frowned. "*Grounds*. Ladies and gentlemen, I find myself . . . on *Bloody Grounds*." Jalen relaxed. "Use one of those," he instructed his phone's recorder.

In the atrium, Marlowe leaned over and whispered urgently. "Do you think Brittlyn was really poisoned?"

"I don't know," Plum whispered back. "It doesn't seem possible!"

If it was poison . . . where had it been? In the cheesecake? Brittlyn hadn't been the only one to eat it. Was it in her drink? Had anyone else eaten the flower on their cheesecake slice?

"It was poison," Sofia murmured. "We should never have come here. It was stupid of us. Greedy. We're paying the price now."

Plum felt gutshot with guilt. It spread through her like a dark dye in water. *She'd* been the one who wanted to come. Who'd wanted to be something more.

"Sofia, that's just your overactive guilt talking," Marlowe whispered harshly. "Besides, you're scaring Plum!" She pointed at Plum.

Plum wasn't scared. Well, not really. She was more shocked. But Marlowe's eyes were saucer-wide.

"Overactive guilt?" Sofia whispered angrily back. "You ever think you could use some? It's guilt 'cause there's a . . . a wrong underneath it! Like how we *lied to our parents*? *Stole Peach's invitation*? Remember that?"

"It was supposed to be a festival!" Marlowe's eyes shimmered. "We just wanted to have some fun!"

Sofia shook her head furiously. Whether she was disgusted at Marlowe, or Marlowe and Plum, or all of them, it didn't matter.

It was Plum's fault.

"Who would kill Brittlyn? If it was . . . was . . . was murder . . ." Plum stammered to her friends. "The police will figure it out. What happened. We . . . we'll leave tomorrow."

Marlowe nodded vigorously. She hugged herself tightly. "On the first boat!"

"If there even *is* a boat," Sofia muttered darkly.

Goose bumps prickled on the back of Plum's neck.

"Wadsworth!" Sean's coarse shout caused Plum to jump. He was still holding his drink. "Oi! Still not talking to us?"

"Hey, guys?" Jude's voice was weak. He had moved back to the door into the dining room.

"Maybe we should post on Pyre Signs?" Shelley suggested from her settee. "Since there's no signal? And no other apps available? We could post on Pyre and ask for the police and stuff?"

"Be my guest," Warix sniped. He pulled his laptop over. "I'm going to try a backdoor hack to lift the data restrictions."

"Oi, maybe you broke Wadsworth with that hacking bollocks." Sean pointed a finger at Warix.

"That's not how any of this works, you wanker." Warix didn't even look up from his computer screen.

Sean frowned menacingly at the gamer.

"And I don't think posting on Pyre Signs is going to help, either," Warix continued. "I'd bet you anything both Wadsworth and Pyre Signs are disabled now."

"What? Why?" Sofia asked.

Warix glanced up at her. His normally snarky expression softened.

"Just a bad feeling, I guess. Wadsworth stopped working *right* when Brittlyn was dying. It's not a coincidence."

Shelley hiccupped and picked up her phone. Next to her, Cici did the same.

"It's stuck on load," Shelley reported. She showed her screen, the fire animation playing on a loop.

"Mine too," Cici said.

"Um, guys." Jude's voice was slightly more firm.

Plum looked back along the conservatory wall. Jude was holding the dining room door open slightly with one hand.

"Didn't someone say they had a phone signal on the dock?" Jalen asked. "Maybe we could call the police from there."

"Guys!" Jude shouted sharply.

All eyes snapped to the YouWow streamer.

Jude lifted a shaky hand. He pointed into the dining room.

The body. He had to be looking at Brittlyn's body.

Finally, Jude turned his eyes back to the room behind him.

"You're not going to like this."

9

They all stood in a tight huddle, even Sean and Warix, filling the doorway to the formal dining room.

"That's . . ." Shelley's voice trailed off.

"That's new," Cici finished.

It was one of the invitations, wasn't it? It was the same heavy card stock with the swirl of oranges and blacks and blues, standing propped open on Brittlyn's stomach.

"Sooooo." Plum drew the word out as her brain sputtered at the inevitable meaning.

"Someone put it there," Jude said. "When we . . . um. Went into the other room."

"It's not an invitation." Marlowe's voice was low and urgent.

"How do you know? Maybe it . . . fell there?" Shelley tipped her head, like she was trying to envision some way the paper just floated down, off the sideboard perhaps, and only accidentally, freakily happened to land tented on Brittlyn's dead body.

They all stood stock-still in the doorway, as if held by a spell.

"*Invitation to Death*," Marlowe pronounced. "Myrna Powell, Henry Harding, Artist's Films, 1936."

"What?" Dude asked.

"The killer left notes on the bodies. That's what that's going to be. Just in case there was any doubt. We're with a killer. There's a killer here. The killer left that note." Her smooth, classic-movie-channel-host voice grew nervous and pressured.

Plum touched Marlowe's arm in reassurance.

"No way," Jude breathed.

"Dude," Dude agreed. He took his sunglasses out of his shirt collar. With his other hand he scrubbed at his bleached hair.

"Only one way to find out," Sean said.

No one moved.

As if they knew once they crossed the threshold, once they picked up the note, everything would change.

"You go get it." Shelley nudged Sean.

"Why me?" Sean asked.

"'Cause you're big and tough?" Cici suggested.

"It's a note, not an MMA fighter," Sean snapped.

"Oh, for the love of Mike," Plum said. "Whoever Mike is."

Plum walked into the room, bent, and picked up the swirled orange, blue, and black card. As if her movement had broken a spell, the others followed her, moving past the threshold and ranging themselves in a line just inside the dining room.

She glanced down, opening the tented fold. The text flowed

out in even lines, indented and stylistically spaced. "It's a poem," Plum told the others.

"Oh!" Shelley sounded slightly pleased. A surprised then dismayed "Oh" followed.

"Go ahead," Sofia urged. "Read it, Plum."

10

Brittlyn wanted to be the woman of the hour;

instead she was choked by those delicate flowers.

Aiming to have absolute influence,

she became the most toxic effluent.

Will you be next? Look around, guess!

Who's the killer—will they confess?

And where was the poison? The flower? That's rich.

Perhaps it was always inside this

horrible excuse for a person.

Plum frowned at the note.

A tittering laugh shivered in the air. Cici stood, both hands hovering over her mouth, trying to hold back the giggle.

"I'm sorry," Cici managed. "It's a joke, right? This is all some practical joke?" She turned, slinging her high ponytail in a parabola as she pivoted, looking in the corners of the room.

"Where are the hidden cameras? You can come out now!"

"It's not a joke," Sofia began gently. "No one dies in prank shows."

"That's supposed to be a poem?" Shelley pointed to the card still in Plum's hand. "It kept breaking meter, and the last line . . ."

"Suddenly you know all about meter?" Dude mocked.

"Just what the hell are you trying to say?" Shelley snapped.

"Dudes," Jalen said, trying to infuse the word with Dude's zen.

"That's my line," Dude said, an only half-joke warning.

At the end of the room nearest the body, Jude put his hand up.

"Yes?" Plum called on him.

"I don't understand the poem. It said she turned in . . . fluent? Like in a foreign language?" Jude looked around for help.

"No," Marlowe said. "*Effluent* means, like . . . industrial waste. Something polluting."

"The killer thinks offing Brittlyn was like cleaning up a toxic dump? Can't say I disagree." Sean crossed his arms high on his chest.

"That's a horrible thing to say!" Shelley turned on him, hands on her hips.

"Well, go on and argue." Sean shrugged. "I'm not a hypocrite, at least."

The room broke into arguing voices, everyone either taking exception to being called a hypocrite or fighting over if that was indeed worse than being an "insufferable boor."

"HELLO?! No one is paying attention to the most important part!" Warix bellowed over the chattering voices.

The room fell silent again as all eyes turned to the gamer.

"The note says *one of us* is the killer!"

Why did he look . . . almost gleeful? Plum wondered. More of that troll-recognizes-troll amusement?

"Dude," Dude said in a disbelieving voice.

Warix held his hands out, palms up. "I'm just repeating what that note said."

Could it be? Not only that Brittlyn had been murdered, but that *one of them* was the one who killed her? Plum felt weak, almost like the muscles that held her up had been robbed of strength by the sudden jolting thought.

"It's worse than that." Marlowe's voice broke the group's shocked silence. "Even if the note is lying, and one of us somehow *isn't the killer* . . ."

"Yeah! It could be lying!" Jude interrupted. His eyes were big with a sudden fervent hope. "It's not one of us!" He fell silent as he realized no one else seemed to share his optimism.

And that they were waiting for Marlowe to finish.

Her blue-green eyes circled the room, lighting on each of the group in turn before finally landing on Sofia, then Plum.

"Everything that has happened on the island is deliberate,"

she said. "No Wi-Fi, no phone signal. No other people here. And no boat. No way off the island."

Jalen's voice was deep and profound. "Listeners." He spoke into his phone. "We're trapped on the island with a serial killer."

11

"It's not a serial killer if there's only one death." Shelley's hands squeezed together. "Right? It's just one?"

"Sure, but how many 'one and done' killers leave notes like that?" Warix scoffed.

"You're saying there'll be more?" Sofia's dark eyes shone.

Warix looked like he was going to say something cutting, then glanced at Sofia's face. He just shrugged.

Plum had to physically stop herself from monitoring her own body, waiting for signs that she, too, had been poisoned. Surely, wherever the poison had been, if anyone else had eaten it, they'd be dead by now.

Plum glanced at Marlowe and Sofia. They both looked fine. Shocked, yes, but otherwise healthy.

"What do we do?" Cici waved her hands, her sparkly pink nails catching the light. "What are we supposed to do now?"

Plum could empathize; she felt similarly confounded. Jalen was holding up his phone slightly—was he recording them?

The rest of the group was still standing in a loose knot, looking down at Brittlyn's cloth-napkin-covered face.

Calling it surreal would be an understatement.

"For starters, don't eat anything that isn't canned," Warix said. "Since we don't know how she got poisoned."

"Yeah, smart." Sean pointed at Warix in agreement. "And what do we do with the body?" Sean asked, his accent making the last word sound like *bo-ee*.

Plum glanced back at the prone form, the faint outline of a nose under the white cloth napkin. To think that just a short time ago, Brittlyn was being mean to them all, and now she was dead.

"I want to leave this room." Shelley's earrings twinkled as she gave a whole-body shiver. "I can still feel her . . . her . . . aura . . ."

"Will you stop that nonsense?" Sean snapped.

"It's *real* and it's *true*, and you should open that thick skull of yours to—" Shelley began.

"Dudes!" Dude yelled, his voice as sharp as a gunshot.

They all silenced and turned to him.

Dude shook his head. "Not helpful, dudes," he scolded Shelley and Sean. He spoke with newfound authority now, Plum thought. What with actually risking death to try to help Brittlyn.

Shelley sniffed and took a few steps away from Sean.

Sean shook his head, a sneer tugging the corner of his mouth.

"We can't just leave her there!" Cici's architecturally perfect eyebrows lifted in disbelief.

"We shouldn't move her," Sofia said at the exact same time.

They turned and blinked at each other.

"On the police shows, you have to leave the crime scene undisturbed," Sofia explained.

"That's when the police are on their way," Warix said. "There's no telling how long we'll wait for rescue."

The word *rescue* hung in the air.

"God, if only someone had a signal!" Jalen said.

Sofia pulled her phone out of her romper pocket. "There's no signal up here, but I sent a text to my sister when we first arrived. Out on the dock."

Dude pointed at Sofia. "I posted my *Killing it!* video of Brittlyn from the dock."

Plum felt a spark of hope. "Yeah!" she said, remembering. "And I did a cross post from the dock when we arrived."

Marlowe cocked a quizzical eyebrow.

Plum gave a little cough and looked down at her feet. "It was the puke bucket," she murmured, not certain how her friend would react.

Marlowe snorted.

Sean took a wide stance, like he was about to storm a beach or run with the football. "We should all go down to the dock with our phones. If we can get a signal, we can call for help from Saint Vitus!"

"Yes!" Jude pumped a fist by his hip. "We'll be saved!"

"It's better than sitting here," Marlowe suggested, turning to her friends.

"Good, let's do that." Cici held up a pink-sparkle-tipped index finger. "To be safe, we should stick together, but not too close on that mountain path!"

"It's not one of us, no way!" Jude said reassuringly. "She said it." He nodded at Marlowe. "The poem's lying."

"I said it *could* be lying," Marlowe said.

Plum looked around the group. If anyone made even a slightly wrong move toward Sofia or Marlowe, Plum would drop them so fast they wouldn't know what hit them.

"If we can just go to the dock and call for help, we can stick together for safety . . . and at a safe distance, until the boat gets here," Marlowe said.

"Good." Sean nodded.

"It's a plan," Dude agreed.

"Listeners, I have a deep sense of foreboding," Jalen dictated into his phone.

"Stow it!" Sean barked at the podcaster.

12

They rushed out through the French doors, past the paved veranda, and onto the pathway that led to the cliff.

Fortunately, the territorial goat from earlier seemed to have bedded down for the night.

The full moon shone spotlight bright, glinting on the silica in the rocks, glittering on the dark ocean before them. They'd been on Little Esau for only about five hours, but it felt like a whole lot longer.

Their group got all the way before they saw it.

An orange glow, bright in the dark. A narrow runway of flames stretched into the ocean.

Plum froze in shock. Sofia and Marlowe bumped into her.

"It's on fire." Plum stated the obvious.

"No!" Sofia wailed. "I was going to call my mom!" She gave a sob, then yelled in anger at the fire blazing in the darkness.

"Impossible!" Sean shouted. He shoved through the others and took off down the cliff path.

Warix stopped next to Sofia. He let out a laugh. "You gotta admire it."

"Admire what?" Shelley asked.

"The game." He turned back toward the house. "Whoever the killer is, they're one step ahead of us. Go ahead and go down there. Try for a signal. It's going to be pointless, but go ahead. I'll be inside." He jerked his thumb back at the villa.

"He's probably right," Cici said. "But I have to see for myself." The petite girl started down the path cautiously, wobbling on her high heels. She looked improbably glamorous, given the setting.

Shelley waited a few moments to give Cici the space she wanted, then also started down the path.

"I guess we should just make sure." Sofia's voice didn't sound hopeful. "That there's no signal on the beach?"

"Maybe if we wade into the water a little bit, we'll get one?" Plum offered, trying to cheer up her friend.

Sofia sighed. "Warix is probably right, but we gotta make sure."

Marlowe nodded.

The three friends trailed the rest of the group, slowly going down the path.

The dock burned brightly in the dark, mocking them.

"Pyre Festival," Jude called back sadly. "Set the night on fire."

13

It was no use.

Everyone but Warix walked around on the stony beach where they had disembarked earlier, holding up their phones. What remained of the dock burned and collapsed into the ocean.

Sofia had started sniffling on their hike down, and it had broken Plum's heart.

It was Plum's fault they were here, stuck on an island in the middle of a wide ocean, with an actual murderer.

It was so far from what she'd planned, it felt like the disco ball inside her had shattered into a thousand pieces, sending jagged, cutting shards into her heart and lungs.

Hearing Sofia cry made it hard to breathe.

"I'm sorry, I'm so sorry," Plum murmured to her two friends.

"Hey." Marlowe's voice was firm yet tired. "It's not like you torched it. "

"I know. But Netflix and ramen for the week back in

Huntington doesn't sound that bad now, does it?" Plum said.

"Stop, Plum." Sofia's voice was raw with frustration.

Plum bit her lip. Her vision got blurry, and she tried to blink back the tears.

Sean paced out into the water, holding up his phone until he was waist-deep. "No luck." He turned and lunged back ashore.

"There's no signal," Jalen said behind Plum.

"We know!" Plum turned around, exasperated.

Jalen gave her an apologetic wince and tilted his phone to indicate that he was, of course, recording. "Whoever has trapped us on this island has set the dock on fire," he pronounced ponderously.

"I'm going to lose it if he keeps doing that," Shelley said. She hugged herself.

"Now what do we do?" Cici asked.

They all turned to Marlowe.

Marlowe realized they were staring at her. "What? I don't know!"

"I thought maybe there's another old movie you might know about," Jude suggested.

"What, an old movie about this?" Marlowe's voice was sarcastic. "Sure, sure. A movie about a fake festival and a group of people stranded on an island with a killer among them? *Oh!*" She turned back to the group with a shocked expression.

"You've thought of one, haven't you?" Plum asked.

"Yes," Marlowe said. "*And Then There Were None,* 20th

Century Fox, 1945. Based on famous mystery novelist Agatha Christie's book."

"Oh! I've seen a remake of that!" Cici said.

They started filing back up the cliff path.

"What does it say we should do?" Sean asked.

"Well, I mean, they almost all die, so I don't think we should use it as a model," Marlowe said. "But one big thing they do that we should do, just to be safe, is search the island."

Plum nodded, grateful that Marlowe's old-movie knowledge was providing them with practical steps they could take.

"Might as well," Sofia said. "It's not like there's gonna be a dance party tonight or anything."

Another spear of guilt stabbed into Plum.

"Sure, but why do we need to do the search?" Dude asked.

"To make sure there's no one else hiding on the island, right?" Jalen asked.

It was hard for Plum to keep from training her eyes on every shadow after Jalen said that. Each lump of rock or squat bush looked like a person, crouching, waiting to strike.

"Yes," Marlowe panted. "To make sure we're the only ones here."

"Better find some flashlights," Plum suggested.

The path was reaching its steepest point. They stopped talking until they crested the cliff and started walking on the moonlit path to the villa.

"Okay, so we'll search the island." Jude nodded. "I won't

be able to sleep now that you've talked about a killer hiding on the island, anyway. We should take weapons 'cause I know we'll meet him!"

"Who?" Sean asked.

"Our killer!" Jude exclaimed.

No one seemed to have the heart to explain to him that the search was necessary, but it wasn't certain they would find someone hiding on the island.

"Okay, so we break into groups of three or more, right? So that not one of us is caught alone with the killer?" Sofia suggested.

"Good idea," Dude agreed.

"She's not the only one who's seen old movies." Sofia jerked a thumb at Marlowe. "That's from *Clue*! It's from the eighties. They're stuck in a mansion, not an island."

"Okay, so we split into groups of three or more." Cici pulled a hand down her long ponytail, smoothing the already perfect strands.

"We'll do the other beach," Marlowe volunteered, gesturing to Plum and Sofia.

"We'll do the grounds and that caretaker shed," Jude yipped. He tossed enthusiastic arms around Dude's and Sean's shoulders, as if it were some kind of game instead of a hunt for a killer.

"And we'll do the villa?" Cici turned to Jalen and Shelley.

Shelley nodded.

"We're going to search the villa, in the hopes of finding a killer," Jalen narrated. "I pray we find them."

"I'll take that as a yes." Cici sighed.

"Better tell Warix what we're doing," Plum suggested. "He said the killer was one step ahead of us. And he was right about there being no signal on the beach down by the dock. Maybe he'll have an idea."

Shelley nodded. "We'll start in the conservatory and get him to join us."

Plum felt a sardonic smile twitch at the edge of her lips. Based on what she'd seen of the gamer, he'd join the group only if he could be in the lead and boss the others around.

But at least they had a plan.

"Okay, check the time. Meet back in the conservatory in an hour. Stay safe. Stay together," Marlowe said.

"We will be safe," Jalen promised into his phone. "Unless the killer has other plans."

14

The moon lit the stone beach, almost as bright as a streetlight.

"Nothing here," Sofia called from the second hive-domed FEMA tent.

"Not here, either," Marlowe yelled. She was crouched low, shining a flashlight into the darkness under a particularly large boulder's overhang.

"Same," Plum called from the opposite side of the small beach. She was moving up and down in a quick search.

Although she knew the beach was small, the search had still gone quicker than she'd expected.

"Let's go back," Plum suggested. "We can help them. Or maybe the others found something."

"You mean someone," Sofia said darkly.

"Yeah," Plum said. "That too."

Sofia led the way back up the path, toward Mabuz Villa.

"I have to say something," Plum said, slowing down. "Before we get back to the conservatory."

"What?" Marlowe asked.

Plum stopped and turned to face her friends.

"I'm sorry." The words weren't big enough for the regret she felt. "It's my fault we're here. I talked you both into coming. It was foolish to start with, and now it's actually dangerous!"

Sofia heaved a sigh. "Listen, while I appreciate the sentiment, and while you're right, I don't have the emotional bandwidth to talk about this right now."

Plum felt a splinter edge into her heart. She'd known it, Sofia *was* upset at her, and she couldn't fix it. "I'm sorry," Plum stammered again.

"Now's not the time," Marlowe said, touching Plum's elbow consolingly.

"I love you anyway, but I *am* mad, and I *do*, you know, blame you, and I'm not ready to try to get over that feeling, even if you're ready to say you're sorry." Sofia lifted her face, closing her eyes to the moonlight.

It was limbo, and Plum felt a new wash of guilt for asking for forgiveness in the middle of the crisis.

Plum was going to make it right. She had to.

Even if she wasn't sure how to do that just yet.

"We have bigger problems right now," Marlowe continued, dropping her hand from Plum's arm.

"Yeah, like trying to figure out how to get off this island and protect ourselves from the killer," Sofia said. She opened her eyes but still didn't look at Plum.

"The first question is, do you guys think we are in any more or any less danger than the others?" Marlowe asked. "Since we're here as impostors? That note seemed pretty pointed toward Brittlyn's actions as an influencer, didn't it?"

Sofia nodded. "It did, and we're nobodies. In a good way."

Plum felt a sinking in her stomach. "We're not nobodies though."

"Jesus, now isn't the time for your ambitions and—" Sofia turned on her in frustration.

Plum took a step back, holding up her hands. "No, I mean, we're nobodies, but we're, um. Somebody-adjacent. And everyone knows it."

Peach.

Marlowe put a hand to her lips in thought.

"Ugh!" Sofia fumed. "The one the invitation was actually for."

"Why are these people targets?" Marlowe murmured. Her blue-green eyes narrowed. "Why Peach? Is there something linking them?"

Plum snorted. "Hardly." She gestured up the path in the direction of the villa. "I'd bet a thousand dollars Peach doesn't know who any of these C-list and no-list 'influencers' even are."

"There has to be a reason. Right? There were only nine people invited. Unless it's just that we're the only ones who showed up?" Sofia asked.

"I don't think so. I mean, that invitation and the website and the app, it was all really convincing," Plum said. She remembered the splashy festival portal, the thrill of finding the same blazing icon in the app store.

Sofia gave her a laser-eye look.

"I'm not just saying that to make myself feel better!" Plum protested. "It was convincing! It wasn't aimed at us, sure, but it made me so certain it was real and was going to be amazing!"

"I thought so, too," Marlowe agreed. "So, what's your point?"

Plum stepped closer to her friends and lowered her voice, even though no one else was around. "My point is, I think there were only nine invitations. Only nine targets."

"And we took Peach's place," Sofia said. Her eyes narrowed.

A cool salt wind pushed at them.

"We're not any safer because we're not Peach," Marlowe concluded.

Plum nodded, feeling a regretful frown tugging at her lips. "In the eyes of the killer, whoever they are, we have to accept that we're every bit as bad as Peach. And, I mean, if the killer is ready to kill nine people . . ."

Her voice trailed off. It was too hard to openly state the dark thought.

Marlowe did it for her.

"What's three more?"

A shiver marched over Plum's skin. The proverbial goose walking on her grave.

The wind gusted again.

"We need to make a plan," Marlowe said. Her voice was firm.

"Yes," Sofia agreed. She stepped closer to Marlowe.

"We can't tell the others that Peach *isn't* coming, for starters," Marlowe said.

Plum stepped closer instinctively, shielding their words from the night and the wind.

"Right, because if one of them is the killer," she began.

"Then they might be waiting for Peach to arrive," Sofia continued. "And us coming, and Peach arriving later—"

"Wasn't part of their plans!" Plum exclaimed softly.

She huddled in closer, feeling a sudden hopefulness.

"Warix said that the killer was at least one step ahead of us," Plum continued. "And that's been true so far."

"But the killer didn't know we'd taken Peach's place. And they don't know we're lying that she's coming later." Marlowe picked up the thought and fleshed it out.

"So for now, let's not tell anyone the truth," Plum said. "We've come this far, so we'll just keep it going."

"In the meantime, we should try to figure out *why* these people. They have to have something in common," Marlowe suggested. "It might help us to figure out which one is the killer."

"Even if the killer lies, the others won't," Sofia said firmly.

Plum looked at her friend in appreciation. Even though Sofia was often anxious, she had a core of steel, that was for sure.

"Tomorrow the boat will come back," Plum said.

"I mean, Wadsworth did say that there'd be another boat in the morning," Sofia said. "Unless the AI's in cahoots with the killer?"

"Whatever *cahoots* is," Plum murmured. "We could keep going around and around on this. I don't know that it's helpful to just go in circles."

"No one really knows the origin of the word *cahoots*," Marlowe interjected. "But it's suspected it's from the French word for *cabin* or *hut*, which morphed into *cohort* and then *cahoots*."

Sofia and Plum stared at her in silence.

"Oh, that was rhetorical, huh?" Marlowe snapped. "Excuse me for knowing the answer."

A snort escaped from Sofia. Then it morphed into a giggle.

"Okay," Plum said, starting to laugh as well. A bit from stress and a bit from how cute Marlowe was when she was mad, with the added ridiculousness of how the wind was tossing her hair around.

"Let's go back and start our investigation," Marlowe grumbled. She turned and stomped up the cliff path.

15

The three friends walked back, lit by the moon high in the night sky. It must have been nearing eleven p.m. or even midnight. Plum didn't want to glance at her cell phone and ruin her night vision to confirm it.

They walked through the open French doors and back into the conservatory. They were apparently the last ones to return from their search.

"The beach is clear," Plum told the others.

"Nothing," Shelley reported. "No one else is here."

"Not on the second floor," Cici reported. "Nothing on the first floor, either."

"I could have told you that," Warix said smugly. He'd apparently declined to join any search party, instead still sitting and clacking away on his computer.

"Look who knows so much," Sean griped, stomping over to the wrought iron liquor cart.

"I don't like to brag. Wait a sec—oh yes I do." Warix smirked.

He propped one of his galaxy-swirl shoes on top of the other, heel on toe, and waggled his feet in punctuation.

"Maybe we should start asking ourselves why you seem to know so much," Shelley said, more annoyed than actually accusatory.

But Warix took the bait anyway. "What's that mean?" he asked, frowning. "You trying to say something, Red?"

Jude moved between the two and held both hands out. His voice was soothing and encouraging at the same time, maybe the exact tone he took when talking to his teen fans on YouWow. "No one suggested it was you," Jude soothed Warix.

"Don't get ahead of yourself," Sean muttered.

"Anyway, no one else is on this damn island." Dude stopped twirling his mirrored sunglasses and propped them on his head.

Plum stared at the older man. He seemed genuinely scared or annoyed, or both. His eyes narrowed in suspicion.

"It's just us," Cici agreed. "We've been all through this house, and you've been all over this rock."

Jalen got out his phone, tapped a few times, and then held it flat below his chin. "We've searched the island to no avail. Now we gather to decide the implications, because if we found no one, it means . . ."

Jalen looked at the others. He made a *come on* gesture with one hand, his eyebrows raised, waiting for any one of them to provide the next line for his podcast.

"That means, if there's no killer hiding on the island . . ."

Jude trailed off like a student trying their best to answer a teacher's extremely difficult question.

"The killer is one of us," Plum finished.

"Not one of us, of course," Sofia murmured to Marlowe and Plum. "Not *us* us."

"No, of course not," Marlowe agreed in a whisper while Plum nodded.

"Indeed, listeners"—Jalen directed his voice toward his phone—"one of the voices you've already heard on our podcast is the killer's. This is *Bloody Grounds*, and it's only just beginning."

"Hey, hold up!" Jude yelped. "I didn't kill anyone!"

"Probably not," Plum conceded. She didn't get much of a chance to continue, because the room erupted in protestations of innocence and accusations, pointing fingers and yells.

"It wasn't me," Jude said in a wounded tone. "I'd never hurt anyone."

"That's what you'd say," Sean snipped.

"Yeah." Cici waved her hands. "Maybe this whole baby-deer routine is an act."

Despite her still-perfect makeup, there was something frantic in her eyes.

Maybe it was in all their eyes.

"Baby deer?" Jude yipped in affront. He darted a sideways glance at the dark window nearby, instinctively checking his reflection.

"I said it!" Cici shouted back.

The room was on the verge of descending into chaos again.

"I know who the killer is!" Shelley announced. She extended her arm, sending rows of bracelets jangling as she pointed at Sean.

"It's *him*!"

16

"What?" Sean's smile was both incredulous and predatory.

"Animal cruelty!" Shelley's voice cracked on the second word. "All the serial killers start with animals!"

Cici spun so fast her ponytail swung out in a high arc. "Exactly! How many Henriettas have there been again?"

Sean shook his head. "There's a big difference between a chicken and a person, ducks."

"See? You even call us *ducks*!" Shelley said.

"You're not making any sense," Sean hissed.

"Don't tell me what I'm doing," Shelley hissed back. Her hazel eyes flashed.

"Dudes," Dude said, in a conciliatory tone. His narrowed eyes still circled the group warily. He held out his hands.

"Yeah," Jude agreed. "Let's not fight."

"Or if you're gonna, make it more interesting at least," Warix drawled.

"That's rich coming from a tosser who tippy-taps on his keyboard all day." Sean poured himself another scotch.

"Some of us are trying to get through the firewall!" Warix shouted.

"Settle down, people," Marlowe called out. "You're falling into a trap they always have in these kinds of movies. Everyone goes at each other's throats. It makes it that much easier for the killer."

"You really think the killer is one of us?" Jude asked anyone, or rather asked everyone.

His transparent hope, and seeming near inability to even ponder that one of them had deliberately poisoned Brittlyn, was painful to witness.

"Dude," Dude said, gently, for them all. "I mean, I don't know, dude."

Of course, they knew; they just couldn't wipe that hope off his face. Like telling a kid about Santa when they hadn't even asked.

Jalen stuck a hand out to Jude's shoulder. His voice was sad, the opposite of his usual polished and unsettlingly eager podcasting voice.

"Yeah, Jude. The killer is one of us."

17

Beyond the dark glass of the conservatory's dome, the moon gleamed. Plum glanced at her cell phone.

Midnight. Was it really only midnight?

Marlowe held up her hands. "The first thing we should do is stick together."

Plum felt a rush of pride and admiration in her best friend as the group turned to her.

"Oh? What old movie has that in it?" Shelley asked.

"All of them," Marlowe said. "Literally every killer-on-the-loose movie ever."

"Right." Cici pointed a baby-doll-pink fingernail at Marlowe in an excited stab of agreement. "Because if we all stick together, even if one of us is the killer, then they won't get a chance to kill the next person."

"Safety in numbers," Sofia agreed.

"The boat will come in the morning," Plum said. "We just have to make it until then."

"You girls are safe." Sean stepped into that wide stance again, arms crossed high on his chest. "I'll protect you."

"Thank you," Cici said sincerely.

"Gee, thanks," Marlowe drawled sarcastically.

Sean tilted his head at her, one eyebrow cocked in a question.

"I mean, thank you? I guess I'll take your word that you're not the killer?" Plum said.

"Other than of countless pet chickens," Sofia sniffed.

"Drop it about the chickens—" Sean began.

"I suggest"—Dude's voice cut over the argument—"that if the goal is that we all stick together, we should all bunk down here for the night."

"Yes," Marlowe agreed. "It's big enough. And all the sofas are here."

"We should also barricade the doors," Jalen said in his narrator's voice.

Plum didn't have to look to confirm that he was recording again.

"We know these drinks are okay, so we can have them if we get thirsty," Plum suggested, pointing to the card table "cocktail reception."

"I can vouch for the scotch on the liquor cart," Sean said.

"And there's a small bathroom right here." Cici crossed to a door set in the wall near the dining room. She opened it, checking that the room was empty, even though they all knew it was from the previous search. She left the door cracked open and the light on.

"And there's one more thing we have to talk about," Plum said.

Marlowe gave Plum an encouraging nod.

"We have to talk about why we're all targets."

18

"What the hell, man?" Dude asked. "I didn't do anything wrong."

Shelley snorted. "Besides film people without their consent, invading their privacy and compromising their dignity as your entire *thing*?"

"Nothing wrong with that. It's funny," Dude replied.

"Not to put too fine a point on it, luv," Sean interjected, "but I ain't a victim."

Sofia waved a hand in exasperation. "Yes, yes, then why were you invited to be one? Why were each of us targeted? What did we each do wrong?"

"It's just a chicken!" Sean gestured with the hand holding his highball glass, sloshing a bit of his scotch over the rim. "How many times do I have to say it? People *eat* chickens!"

"I've got nothing to hide," Warix interrupted. "If we had the internet, I'd even show you my best-of clips."

"You're a gamer, so I don't really know what about that

makes you a target," Cici started. "I don't know much about gaming."

Warix shrugged. That sharky smile quirked at Cici. "That's okay, babe. I don't know anything about makeup."

It sounded like the insult it was meant to be.

Plum imagined she could hear the grinding of Cici's teeth as her jaw squeezed tight.

Marlowe caught Plum's gaze, then rolled her eyes upward. Plum tightened the tendons in her neck, making a quick gag-face.

"Gamers get in a lot of fights," Warix continued. "Like personally. It can get ugly, but that's what makes it so fun. I'm basically famous for going in and wrecking shit. *Leeroy Jenkins!*–style. And then I mock the people who get mad. I don't know how I get other gamers to ever believe me that I'm going to play nice this time or be part of the team. But they do. Or they're building their own followers, so they take the hit for the likes. It's just part of a larger game."

Plum tried not to feel a self-satisfied surge at the dismayed expression on Sofia's face. She and Marlowe had seen Warix for who he was—now Sofia was finally seeing it, too.

"But there's no law against being a jackhole, so who cares?" Warix reclined even farther, putting his feet up again. "Right, Dude? It's just comedy."

Dude looked slightly miffed to be categorized with Warix, then shrugged. "If it makes people laugh, it's not all bad, is it?"

Warix took one hand off the back of his head and pointed at Dude. "Exactly, exactly."

"Okay, for the sake of being quick and trying to have the least drama," Plum said, "how about let's not be defensive about why we might be here? Just tell us your best guess about *why*. Who you might have pissed off online or whatever. Maybe we can find commonalities? And that might help us figure out who's doing this."

Marlowe nodded and touched Plum's arm in approval. "Brittlyn was considered a bad influence because of her gun-troll stuff." Marlowe held up a finger, then a second one. "Warix is probably here because he's a game troll."

Warix shrugged and nodded.

Marlowe held up a third finger.

"Dude, you know why. Third verse, same as the first."

Dude shook his head in vague disagreement but didn't argue.

Marlowe held up a fourth finger. "Sean, does anyone know about the other Henriettas? Or is there something else you can think of?"

Sean frowned and shook his head. "I've not done anything wrong. And, yeah, I get animal-rights activists sometimes, worried that Henrietta doesn't like her carrier and whatnot. It's all tosh."

Marlowe turned to Jalen. "And I'm guessing your podcast is, um . . . how shall I say this?"

Jalen held up a hand. "It's okay. I've already heard it. It's in poor taste, ghoulish, profiting off the tragedies of other people, exploitative, yada yada yada." Jalen made a beak shape out of his fingers and mimicked talking with it. "But—before *Bloody Grounds* . . . I had a YouTube show, *Epic Fail*. We played a bunch of viral videos, made fun of them. Stuff like that."

Plum stared at the podcaster. He was starting to seem like the inverse of Warix. The gamer was exactly what he'd seemed to be from the start. But Jalen didn't look like the kind of person who would host a ghoulish podcast or a mean YouTube show.

And yet, here he was, openly admitting it. So didn't that absolve him of suspicion for the murders, at least?

"Sounds like there's lots of possible people who wanted revenge on you, dude," Dude said, his voice dry. "Guess I don't look so bad now, huh?"

"So that leaves Cici, Shelley, and Jude," Marlowe said.

Cici cocked a hip in defiance. "Aren't you forgetting someone?" she asked.

Plum glanced at Sofia and Marlowe. Then she stepped forward.

"No," Plum answered, looking down. "I'll tell you why we're here. Why I've made my two best friends targets as much as myself."

19

Plum took a deep breath.

"I'm here—we're here—because I wanted to do something fun." Plum made herself look up from the floor even though it was where her eyes wanted to stay. "I wanted to be important. Like my sister, Peach. I wanted to see what it felt like to be her." Plum sighed. "If I'm being completely honest, I wanted to pretend to be her. You know. For a change."

"What's wrong with the way you are?" Marlowe asked gently.

"There's nothing more valuable than being yourself!" Jude exclaimed. He hopped on one foot and pumped a fist. "Be authentic! That's what I always tell my fans!"

Plum smiled at his attempt to cheer her up and didn't call out the fact that he seemed to vacillate between personalities when he was "on" versus when he was "off."

"Thanks, Jude." Plum turned to Marlowe. "And, yeah, I know I'm supposed to be happy with who I am. It's just it's hard when you feel like you're left out of everything. And you go online, and there's your sister . . ." Plum didn't know how to express it. The feeling of looking in through a window. Of being invisible. The empty feeling inside, even as she could scroll and scroll and feast her eyes on the life Peach had created for herself.

Away from her.

"And I miss her, too," Plum went on, glossing over the hardest part. "She doesn't miss me though. Why should she?" It was hard to keep the bitterness out of her voice.

"Oh, Plum, I'm sure she misses you!" Sofia said. She put a hand on Plum's arm.

Plum felt a surge of reassurance, but she still mumbled, "Sure doesn't act like it."

"Well, when she arrives, I bet it'll be tomorrow, you can talk it out with her!" Cici said firmly. The petite YouTuber walked over, followed by Shelley.

"Yeah," Shelley said. "You can tell her how you feel! She's an Aries, right? Tomorrow is a good day to make a new start for Aries. And then we can all leave on the boat!"

"I . . . I don't know," Plum stammered, trying to avoid actually lying, since she and her friends had agreed that they wouldn't reveal that Peach wasn't actually going to be joining them on the island.

"No, we've got your back!" Jude walked over to join the group of girls standing in a loose circle around Plum.

"Um, thanks, but I don't know if—" Plum began. "Anyway,

the point is, my friends shouldn't be here. They don't deserve any of this. So, um. Yeah. I guess pressuring them into coming with me is officially the worst thing I've ever done."

"Besides start a fight in eighth grade and get sent to the principal's office?" Sofia wore a slight smile. Plum felt the knot of tension that Sofia was mad at her loosen slightly with the memory and the smile.

"Nah, that doesn't count," Plum said. "I'd do that all over again."

Sofia laughed and bumped into Plum's side. "Dork."

Plum bumped her hip back into Sofia's. "Goober."

"I've never been sent to the principal's office," Marlowe interjected in a slightly haughty tone.

Since she'd been feeling it herself, Plum had no trouble spotting the tone underneath. Marlowe was jealous. She felt left out.

Plum lunged over and drew Marlowe into a one-armed hug.

"Aw, poor Lowe!" she cooed. "If we get out of this—no, *when* we get out of this—we'll make that a goal when we get back home."

Sofia snorted. Her sharp chin jutted out as she pursed her lips in a teasing *yeah, sure* pout. "Don't act like such a badass, Plum," she said. "I still remember you freaking out about getting grounded."

"Well, so were you," Plum said.

"What'd you do?" Jude asked curiously. "I got sent to the

principal's office once for leaving campus without a pass. But it was to do a fan meet at the mall, so it was worth it."

"Oh yeah?" Cici asked. "How many fans?"

"Five!" Jude chirped. "We got pretzels and walked around! It was great!"

"Well, this one here," Sofia said, jerking a thumb at Plum, "got into a fight with two girls who were giving me a hard time."

Plum actually felt herself standing taller. Yeah, sometimes she did things right. It could happen.

"I dumped my water bottle on that one girl's head," Plum said, laughing. "She was being such a bigot, trying to cause trouble."

"You dumped water on her head? That's so cool!" Jude exclaimed, swooping his hand toward his crotch.

"Yeah, it was, actually." Sofia gave Plum a soft smile. "Although I didn't need any help. For the record."

"Yeah, you're both regular badasses," Marlowe teased them.

Plum felt the warmth from her two best friends, and even a reflected warmth beyond that, as Cici, Shelley, and Jude were also smiling.

Then she looked out to the remaining group, watching them.

Sean and Jalen looked bored.

Warix looked annoyed. "Are they going to start braiding each other's hair now?" he asked. "'Cause if so, note to the killer"—he looked around the room, open pleading in his eyes—"go ahead and kill me now. Seriously."

20

"I guess it's my turn," Cici said, taking a deep breath and turning to face the others. "I've been thinking about it a lot, and I'm pretty sure I know why I'm here." She lifted her chin. "It's because I make people feel bad about themselves."

Across the room, Warix guffawed and sprayed a mouthful of Diet Hillside Dew onto the conservatory floor.

Sofia glared at him.

"Sorry," Warix said. He smiled that sharky smile as he wiped his chin. "Do go on, please."

Cici didn't acknowledge him. "I get a lot of haters. Men who tell me I'm so beautiful, but then when I don't respond or when I don't respond the way they want, they cuss me out. Tell me I'm being stuck-up or whatever." Her tan shoulders bobbed once, dismissing the mean comments. "That's part of being a woman online, unfortunately. Worse than that though are all the girls who come at me, telling me I'm beautiful."

"'Don't hate me because I'm beautiful'?" Sean mocked.

Plum could tell he was quoting something, but she didn't know what. "Really? That's what you think you've done wrong? Be pretty?"

"No, it's not that." Cici gave him a dirty look, then got more serious. "They hate themselves. They'll start out saying, 'You're so beautiful, oh, I love your hair,' or 'Your eyes are so pretty.' Stuff like that." Cici sighed and looked at her hands. "Then they'll just start talking about everything they hate about themselves. It's like my videos feed self-loathing. They'll say they're ugly or they're fat."

"I mean, they probably are," Warix said consolingly.

Marlowe whirled on him. "Shut up, you pig!"

Cici just ignored him. She carefully swiped a pink fingernail under her eyes, removing gathering tears before they could wreak havoc on her mascara. "I love makeup. I do. I love doing tutorials and videos. But sometimes I think my videos are doing more harm than good."

"Huh," Sofia said. There was an assessing look in her eyes.

"I didn't make the world, I just live in it. But sometimes I think I should be doing a better job moving through it. You know? And I should do a better job talking about it. About body positivity and just . . . everything." Her big brown eyes circled the smaller, more supportive group.

"Wow," Jude said sincerely. He gave his head a little shake, flopping his hair over his eyes in a very practiced way. "I don't understand a lot of what you just said," Jude admitted. "But it sounded really important." He brought his hands up and pressed his fingertips together into a vague prayer-hands shape. "Thank you for that, for your truth and stuff."

There was a mocking snort behind them.

No one turned to see who it was.

It sounded like Dude. Or Warix.

Or Sean.

"Fine, okay, I'll go." Shelley put both hands on her hips and spoke in a rush. "I'm probably here because I stole a bunch of my posts from what I thought was a defunct website, okay? I'm not proud of it."

"Wait, wait." Sean moved rapidly in spite of all the scotch he'd been drinking. "You're telling me that you, Little Miss True Belief, *stole* your BS?"

"No! Well, yes. Some, okay? I'm sorry I did it. I paid some fees. It's done and in the past now."

"Well, maybe not, if that's why you're here." Sean drained his glass.

"In my defense, if you'd like to know, I found this very obscure old website. It was so cool, mainly about Santeria—but the website was clearly over. I mean, you should have seen it, it was practically an antique, okay? Such bad design, too much text, horrible fonts, the whole deal."

Marlowe glanced at Plum, her eyebrows lowered over a frown. Plum knew why: it was Shelley's casual mention of Santeria, and the inevitable conclusion that Shelley had helped herself, cherry-picking from a tradition that wasn't her birthright, likely without sensitivity or respect.

Worse, that she had actually profited off it.

"Sure, but you didn't steal the website design," Warix said from the sofa.

Shelley turned. "I'm just saying I thought no one would be hurt!"

"No, you thought no one would notice," Cici said softly.

Shelley looked dismayed. "Yeah, okay, that's right. The woman whose website it was, I found out she was dead. So I didn't think it was a big deal. But her daughter found my blog, and . . . it got ugly." She shook her head. "I tried to apologize! And I told her I'd pay for the use of her mom's writings—and I totally did! But it wasn't enough. The daughter, she said some really nasty things about me."

"Like what?" Jalen asked, moving closer and looking like he was trying to be inconspicuous with his cell phone placement.

"She said I shouldn't use any of Santeria, not just her mother's writings. Because I wasn't serious about it. Like that was her call to make! She said that I was appropriating the work of her mother, the traditions of her ancestors, and was being disrespectful, and she wouldn't listen to me about what I intended, and anyway. It was a real pain in the ass."

Plum felt like her neck might get a cramp because she kept having to tip her head to make sure she was hearing Shelley correctly. Shelley, who didn't actually sound sorry about what she did but more affronted that anyone had called her to account.

"Gross," Marlowe said flatly.

"So . . ." Shelley announced into the uncomfortable silence of everyone looking at her. "That was a few months ago, and it's the worst thing that's ever happened to me." She gave a little sniff. "Until now. Like you're all so pure!" She stomped away and flopped down on a settee. "Does anyone else have anything to share?" Shelley asked, her voice high, shivery with tension, eager for anyone else to admit their fault next.

Jude's hand edged into the air. "Um." His voice was nervous. "I'm the only one who hasn't gone."

"Go on, kid," Dude encouraged.

Jude couldn't take his eyes off the marble tiles between his feet. "You're going to hate me," he whispered. A shimmering of bright tears gathered in his blue eyes. "It's so bad." Jude nearly twisted his hands together. "You don't know, okay? It's the worst thing."

"It's okay," Plum said gently. "We've all done something wrong." There didn't appear to be a common thread among them, but maybe Jude's transgression would be the one that linked them together. She had to find out. If there was even the slightest chance it could save them. Could save Sofia. And Marlowe.

"Ohhhhkaaaaay," Jude breathed. "King—my manager—was going to drop me as a client, so . . . I bought some of my followers."

21

If their eyelids could all make noise, Plum thought, like if they all made a single piano plink—then the silence that greeted Jude's statement would have been filled with a bunch of piano notes.

"Yeah, I mean, that's okay, man," Dude said bracingly. He squeezed the teen's shoulder.

"No, it's not!" Jude wailed. Tears openly poured down his face. "It's a lie!"

"It is, but it's not a big one," Cici reassured him.

Jude sniffled. "I'm such a fraud!"

Marlowe gave Plum and Sofia a look and tipped her head. The three friends retreated slightly as Cici and Dude kept trying to console Jude.

Marlowe spoke in a low hush. "Here's what I heard. Everyone here falls into two groups: opportunists and liars. Some people—like us, sadly—are in both groups."

"So the link is . . . lying?" Sofia asked.

Marlowe nodded. "So far. It doesn't seem like enough. Lots of people lie. Lots of people are opportunists."

"There has to be more," Plum agreed. "This is just the starting point."

Marlowe held up three fingers. "Three trolls: Warix, Brittlyn, Dude."

Sofia held up three fingers of her own. "Three liars: Sean, Shelley, and Jude."

"Cici might count as a liar," Plum murmured. "To the killer, at least. I'm not saying I agree, just the deception of makeup, maybe. 'Lying'—you know. 'You don't look like your picture.' "

Marlowe nodded. "Which leaves Jalen out, but he's a monster, right? If he's a ghoul? So maybe that's the troll pile."

Plum nodded. "Where would Peach be? If she were here?"

Marlowe shrugged. "Your guess is as good as mine."

Plum sighed. It hurt in that same old familiar way. That she didn't know enough about Peach's life to know what possible wrong could have brought her into a killer's plan. "I don't know," Plum admitted. "But I've got one more for you."

She held up a finger and turned it on herself. "I'm both. A monster, because I was so desperate to be somebody. And a liar. Pretending that Peach was coming. Or that I ever had anything to do with her. Reflected glory like sucking on rotten marrow." Plum couldn't take her gaze off her feet. "I'm such a jerk. I'm going to get us all killed."

22

The conservatory was mostly dark, the only light coming from the full moon filtering through the tinted glass dome and from the cracked-open bathroom door. The gentle shushing of faraway waves and the whistle of wind outside were the only sounds.

The group of ten Pyre Festival guests were ranged around the room, trying to sleep.

All together. For safety. In the same room with a killer.

If they only knew who it was.

"This is so surreal," Marlowe whispered.

"Try to get some sleep," Plum whispered back. Even as her eyes were wide open and every inch of skin along her right side was achingly aware of Marlowe's warmth.

"You try," Sofia huffed in annoyance. "I'm going to keep watch."

They were nestled together on the higher level of the tiered conservatory floor so their "backs could be against a wall," as Marlowe had suggested.

After finally reassuring Jude that no one really cared, even if he had bought all his followers, the group decided to go from room to room in Mabuz Villa, conducting a final search for the killer—if it wasn't one of them—and retrieving flat pillows and threadbare blankets from the beds.

Shelley had screamed a few times—whenever they opened a door, basically. But at last they had collected what they needed and returned to the conservatory, where they set up their makeshift pallets for the night.

Jude was the next closest to their huddle, farther along the wall.

Cici and Shelley appeared to have formed an alliance of sorts; they'd pushed two of the fainting couches together near the floor-to-ceiling windows.

Jalen and Warix were in opposite corners along the same wall, with the door to the small bathroom between them.

Sean had defiantly refused a blanket and taken only a round pillow from one of the armchairs. He was the only one bedded down in the sunken portion in the middle of the room, near the large globe centerpiece and the liquor cart.

Plum didn't suppose you'd need a blanket if you'd been drinking as heavily as the reluctant chicken owner had.

Speaking of which—or of whom?—Plum didn't know which pronoun to use, but whichever one it was, Henrietta still snoozed in the aviary with her head under one wing.

Dude had set up his bed on the floor beside more windows,

down below the French doors that separated his area from Shelley and Cici's couches.

"This is a nightmare," Sofia whispered.

"I'm sorry I got us all into this," Plum whispered back.

"It's not your fault!" Marlowe muttered emphatically.

"Still not ready!" Sofia whispered with equal emphasis at the exact same time.

Sean's normal speaking voice cracked into the air like a slap. "So, it's a slumber party is it, ducks? Gonna whisper secrets all night long?"

The reprimand scrubbed at Plum like the abrading bristles of a wire brush.

"Yeah, is that all right with you, buddy?" Marlowe sniped back. "Just have another nightcap, eh?"

"Hey, let's not fight," Jude began.

"Shut up already, everyone!" Dude yelled over their voices. "I swear to God, the next person who talks I will personally kill myself."

There was a moment of silence.

"You'll kill *them* yourself, or you'll kill *yourself*?" Jalen asked as he plugged his cell phone into its charger.

Shelley snorted a laugh from her fainting couch by the window.

"Loooooosers!" Warix called, laughing raucously.

"Shut up! Shut up, SHUT! UP!" Dude screamed. He was suddenly standing on his pallet, his fists balled tight.

"Whoa, pressure getting to you, buddy?" Warix taunted. He looked comfortable in his corner.

"Could you all be quiet, please?" Cici yelled from her couch.

"Need your beauty sleep, huh?" Sean laughed more than asked.

"You're drunk," Cici stated, for all of them.

"Is that against the law now?" Sean demanded.

"We have to get Henrietta away from him," Sofia whispered to her friends urgently. "Tomorrow. Before he gets on the boat. Before he kills her, too."

"All right," Sean called to the room. "Listen up, kids! I'll be quiet now, I promise!"

"Damn right you wi—" Dude snapped, but he didn't get a chance to finish the sentence. A loud pop—or rather a series of pops—went off from the center of the room.

Cici shrieked.

Shelley yelped in pain.

The acrid scent of gunpowder, like after Fourth of July fireworks, filled Plum's nostrils.

There was a rumble, a huge scrape, and a percussive bang, so intense the floor shook.

Then there was a deep scream, cut horribly short by gurgling.

And then silence.

23

The lights flicked on. Jude stood by the wall switch, his hand still resting on it.

A thin haze of smoke hovered against the domed ceiling of the conservatory.

The center column was missing. Or at least the arrow-speared metal globe statue atop it was missing.

Cici let out a piercing scream.

Plum, Sofia, and Marlowe fought out of their blankets and rushed around the edge of the room until they reached the fainting couches.

Shelley was holding her upper arm, a small stream of blood trickling through her fingers.

Cici wasn't looking at her bunkmate. Instead her wide brown eyes were fixed on the center of the room.

"You okay?" Jude asked Shelley as he skidded to a stop behind Plum and her friends.

"I'm okay." Shelley winced.

Plum turned, following Cici's gaze.

In the center of the room, near the liquor cart, Sean Bentham was trapped.

The central statue of the conservatory, the large metalwork globe, had toppled.

The arrow that bisected the globe had speared Sean in the chest, going clear through him and bending against the marble floor underneath.

Blood was everywhere.

Sean was slumped forward, as if he'd been in the act of sitting up when the spear pierced his chest.

With the open bands of the metal-stripped globe around his torso, it looked like, well, it sort of looked like—

Plum wanted to laugh in disbelief but ruthlessly crushed the instinct, knowing it wouldn't be exactly healthy to start laughing right now.

But it looked—

"He's in a cage," Jude said.

At least Jude wasn't laughing. "Is it just me?" Jude turned wide blue eyes to the three friends. "Doesn't it look kind of like he's in a cage?"

"Yes," Sofia agreed, her voice soft with either disbelief or horror.

Or both.

Silence reigned as they all considered the implication of Jude's observation.

"He's in a cage because . . . because of—" Sofia couldn't finish the sentence.

But they all finished the thought in their heads, and as one, the group turned to look at the birdcage, where the floof-headed hen slept.

A white piece of paper stood out in stark contrast to the bamboo and wire, affixed to the door.

"That's new," Jude said, his voice conversational. Deceptively calm.

24

Jude crossed to the cage and gently took the paper from the front of it.

"It's a poem," he reported. He glanced up at the group and although it wasn't the right timing for this sort of observation, Plum couldn't help but think how very male-modelish he looked, with his perfect hair swoop, chin lowered, and vibrant eyes glancing out at them.

Plum realized that woolgathering about the relative attractiveness of other possible victims or killers in this scenario was just as bad as an unhinged laugh, so she forced herself to focus.

"What's it say?" Shelley asked.

Jude cleared his throat.

He traveled the world, he went round and then some,

just him and his girls, the chickens, a sixsome.

Listen up, dummies, it's not about the birds,

just that this guy was the biggest of turds.

You all are found guilty. Your sentence is death,

and when you lie lifeless, only then will I rest.

Was the influence worth it? Do you regret it one bit?

Or are you, like Sean, a complete piece of

human waste?

Nah, I won't rest. I'll keep killing some more.

It's just so fun, keeping the score.

"Huh," Jude said. His lips moved silently as he reread the lines to himself. "I think he meant *shit*—there. In the middle."

"Um, duh," Dude said, but his tone was tired more than harsh.

"Can I say he's a serial killer now? Huh? Can I?" Jalen nearly shouted. Behind his glasses, his eyes were bright with the edge of panic. "We did everything right, and still another one of us got picked off—WHAM!" He clapped his hands together percussively.

"How did it happen, anyway?" Shelley timidly asked. She was still clutching her arm where a piece of flying rock or metal had cut her.

"Hey, let's help you with that," Sofia offered first.

For a few moments, the survivors were mostly absorbed with making a bandage from one of Shelley's fluttering scarves, mentioning the necessity of actually finding that first aid kit, and splashing seltzer water across the shallow cut.

Cici helped Shelley tie the bandage. There was a slight

smudge of grime on one cheek, like the makeup YouTuber was on the set of an action movie and had been artfully "mussed up" while still needing to look essentially perfect.

Plum shook herself to stop the distracting, frankly unhelpful observations.

"This doesn't make any sense." Jalen paced in front of the birdcage. "It's a bad reason to kill a person!" His voice rose to a shout. "Nothing about this makes sense!"

"That's because it *doesn't* make sense!" Warix shouted back.

Jalen stopped abruptly, almost like Warix's shout had slapped him. "Right," he said. "Right, right. Serial killers aren't normal people. Right."

"What caused it to fall? Do you know?" Cici asked.

"I don't know. It happened right after the second set of explosions," Shelley replied.

Plum rocked back on her heels. "Oh," she said in sudden understanding.

The others glanced back at her for an explanation.

"Just that's how it fell," Plum explained. She pointed to the now-empty plinth in the center of the conservatory. "Those pops were some kind of dynamite or squibs or whatever you call it."

Warix leaped up onto the raised edge of the planter and plowed through the dead plants until he reached the column.

"Be careful!" Sofia called. "What if one of them didn't go off?"

Warix shook his head. "Then our killer will have to work fast to post another poem," he said.

"Speaking of that, how could that poem have been put on the cage?" Plum asked.

"Who was closest to it?" Cici asked.

"We were," Marlowe said calmly. "Us and Jude."

"We didn't do this!" Plum gestured at herself and her friends.

"I didn't either!" Jude said emphatically, shaking his head, then giving it that practiced toss that tousled his pompadour just right.

Plum wanted to believe him. The thing was, she wanted to believe every other person as they stated their denials that they hadn't done it, either.

"But anyone could have done it," Jalen announced.

Warix held up a small wired box. One edge of the plastic was deformed, blasted outward.

"Remote-controlled," Warix announced, holding out the tape-wrapped wires. "Under the globe, so we couldn't see it or the explosives, and ringed all around the bottom of the edge. Plus, I bet the bolts were cut or loosened."

Marlowe nodded and moved into the center of the room, next to Jalen. In her pencil skirt and pin-tucked blouse, she looked like an old-timey detective or girl Friday, there to wisecrack about the crime. "Anyone could have set it off," she agreed. "Our killer is smart. They would have ditched the remote immediately."

"They probably set it off when they put up the poem," Shelley offered. "There was so much chaos, and it was dark and smoky—any one of us had enough time to do it unobserved."

"Our killer planned for all this," Marlowe said.

"I wish you wouldn't call them that." Plum's head was swimming. Maybe it was the lingering scent of gunpowder. Maybe it was the sight of her gorgeous best friend standing casually where moments before an actual explosion had gone off. Maybe it was the franks and beans backing up on her. But Plum felt like she was going to be sick.

"Call who what?" Marlowe asked solicitously, frowning at Plum in concern.

Plum closed her eyes, concentrated on her breathing. "Call them 'our killer,'" she said. "You make it sound like we're all next."

25

"I understand that it could be any one of us." Jude frowned, his eyebrows pulling together in an expression of confusion. "And I understand that the dynamite stuff was remote-controlled," he continued. "But what I don't get is, how could the killer be sure they would be killing Sean?"

Plum and her friends turned to look behind them. Sean was still there, impaled within the center of the metal-banded globe. His body sagged forward into the spear heavily.

"We should do something about that," Jalen said. "Cover him, at least."

"Knock yerself out," Warix said mockingly, not moving to help.

"Good question, Jude," Shelley agreed, ignoring Warix. "How did the killer make sure that Sean would be the one to get the . . . um . . . the spear?"

"Right, what if I had set up my bed there?" Jalen asked. Then he pointed to Shelley. "Or you?" He turned to point a finger at Plum and Sofia. "Or you girls?"

"Maybe the killer didn't care," Cici suggested. "Maybe it was just bad luck." The petite brunette crossed herself.

"No." Marlowe shook her head. She glanced down at the dead man. "This was meant for Sean and only Sean."

Jalen picked up the threadbare coverlet he'd been lying on and approached Sean's body trapped in the globe. "If you don't mind, I'll just . . ." Jalen's voice trailed off as he threw the coverlet over the globe.

The blanket covered only a portion of the grisly scene, like a horrible, moth-eaten tablecloth covering a magician's unwanted surprise underneath.

But it was at least just large enough to cover Sean's impaled torso within the globe. The dead man's muscular legs stuck out, like some macabre practical joke.

"Unless our killer is carrying around a sheaf of murder poems where each one of us could be the victim of whatever death trap is next, then no, this was definitely meant for him," Marlowe stated firmly. "Never mind the, um . . . perfection of it. The, um. Imagery. The animal-cruelty guy in a cage. The lady always calling out delicate flowers choking on one."

"Yeah," Jalen agreed. Then, in the same breath, "Man, this is going to make an epic podcast."

"If you get out of here alive," Marlowe replied.

"Yeah. If that," Jalen agreed.

The group fell silent, trying not to think about Marlowe's last statement.

26

The covered globe in the center of the conservatory looked simultaneously disturbing and unintentionally hilarious. Plum was fighting giggles. She snapped her mouth shut.

Best not to look at it.

"I get that it was supposed to be for him," Jude continued, that frown still on his face. "I'm just trying to figure out how in the world the killer could be certain that trap would get Sean?"

"Beats me." Shelley sat down heavily on the fainting couch. She kicked at a small chunk of marble by her foot. "I'm still trying to figure out how you guys think *my* poetry is bad."

"Why does it matter?" Dude asked. He held up a placating hand to Shelley. "I mean Jude's question."

"Because." Jude's forehead stitched tighter, a network of lines appearing like thought-generated venetian blinds. "If we can figure that out, then maybe we can avoid the next one."

A shiver marched over Plum's skin. What would the next death trap be?

"Next one!" Shelley stood up. "Why does there have to be a next one?"

"Just seems like the way this is all shaping up," Plum muttered. Although she didn't understand it, either, there was no doubt they were trapped on an island with a killer. One who wanted to keep killing.

Plum looked at the shrouded globe. She glanced at the semi-toppled plinth in the middle of the room, the marks where the explosions had loosened the globe and set it rolling. She moved down the three steps into the sunken center of the conservatory.

"To make that globe kill Sean, the killer had to be certain Sean would place his bed right there," Marlowe said.

Plum edged closer to the globe and the liquor cart next to it. She reached out and lifted the crystal decanter filled with amber liquid. "Scotch," she said. "The cart."

Behind her, Warix made a snorting noise that sounded both surprised and amused.

"That would do it," Dude agreed. "He was the only one drinking. I mean, after Brittlyn."

Plum placed the decanter back on the full liquor cart and dropped both hands onto the handlebar. She tugged. The cart didn't move an inch. "It's stuck," Plum reported. She planted her feet and gave an almighty yank. The cart didn't move even a centimeter.

"It's bolted to the floor," Jalen suggested. He joined Plum

next to the cart and bent to examine the solid metal wheels. "Yep."

"So, the killer knew that Sean would drink the scotch, so much that he would bed down there," Plum said.

"Might as well have painted a bull's-eye on the floor," Warix said, his voice grudgingly filled with something that sounded like admiration.

"What does that mean for us?" Cici asked. She drummed her baby-doll-pink nails nervously on her arms. "How do we avoid a trap set for us, with that knowledge?"

"It means," Plum stated slowly, "that the killer knows how to lure us. Knows our personalities enough that if there are more traps, each one will be set with just the right bait."

"I'm going to get Henrietta out of that cage now," Sofia said.

"Good idea," Plum agreed.

27

"What do we do now?" Dude paced back and forth near his bedroll. "So, what if the killer knows I like to drink my coffee black, knows I like to play Monopoly, whatever—what do we *do* now?"

"We should examine the room," Plum suggested. "Look for any other dangerous areas or potential deadly situations."

"I can't stay in here with that body," Shelley moaned.

"Okay, listen." Plum held up her hands and waited for everyone to get quiet. "We move to a different room. Which room is around this size?"

"The ballroom," Warix answered. "It's where the server is, I saw it earlier. The ballroom's mostly empty!"

"Okay." Plum nodded. "We take the sodas and our beds." She glanced at Sofia. "And Henrietta, of course," Plum said.

"Naturally," Sofia said, holding the sleeping chicken tighter to her body.

"We go set up in the ballroom," Plum continued. "We stick together. Nothing else has changed."

"Except for Sean," Cici quipped, but it wasn't a disagreement, Plum decided. Just frazzled nerves.

"We search the room, we barricade ourselves in there, we make sure we're not near anything hazardous," Marlowe said.

"Right," Plum said. "And we wait for the morning."

"The boat." The deep frown lines on Jude's forehead eased. "Then we all leave on the boat."

"We'll all go to the police together once we get back to Saint Vitus," Sofia said.

"Does everyone agree?" Plum asked, looking at each person in turn.

Dude nodded. Warix shrugged agreement. Jalen nodded. Cici sighed and shook her head, but finally said, "Yes."

Shelley had already begun gathering her things.

Together, Plum, Sofia, and Marlowe gathered their bedding.

Sofia opened a small chest and found a heavy cut-velvet shawl. Henrietta squawked when Sofia wrapped it tightly over her wings and under her feet, and then knotted it at her chest. But the minute Sofia had picked up the chicken-bundle again, the hen settled back to sleep.

"Good idea," Marlowe told Sofia, nodding at the bundled bird.

Sofia shrugged. "I figured it might keep her calm while we sleep, kind of like a weighted blanket."

"I could use one of those right about now," Plum said.

"No kidding," Marlowe agreed.

Together the group walked across the atrium and through the double doors of the large ballroom. Heavy gilt mirrors hung on the wall, scattering the amber light of wall sconces and two glittering chandeliers.

"They're not exactly *Phantom of the Opera*–sized," Marlowe said, pointing at the chandeliers, "but best not set up under them anyway."

"Yes, and avoid the mirrors," Warix said. He was already unrolling his blanket and pillow behind the doors in another corner.

They all spaced themselves around the room, most of them setting up in a scattered row in front of the large windows. Warix set up his pallet next to the small server and wireless router, which sat on the floor near the door to the hall.

Sofia settled down next to their window, Marlowe next to her and Plum on the inside of the room. Henrietta gave a short series of clucks, then closed her eyes when Sofia lay back next to the hen. The black hen's beak started grinding softly—a contented noise—and rather comforting, Plum decided.

There wasn't much more conversation as they all settled down for the night. Again. By unspoken agreement, they left the wall sconces on.

"Maybe that's all," Marlowe whispered to the two other girls lying on the floor with her.

"What do you mean?" Sofia asked.

Marlowe's blue-green eyes glittered in the semi-dark. Her answering whisper was urgent with hope. "Maybe no one else has to die."

The Second Day of Pyre Festival

The Island of Little Esau

A Trap and a Knife

1

The morning sun glared down on the ocean, sending glittering sparkles lancing into everyone's eyes. All that remained of the burned dock were the jagged support struts, spaced out at even intervals in the water.

Marlowe wore her serving-platter hat and cat's-eye sunglasses, looking impossibly chic as always as she watched the horizon.

Plum felt stale and wrinkled.

"Is that it?" Cici asked, pointing out into the ocean. Like Marlowe, she looked very put-together and not at all like she'd spent the better part of the night starting awake at the slightest noise, scared that a killer would creep up in her sleep.

Then again, maybe that was just Plum who did that.

And Sofia. Bless her sweet friend, the few times Plum *had* managed to doze off, Sofia had shaken her awake with an urgent "Did you hear that?" or "What's that?" Both times, there was no satisfactory answer. They'd spent the majority of the night straining to hear a stealthy footfall or to see better into the dimly lit ballroom.

"I don't see anything," Warix replied to Cici.

They all fell silent, not wanting to think about the boat not arriving.

"Dudes." The word was sad.

"No, don't say it," Jude said. "It's coming." He puffed his cheeks out, holding the breath of hope in his lungs.

"Dude . . ."

"No, seriously. You just got to believe, right?" Jude didn't look anyone in the eye. "Good things happen if you believe. Make room in your heart. It's what I tell my fans. Believe and achieve."

"Normally I would agree with you," Shelley began gently.

Behind them, their suitcases sat forlornly on the tables where the day before a lavish buffet had been set out. A buffet with food, but no water.

It had been a sign. A warning.

And none of them had seen it, so eager to be somebody. To be a part of something amazing. Storied. Legendary.

Plum more than the rest of them. So foolish, so desperate.

Jude was still talking. "Like, if you believe good things, they come to you—the law of attraction, right?" His voice dipped into his webcam patter, the pop accent, the oh-my-God tone. "For example," Jude said urgently, and he met Plum's eyes. "If I think, *Hey, that boat's coming for me,* then it'll come. Or something will come! We won't be trapped here!"

"I guess that's maybe partly—" Plum began gently.

"And! If I think, *I am not getting murdered on this island!* then it's going to be true, right?" Jude interrupted. His eyes moved to them each in turn, blue pools full of hope.

Sofia repositioned Henrietta on her hip. "I don't think that's quite how it works."

Jude shook his head. He closed his eyes and tipped his face up to the sun, extending his arms fully like he was seeking a blessing from the sky. "I'm not getting murdered on this island," he said with absolute certainty.

Warix laughed.

"Dudes," Dude began again. "I think it's time we faced it."

"No one's coming," Shelley moaned. "The boat was a lie."

"Nooooo." Jude shook his head, his face still tipped up to the sky, his eyes still closed. "Don't listen to them," he pleaded to . . . the sun? God?

"Of course no boat's coming," Warix scoffed.

It was the last straw.

Under the blazing sun, with sweat stinging her eyes, fried on sleeplessness and fear, Plum whirled on the gamer. But Cici beat her to it, clomping her platform sandals up to where Warix sat on one of the empty tables.

"Oh yeah?" Cici snapped. "You know so much, how come you brought *your* suitcase down here?"

Warix shrugged. "Just in case I was wrong. It happens sometimes."

Cici's eyes narrowed. "You thought you were leaving, too. Drop the act."

"Hey!" Jude yelped as he threw his arms wider. "I just remembered!" he yelled. "WE ARE GETTING RESCUED TODAY!"

"Dude, you've got to stop," Dude said, his voice growing an edge. He dropped his head, the blond spikes of his hair lowering almost like horns.

"No! I mean it! Not a universe thing!" Jude pointed at Plum. "Peach Winter is coming! It has to be today! She'll have a big charter boat or something, maybe one of those water planes, and she'll come and we'll be *saved*!"

Beside her, Plum heard Marlowe curse softly under her breath. Sofia stepped closer to Plum's shoulder. Henrietta squawked slightly.

"Um, about that—" Plum began.

Everyone turned to her, their eyes weighted with hope.

"S-so," Plum stammered.

Shelley began to shake her head. "Don't say it."

"It's just that, um, she's not coming," Plum said.

Marlowe wrapped an arm around Plum, squeezing her tightly in support.

"What? Why not?" Jude asked. "You said so on the boat yesterday!"

"I lied," Plum stated. She couldn't stand the feeling of nausea in her stomach, the pinpricks of it in her cheeks. "My sister doesn't even know about Pyre Festival," Plum explained in a rush. "Because I took her invitation."

There was a moment of shocked silence, one part growing anger, one part disappointment.

"Dude."

The word held all the accusation and recrimination in the world.

2

"Why?" Cici asked. "Why would you do that?"

"Why wouldn't we?" Marlowe's defensive answer was so fast that Cici stepped back. "I mean, you're all here!" Marlowe stepped forward forcefully. "The same reason you're here, well, that's why we're here!"

"*We* were *invited*." Cici crossed her arms and cocked a hip. The pendulum of her ponytail swung wide.

"Yeah!" Jalen seconded her. He gestured to the others. "We're influencers."

"I'm not mad," Shelley chimed in, dipping into her airy yoga-app voice again. "I am just wondering, Plum, what you thought would happen when you got here. Like if it was a normal festival and stuff."

"I thought . . ." Plum shrugged. "I thought no one would notice me. Like always."

On the beach in front of her, Marlowe turned to face Plum, shock on her face.

Before her friend could say anything affirming, Plum plowed on. "We thought that it would be crowded! There was supposed to be the villa, plus the extension rooms, remember? The yurts, the yachts."

"Someone would have noticed you're nobody," Cici said. "When you got to the festival."

"Not if the festival had been everything they'd said," Sofia answered. She somehow looked fierce, despite the chicken in her arms. It reminded Plum of the first day they'd met. How Sofia had been ready to take on the bullies.

"Anyway, none of that matters now, does it?" Jalen asked. "We have to figure out what to do next. Does anyone have someone who's expecting you to check in? Because that might trigger someone to send help?"

Shelley held up a hand. "I have some clients who will be expecting to hear from me," she said. "But not until after the festival."

"That's the problem," Dude said with a sigh. "Every one of us is where we're supposed to be, and no one will worry."

"What about the Pyre Signs app?" Cici asked. "Is it working? Do we know anyone looking for our updates?"

Warix shook his head and gave a dark little laugh. His sharky smile wasn't even remotely cute anymore. Instead it was smug as he punctured their hopes. "Oh, you guys haven't figured that out yet? Even if it was working, it's a closed loop. It's not actually broadcasting. That's why we haven't been able to post anything. It's deliberate isolation."

"But people clicked like on my post yesterday," Jude protested, fiddling with his phone.

"They're all bots," the gamer explained. "Not one is real. I'd bet you that if we compared posts, we'd see the exact same accounts engaging with us."

Plum felt a sinking in her chest. She knew the killer was prepared. Had planned and readied themselves for their murder spree. But she kept forgetting the absolutely elaborate steps the killer had had to take to get them all there, to lull them into a false sense of security, and to keep them isolated.

"It's just like the AI," Plum said. "All a cover to keep us from suspecting anything. Lulling us."

"Ah, man. Wadsworth," Jude said softly, almost like he was grieving the absence of the disembodied voice.

"I want to say something," Marlowe began hesitantly.

The others turned to her.

"Now you know that we weren't actually supposed to be here. That we took Peach Winter's place."

Sofia nodded.

"So none of us could be the killer," Marlowe explained. Her hand circled, indicating herself and her two friends. "We've been best friends for years. We're not influencers. The killer can't be one of us."

Shelley nodded in agreement.

Cici didn't look as certain.

Warix laughed mockingly. "Sure. Why don't we just take your word for it? Why not. Hey, I'm not the killer, either, guys."

Sofia glowered at him.

Warix held out a hand. "I'm just saying. You telling us who you are, how you got here, why you *couldn't possibly* be the killer?" He shook his head. "It means absolutely nothing. For all I know, one of you is the killer. Or all of you are. Maybe you've got some grudge against us, and you're picking us off one by one, just pretending to be nobody special, all part of your cover."

"No, she's really Peach Winter's sister," Jude piped up, pointing at Plum. "I've seen Peach share her picture on Instagram."

"It doesn't matter!" Warix yelled. "Serial killers have family, right? It's always someone there going, *Huh, gee, we've been neighbors for ten years. I never would have guessed they were killing little old ladies and burying them in the basement!*"

"I mean, that is also true," Jalen agreed. "That's exactly how it always goes."

"Ugh!" Cici yelled. "This sun is melting my Etoile makeup. If we're stuck here, might as well go back to the villa." She crossed to the table where her bags waited for the boat that wouldn't be coming. Cici yanked them off the table and began the climb back to the villa.

Shelley, Warix, and Dude followed her.

Jude and Jalen hesitated.

"For what it's worth," Jude offered, "I don't think any of you girls is the killer." He smiled at them brightly.

"Thanks," Plum said tiredly.

"Me either," Jalen offered. Then he lifted his phone under his chin. His voice dropped into profundity. "Statistically speaking," he announced, "most serial killers are men."

Without thinking about it or conferring among themselves, Plum and her two best friends took a big step back from Jalen and Jude.

"Sorry," Plum said. "That was instinctive."

"No problem," Jalen said. He turned off his recording app and stowed his phone back in his pocket. "I'm not the killer," he said with a sigh. "Although that would make one hell of a podcast, wouldn't it?"

3

They grabbed their bags and started a slow march back up to Mabuz Villa.

"We have to talk," Marlowe began, glancing over at Plum.

Her kitten heel sandal sank into the sandy soil. Marlowe made a squawking noise, a cross between "Ah!" and "Gak!"

Plum leaped forward at the same time as Sofia. Together they managed to catch Marlowe before she toppled sideways. Sofia didn't even drop Henrietta.

Marlowe smiled at her friends. "Good catch," she said gratefully.

"I do my best work while holding a chicken," Sofia said.

"Are you okay?" Plum asked her friend.

Marlowe flexed her foot. "I'm fine. Though my ankle hurts a little."

Plum hadn't let go of Marlowe's arm. And she hadn't let go of where her other hand had steadied her friend, resting on the small of Marlowe's back.

Plum couldn't help but feel the softness and warmth of Marlowe's skin under her hand.

And she couldn't help but breathe in Marlowe's unique smell, just the faintest trace but still discernible, even out here with the sea air all around them. It was a scent she noticed and recognized more than she could describe. Warmth, skin, some kind of hormone or sex pollen, no doubt, because Marlowe smelled so *good,* but it wasn't like she smelled of anything . . . not like vanilla or any other scent, but something maybe electrostatic, or noticeable only to Plum, a scent that felt like a banked fire, like home, like ignition.

Plum realized Marlowe was talking to her.

"—you?" Marlowe was frowning. She'd taken off her cat's-eye sunglasses, her beautiful blue-green eyes penetrating.

"I'm sorry?" Plum asked, still somehow unable to let go of Marlowe.

Don't make it weird, Plum told herself. *Let go of her arm. Drop your other hand from her back. She's your friend and she's not in danger of falling anymore.*

Plum's hands didn't let go.

Marlowe's own hand turned and curled up, resting on Plum's waist. "You said before no one ever notices you. Do you really feel like *I* don't notice you?" Marlowe repeated.

Jalen and Jude were standing nearby, waiting for them to continue the climb or possibly even listening in, waiting for Plum to explain herself.

"Um, you don't count," Plum answered Marlowe. She tried to put a smile in it and explain. "I mean, you're my friend." Plum dropped her hands and stepped back.

Marlowe's eyes shone. She turned her head and fumbled her sunglasses back on.

"Oh my God, Plum." Sofia's whisper was nearly a hiss.

"What?" Plum whispered back. Did Sofia sense something? It was hard to think. Her brain felt like molasses.

"Huh," Jalen said. His eyes slid between Marlowe and Plum.

"What?" Plum asked.

"Nothing." Jalen turned away, pretending to be as absorbed in the horizon as Marlowe. "Just, what a predicament," he added. His hand touched Marlowe's shoulder briefly. Consolingly.

"Don't worry, Marlowe," Plum said. "We'll figure a way out of here."

The broad brim of Marlowe's serving-platter sun hat dipped as she nodded briskly.

"Let's just get out of the sun before it completely cooks what's left of Plum's brain," Sofia said to Marlowe in a strangely consoling voice.

Plum felt tears jump to her eyes as the rest of the group started climbing ahead of her.

Everyone was mad at her. She'd brought her friends to this death trap festival, *and* she'd lied to everyone about her sister. She couldn't just expect everyone to get over that.

She trudged up the path behind her friends.

4

The group climbed the rest of the cliff path in silence and took shelter from the heat back inside the empty ballroom where they'd slept.

Plum couldn't shake the horrible feeling that she'd done something wrong. Apart from coming in the first place, convincing her two best friends to come, and lying to everyone about her sister coming.

"Now what do we do?" Jalen asked.

"We should build a signal fire for help," Cici suggested. "If a boat comes by or something."

"Yeah!" Jalen said. "There's driftwood and scrub brush. It should be a piece of cake."

"We can't leave it burning all the time. There's not that much wood on the island. Unless we want to burn the furniture?" Sofia asked.

"It would be easier to just have the signal fire built and ready to be lit," Jalen suggested. "Maybe we can find some lighter fluid or something."

Plum nodded.

"Warix, is there any hope with the internet block?" Dude asked.

Warix sighed and arched his back in a stretch. "I don't think so, but I'll take another look." He fished into his pocket and pulled out a Zippo. "Whoever goes to the signal fire can have this."

"I've got one, too," Dude offered.

"There's no point in making a signal fire if we don't schedule watches ready to light it if a boat goes by," Plum said. "So we should break into teams and take shifts."

"No way am I sitting out there in the sun." Cici glanced down at her forearms, as if imagining the sunburn already.

"How about we get a FEMA tent?" Shelley suggested. "While we're down there, we can try to write a message on the beach. Just in case a helicopter flies over."

"Good idea!" Jude cheered.

The pop of a can opening echoed in the room. "Dudes," Dude said, looking down at the can of Diet Hillside Dew in his hand. "I don't know if I can drink much more of this syrup. Anyone else hungry?"

The entire group agreed to the plan and split into three groups to accomplish the different jobs.

Cici, Shelley, and Jude would go down to the beach and attempt to write a giant *HELP* in the rocky beach before bringing up the tent. Dude, Jalen, and Warix would build a fire on the cliff overlooking the stubs of the dock. Plum and her friends would go to the kitchen and heat up more franks and beans for everyone.

Sofia would have to eat another meal-replacement bar. It was so unfair, Plum thought as she stood next to Marlowe at the stove.

But while they were in the kitchen and Marlowe was opening the cans of beanie weenies, Plum found a large metal container of lamp oil. "This will go right to the signal fire," Plum crowed, holding it up.

Sofia cheered.

They settled in to wait for the franks and beans to heat.

"If it had to be shelf-stable food, why couldn't it be ramen?" Marlowe sighed, leaning her head on Plum's shoulder as she stirred the beans.

"Guess I'm forgiven, huh?" Plum said to Marlowe. "I didn't mean to make it sound like you didn't count earlier. Just that since you're my friend—"

Marlowe lifted her head slightly, almost like she regretted resting it on Plum's shoulder in the first place, and held it up.

"Relax, would ya?" Plum urged, and gave in to her desire to touch Marlowe's hair as she gently pressed Marlowe's head back into the crook of her neck. "I'm just trying to say I'm sorry."

The weight of Marlowe's head returned. "Don't worry about it," Marlowe sighed. "It's fine."

Plum still couldn't shake the feeling that she was missing

something glaringly obvious. Once she wasn't so hungry, maybe she'd figure it out.

They brought the pot of beans and bowls and spoons into the ballroom.

"Who has first shift?" Cici asked.

"We'll pick after we eat." Warix was already scooping out a bowl of beanie weenies.

The others settled on the floor. Sofia and Marlowe spooned out bowls of food and passed them around until everyone was served.

"Mmm! Even better the second time!" Jude held up a spoonful of franks and beans and sniffed at it as if it were a bite of filet mignon he was anticipating.

Dude sat next to Jude on the floor of the ballroom. He shrugged. "I'm just happy to be eating, dude."

"Me too, Dude," Jude said.

"You ate these a lot as a kid, Jude?" Jalen asked, leaning forward to look around Dude.

"Dude, yeah!" Jude said.

"I guess they grow on you, dude," Dude said.

"If they didn't, we'd be screwed, Dude," Jude replied solemnly.

Across from them, Shelley let out a sudden snort of laughter.

The three guys stopped eating and looked up questioningly.

Shelley was wiping her mouth and trying not to spit out her

remaining beans. "Just," she said, her hand muffling her words somewhat, "just . . . you think *my* poetry is bad."

The guys gave her a blank look.

Shelley put her elbows out, arms wide in a bro-y gesture. "Dude!" she mimicked Dude. "Dude," she mimicked Jude. "Jude!" She pointed at Jalen. "Dude!" She looked back at Jude. "Screwed dude." She dissolved into laughter again, leaning over and clutching her stomach.

The dudes just glanced at each other.

"That's just rich," Shelley said. "You mocking me."

Dude gave a small sniff. "You can drop the attitude—" His voice cut off suddenly. A surprised then wry expression crossed his face. "Dude," he added, and started laughing with Shelley.

Maybe it was stress. Maybe it was the fact that they were all finally eating, filling their hollow bellies, but it wasn't long before they were all laughing, sitting in a loose circle on the floor of the ballroom, eating their lunch.

Plum's eyes roved around the circle, a surprise warm glow in her chest. They were all in this together. Weren't they? It was impossible to imagine that anyone sitting on the floor and laughing, sharing this meal, could be capable of killing two people.

Plum's eyes landed on Jude. Marlowe had said he was too clueless to be the killer . . . but what if it was an act? Jude laughed at something Dude said. A clump of half-chewed beanie weenies landed on his leg.

No way.

Plum's eyes circled to Jalen. If he planned to kill them all, surely he wouldn't have shown such relish talking about his murder podcast? It gave him a sort of expertise, if he studied killers. Surely he would have hidden that if he *actually was* the killer?

And Dude. Sure, he could be abrasive, but he had the most followers out of any of them. Sure, follower count wasn't a lie detector, but didn't it show that he was dedicated to his life as an influencer? And besides, he'd tried to give rescue breaths to Brittlyn when they'd already thought that she'd been poisoned. He'd put his life at risk to try to save hers.

Plum's eyes moved to Warix. He was a jerk, but he was also clearly who he said he was. A gamer who didn't bother to fake or hide his jerky side. He might have the most technical know-how out of all of them, so it *was* possible he was the one behind it all. Who knew how to set up a fake AI butler, trigger explosives, and the like.

Okay, maybe it was Warix.

Plum's eyes slid past Warix and landed on Shelley and Cici, sitting together.

Shelley had gotten injured when Sean was killed in the conservatory. There was no way to be that close to the explosion and know it was safe. Surely the killer would have positioned themselves farther away from danger?

And the same went for the petite beauty maven. Cici had

been right next to Shelley, the two of them the closest to the trap, apart from Sean.

Plum glanced at her friends and felt a lancing of pain. They shouldn't be here. If it wasn't for her—

"Hey." Marlowe leaned over, her flawless face suddenly filling Plum's vision. "What are you thinking?" Marlowe asked.

"We shouldn't be here," Plum whispered. "You shouldn't be here."

"Don't start that again." A gentle frown stitched between Marlowe's eyes.

Plum heaved a sigh, then nodded. There was no point going into it again. There was no going back and fixing it, no stopping them before they all arrived on Little Esau. Although that wouldn't stop her from holding the regret in her heart until the end of her days, Plum thought.

"It's just," Plum whispered, and gestured to the rest of the seated circle. "It's like you said. I can't imagine *any* of them doing it. Except maybe Warix. But even that's a stretch."

Marlowe looked away, glancing around the room. "Yeah," she breathed. "But someone's behind it. Two people are dead."

"We have an advantage over everyone else, at least," Plum whispered.

"How so?" Marlowe smiled.

"Well, we *know* none of us are the killer." Plum glanced to Sofia, who sat, carefully tending Henrietta. The hen was loose from her compression wrap and was lackadaisically pecking at beans that Sofia held out.

Marlowe's wry half smile cocked at Plum. "You sure about that?" she teased lightly.

Plum's heart did a flip-flop. She swatted Marlowe's shoulder. "Don't joke," she said, but couldn't help smiling. It was definitely the stress, she decided.

Stress, that could make her heart flutter and stomach swoop when Marlowe was joking—*actually joking*—about being a killer.

Stress. That was all it was.

5

After they finished eating, they all lay back on the floor. In a few minutes, they'd send the first group out to the cliff and the unlit signal fire to watch for possible boats.

But for the moment, with the afternoon sun streaming in though the leaded windows, it was easier to feel safe, or at least safer, than in the dead of night. And maybe Sean and Brittlyn were the only targets. If they could just hold on long enough, they were bound to be rescued.

"What do we do now?" Jude asked, wrecking the moment of peace.

Dude groaned for all of them. "We've got to set a watch schedule, dude."

"And, um, we can't . . ." Shelley cleared her throat. "We can't just leave those bodies much longer. Can we?"

The unwanted thought of heat and decomposition bloomed in Plum's mind.

"Ew," Sofia said. "No, but ew."

"There's a walk-in fridge in the kitchen." Warix spoke around his finger as he methodically chewed off his nails. "If you don't mind bodies where you cook," he added.

"Okay, that was vivid." Shelley closed her eyes and gave a shiver. The bangles on her wrists chimed with the movement.

"Just sayin'." Warix shrugged.

"Okay, who's going to sit with the signal fire?" Jalen squinted out the windows. "We shouldn't take any chances leaving it alone. It would suck to have gone to all the trouble of building it and not be there to actually light it if a boat goes by."

"Several someones would be better," Shelley offered. "For safety and to help watch."

"We could take turns," Jude offered. "In our groups from before. Right? That's a good idea, right?"

Dude reached out and squeezed the boy's shoulder. "Yeah, dude. Good thinking."

"Yeah!" he chirruped happily.

It was disconcertingly like Jude had become their mascot somehow. As if without talking about it, the group had all agreed that there was no way he could be the killer.

Sofia leaned over to Plum and Marlowe. "Actual cinnamon roll," she whispered.

"A dumpling," Marlowe agreed.

Plum nodded. "Must protect."

A jarring two-note digital tone, almost like an AMBER

Alert, suddenly went off all around the room. Plum and her friends jumped.

Across the circle from them, Shelley clung to Cici.

Cici looked perplexed. She pulled out her cell phone. "They're all going off," she yelled over the alarm.

Plum dug her phone out of her back pocket. The screen was alight with a video clip of a blazing fire.

6

The fire was so realistic Plum almost dropped her phone for fear of singeing her fingertips.

"What the hell?" Cici jabbed at her phone.

Jude looked incongruously happy. "Wadsworth?" he called into his phone. "Is that you?"

His face fell when the virtual butler didn't respond.

On all their screens, the flames burned.

"It's . . . a fire?" Dude asked.

Marlowe looked up. "No, it's a pyre."

Sure enough, when Plum watched the video clip, the camera pulled back from the dancing flames at the end. The fire wasn't shaped like a campfire. Or a bonfire.

It was oblong. The length of a body.

"Oh no," Cici breathed. "Oh, ew, is that . . ."

"That looks like a body." Shelley's voice was thin with disgust.

"Whatever it is, I can't get it to shut up." Warix was holding a button on the side of his phone, his mouth a grim line of determination.

Around the room, each person had stood when the alarm sounded. Ready to spring into action, ready to run, ready to do anything.

They all just stood there with their phones in their hands.

The alarms suddenly cut off. The quiet was so deafening Plum felt as if her ears had popped.

The video looping on their screens changed. Each person in their group stood transfixed.

The shot changed, the screens filling with hectic flames—then the screen turned blood-red.

Words appeared on the screen, typing out one letter at a time.

D A N C E

P U P P E T S

"Um." Jude's voice was frightened. "What?"

"Well, that makes no sense," Cici snapped. She cocked a hip and waved her phone in exasperation. "Is it a band?"

"No." Plum shook her head.

"It's a message for us." Sofia picked up Henrietta, wrapping the hen in the now-soiled scarf.

"Those *bastards*," Shelley hissed. She held out her phone, displaying the red screen. "We downloaded *malware*."

Warix laughed. "Clever."

"I'm uninstalling it," Cici said. "If my phone stops this junk, I'm uninstalling Pyre Signs and running my antivirus."

Warix actually snorted. "Like uninstalling the app will be enough to disable the malware. It was a Trojan horse, and now it's in all our phones."

"Do you *mind* not being so *negative*?" Shelley's scarf skirt flared out wide as she whirled on him.

"But what does it mean?" Jude asked, an edge of panic to his voice. "Dance puppets?"

As if his question was what their mysterious killer had been waiting for, the room was suddenly filled with the scratch of a needle and the rasp and hiss of an old-fashioned record playing.

A jaunty band started to play.

"Oh!" Marlowe smiled reflexively.

The music grew louder.

Plum looked up. There were speakers all around the room, fastened to the ceiling, tucked in corners.

A man started singing a song about smoke, cigarettes, the dark all around. It was probably supposed to be romantic, but to Plum it sounded ominous. Gooseflesh rose on her arms. The brass section on the old-timey recording pumped a shrill, syncopated bridge.

Warix started thumping the panels set in the walls around the edges of the room.

Cici and Shelley huddled together, looking at their phones.

Jalen held his fingers in his ears.

Just then the music shifted. A heavy beat pounded over the jazzy 1920s tune.

Marlowe shrieked.

At the same instant, Plum felt the phone in her hand vibrate. She looked down. The letters deleted and reappeared in time with the beat of the club music flooding the room.

DANCE, PUPPETS!

Plum felt her heart plummet. Nothing was over. Brittlyn and Sean weren't the only targets.

The killer was toying with them.

Coming for them all.

As if to confirm her darkest thoughts, the letters on the screen changed.

DIE, PUPPETS!

7

Warix kept knocking at the panels as he made his way around the room.

The music grew louder. Marlowe winced and ducked her head.

Plum stuck her fingers in her ears. Jude shook her shoulder. When she turned, he pointed.

Warix had taken one of the panels off the wall. Behind it was a high-tech array of wires and blinking lights.

The music suddenly stopped. Warix spun, holding up a wire in triumph. "Ha!" he yelled.

Plum's ears still rang.

"I knew it was going to be in here!" Warix continued. "When the phones started going off!" He was still yelling.

Plum felt like her eardrums might burst, the noise throbbing in a *wub-dub* rhythm, almost unbearable, growing louder.

"WAIT!" Cici yelled, her hands shooting out to grab Shelley's and Dude's hands.

Dude pulled away from Cici's hand like a toddler trying to escape their mother's grip.

"BE QUIET!" Cici shrieked.

That was when Plum realized the throbbing thumping in her ears wasn't because of the loud music.

"It's a helicopter!" Shelley yelled. She clapped her hands. "We're saved!" she screamed. "It's landing, right?"

"Go light the signal fire!" Dude yelled.

Warix was the first to reach the French doors. He threw them open just as the cacophony of the blades sounded like it was directly above their heads.

"Where could it land?" Cici asked, but no one was listening. Everyone else, including Plum, Sofia, and Marlowe, rushed out onto the terrace.

The *twap-thwap-twap* started to recede.

"It's leaving!" Shelley wailed.

There was a rush of wind, from the helicopter blades, or simply from the ocean; Plum couldn't tell. She craned her neck. "Hey!" Plum yelled.

"Is it looking for a place to land?" Jalen suggested as the helicopter banked.

"No, it's heading back to Saint Vitus!" Dude yelled.

They all started screaming, jumping up and down, waving their arms.

The tail rudder of the helicopter moved away from them.

"There's no way the pilot can see us!" Sofia shouted.

Henrietta was struggling in her friend's arms, flapping and squawking with the commotion. One wing got free from Sofia's grip and buffeted her in the face.

Plum didn't know the cruising or highest speed of a helicopter, but the one that had just flown over the island was growing smaller with startling rapidity.

"No!" Marlowe moaned.

"The signal fire!" Jalen yelled. He took off after Warix.

"Yes!" Jude took off after him.

"Dudes! I have the lighter!" Dude yelled, trailing the two younger men.

"Do helicopters have rearview mirrors?" Shelley asked. "How are they going to see us with the island behind them?"

"I don't know," Marlowe murmured. "But what else are we supposed to do?"

"Why did it even fly over?" Cici asked.

Sofia had Henrietta firmly under control again, although there were a few scratches on her arms from the panicked bird.

There was a bright crackle of orange from the cliff edge. As if drawn by primitive instinct, the remaining group on the terrace started walking out toward the fire.

The fire had immediately doubled, then tripled in size.

The helicopter could only barely be seen. A disappearing speck in the sky. All their hope for rescue, gone.

Plum grabbed Sofia's and Marlowe's hands and squeezed. Cici and Shelley sighed, looking disheartened and completely exhausted. Marlowe squeezed Plum's hand back and bumped her hip. "We better go join the others."

Plum's heart flip-flopped in her chest, but she tried to jam any feeling down. Not the time for this. Instead she nodded and caught Sofia's eye, and together the group joined the others at the signal fire.

"Damn," Warix cursed. "It's gone."

They all stood in a loose ring, watching the empty horizon. The fire crackled merrily.

"We're going to have to build another bonfire." Dude sounded despondent. "When this one burns out. Just in case. Another helicopter or boat . . ."

He couldn't finish his sentence, he was too sunk in sorrow over their missed opportunity.

"If it was a sightseeing company, they'll be back," Plum said, to encourage herself as much as anyone else.

"Right." Cici nodded so vigorously her ponytail bobbed. "And I bet we weren't the only ones who heard about Pyre Festival. Maybe others are curious—they'll come out."

"There's always party crashers!" Shelley said.

"MEH!"

Shelley jumped and Cici let out a stifled cry as a goat's head lifted over the scraggly brush about six yards away. The large shrub was the last growing thing before the outcropping fell away into nothingness.

The goat tilted its head to one side, fixing their group with one profoundly creepy eye, a bright yellow iris with a horizontal slit of pupil. Judging by the stains on its beard, it was the same goat from before. It lowered its head, disappearing into the bush again as it ignored them to continue to graze.

Behind them was a soft rumbling sound and a frustrated woman's voice. "Ugh! Where is everybody?"

The voice was familiar.

Plum held her breath and turned around.

On the marble terrace behind them, a slender and eminently stylish young woman was struggling to pull a large suitcase behind her. She wore a broad navy sun hat, almost as large as Marlowe's, and platform sandals tied with crisscrossing white fabric bands that twined up her golden-tan calves. Her off-the-shoulder minidress looked almost like a high-fashion impression of a kitchen-window curtain, diaphanous, studded with eyelets, and such a bright white it was almost beyond the Pantone color spectrum.

"Peach?" Plum breathed.

"Oh my God," Jude exclaimed in a loud voice. "Peach Winter!"

Peach turned to their bedraggled group with a bright smile. The smile wavered, then widened when she saw Plum.

"Oh my God," Sofia said.

Marlowe started to laugh weakly. "This is absurd," she gasped.

"Plum Winter, you surprising little minx!" her sister called from the terrace.

Peach Winter sent a dazzling smile to the ragged group. She tossed one arm in the air and held the other out wide, as if posing for a picture. #LivingTheDream #Blessed. "Pyre Festival!" she chirruped. "But I don't have to tell you, do I?" Peach singsonged at Plum, seeming completely delighted that her little sister was there. "Bet you're surprised to see me!" Peach smiled, then curtsied lightly, a little dip of *ta-da* and *yes, it's me* all in one.

"I saw your post, Plum! The bucket and the boat!" Peach explained, mistaking their blank faces. "I wasn't going to come, but then I saw that you were here, and I looked up the website, and thought, *Why not?* So Andre loaned me his helicopter and here I am!"

"Call him to come back!" Shelley insisted.

"I would never! And he doesn't have a phone anyway, because he's on a tech cleanse. Isn't that so vital? So proud of him." Peach fluffed her hair and glanced at her own cell phone at the same time.

"Yeah, well, we . . ." Plum began. "The thing is . . ." Where to begin? How to explain?

"Plum, you bold little thing. I didn't know you had it in you!" Peach came forward and twined an arm around her sister's shoulder.

In spite of missing possible rescue, Plum still felt the warm rush of affection she always felt for Peach. "I did have it in me," Plum said, thinking of the feelings that had driven her here.

The feeling that nothing was enough, that she was desperate to do anything, be anyone, just to get away from herself. Away from her boring life.

But now all that had changed. The things of real importance had been thrown into stark relief by actual life-and-death. Her friends' lives, and her own life, were in danger every moment they stayed on this island.

Peach gave a vague yet benevolent smile and fluffed her hair again. "Aaaannnyway," she began.

"Hi!" Jude waved at her. "I'm Jude Romeo!"

"You're adorable," Peach declared.

Jude fizzed with delight.

"I don't believe this." Dude's voice was exasperated as he stalked away.

"Another victim has entered the fray," Jalen narrated into his phone.

"Peach, you met Marlowe and Sofia that one time at Christmas, remember?" Plum interjected, indicating her two friends.

"Hi. Been a while," Marlowe murmured.

Sofia gave a small wave. Plum continued. "So, we came here together, but the thing is—"

Peach interrupted again. "That's so sweet! Isn't this fun?" She smiled around at the entire group. "Pyre Festival!" She held her phone up, frowning. "Does anyone have a signal?"

"No," Plum answered. It was going to be a long explanation.

"The thing is—" Plum began, trying to think of the best place to start.

"Oh my God, tell me everything," Peach said, but held up a finger. "But first . . . where's Diplo?"

8

"Before you tell me, Plum, you can't just post a puke bucket, okay?" Peach scolded. "You're at Pyre Festival. You should post, you know . . . aspirational stuff."

"Okay, except there's a—" Plum stammered.

"For example," Peach continued. "On the helicopter out here, did I post a picture to Instagram wearing that frankly unflattering headset? No! I posted my legs sticking out from the door over the water. And on TikTok I posted a pan from my legs to the water sparkling below the helicopter with that new song by DanceBeast."

"That sounds nice. I would click love," Jude said affirmingly.

Peach indulged the teen with a smile.

"Also! Look at that date!" Peach held out her phone, sharing Plum's puke-bucket Instagram post. "You haven't updated in two days!"

"Listen, now's not the time, because—" Dude began, pushing his sunglasses up on his forehead. With them perched there, it almost made his bleached hair look like one of those anime novelty wigs.

"No excuses!" Peach held out an imperious hand. "I think no one really appreciates how much work goes into what I do. I know, I make it look easy with my fabulous lifestyle, but it's *work, kid*. Dubya-OH-Rrr-Kuh! *WORK*." Peach's eyes were wide in emphasis.

"Hey, so, I don't know you," Dude began again, gently inserting himself into the moment. "But we've all been lured here under false—"

"Who are you again?" Peach asked.

"I'm Dude," Dude explained. "From *Killing it, dude*!"

Peach just stared at Dude blankly.

"Y-you know," Dude stammered. His voice went from normal to ragged in an instant as he yelled, "KILLING IT, DUDE!"

Peach glanced at Plum, clearly seeking either guidance or rescue.

"It doesn't matter." Dude avoided their eyes as his mouth turned down. "What I mean is . . ." His voice grew harder. "What you don't know is no one can post anything because there *is no internet*."

"Yeah, and also, small matter, really." Shelley's smile was pressured in such a way that it seemed like she would break off into peals of unhinged laughter at any moment. "Like, no biggie, but also there's a killer on the island and they've killed two people so far. Ha!" Shelley clapped her hand over her mouth.

"Yeah, we bury the lede around here," Warix said. "Also, if you downloaded Pyre Signs, your phone is wrecked."

Peach started to speak, then snapped her mouth closed again. The broad brim of her sun hat wobbled like pudding as she swiveled her head to look at Warix. "No internet?" she asked, as if pondering the unfathomable.

"Nope!" Jude said brightly, still fizzing that Peach had called him "adorable."

"No internet and *two dead bodies,*" Dude emphasized.

Peach gave Dude a vague, confused smile. She turned to Plum. "No internet?" she asked again.

"They're telling the truth, Peach." Plum said. "Try your phone and see."

Marlowe and Sofia wore the same expression of disbelief, their eyes almost comically wide at Peach's inability to focus on the *murdery content*.

"And if you've got a signal, get a boat or something sent out, pronto," Cici added.

"Sure thing, babe." Peach put the phone to her ear, waiting. "Love your makeup, by the way." She waited.

The ocean glittered all around them.

Peach held out her phone, glaring at it. "This is impossible." She raised her phone up, first to one side, then another. "This phone is supposed to have network coverage *everywhere*."

"Okay, and *also* there's a *killer* on the *island* here with *us*," Sofia said, over-enunciating every third word.

Peach stared at her. "So you're actually being serious . . . ?"

"That's what we've been trying to tell you, dude." Dude nodded at Peach, a gentle bob of encouragement for the influencer processing the information.

"Look, I know this is a bizarre situation to just walk into." Jalen held up placating hands. "But it's true. We're not pranking you." He gestured at Plum. "Trust your sister."

They all stared at each other in silence.

Peach blinked.

"Would you like to see the bodies?" Marlowe asked solicitously. As if she were offering a beverage or a snack instead of offering to take her to view two corpses.

"No, that won't be necessary," Peach replied.

"Speaking of the bodies, maybe we should finally move them," Warix suggested.

"We have to figure out our watch schedule first," Dude reminded the others.

"You're holding a chicken," Peach stated, her voice flat, an unspoken *you realize* transmitted in her tone.

"Yeah." Sofia spared Plum's sister a glance. "Her owner died on the first night."

Peach rocked back on the heels of her platform espadrilles.

"Trippy, ain't it?" Dude's voice was more amused than mocking.

"Excuse me," Peach began, her voice both wounded and shocked. "I'm just trying to take this all in." Under her golden tan, she looked pale.

"You and us both." Jude sighed.

Peach rounded on Plum, an accusing finger outstretched. "Only *you* would crash a *murder festival.*"

9

Eventually the group went back inside. After a brief conference, they decided to split into their groups to do different jobs. Although the signal fire was still burning itself out, Cici, Shelley, and Warix went to watch at the cliff and collect more wood to be ready to start a new one.

Peach, Plum, and her friends would rest in the ballroom, readying for their watch shift at the cliff.

Dude, Jalen, and Jude left to move the bodies into the walk-in refrigerator.

It felt good to have a plan, even if Plum couldn't shake the memory of those ominous words appearing on her phone screen.

DANCE, PUPPETS!

DIE, PUPPETS!

She gave herself a shake.

"They're actually putting bodies in the refrigerator," Marlowe whispered to Plum, sitting beside her on the ballroom floor. "That's actually a thing that is happening now."

"Yeah," Plum replied. "I'm sorry."

She couldn't help feeling responsible.

"It's not your fault," Marlowe replied. "I just can't believe it."

"Me either," Plum said.

Without saying another word, their hands found each other's, twining together and squeezing tight.

A hoarse shriek echoed into the ballroom.

Plum and Marlowe raced into the hallway. Behind them, Plum could hear Sofia exasperatedly calling to the chicken, and Peach's panicked "What was that? Who was that?"

They ran down the hall, through the large atrium, under the swirling arch of the round staircase.

The scream was coming from the dining room.

Without stopping, Plum, Marlowe, and Sofia (holding Henrietta) piled into the doorway.

Jude, Dude, and Jalen stood in a loose semicircle facing where they'd left Brittlyn's body. They looked totally shell-shocked.

Plum noticed two specific things simultaneously. One: Jude was the one who'd screamed. He stood a little beyond the other two, as if he'd backed away from them. He looked utterly terrified.

Two: Brittlyn's body was gone.

"Her body's gone," Jalen said, stating the obvious thing somewhat obviously into his phone.

"Maybe she wasn't . . . dead?" Dude offered waveringly.

"You said she was dead!" Jalen rounded on Plum.

"We *all* said she was dead!" she said.

"Dude!" Sofia pointed at Dude. "You did CPR! Did she seem dead to you?"

"This is ridiculous!" he spluttered. "*Of course* she looked dead to me! She looked dead to all of us!"

"Someone moved her," Jude said.

"Dude, when? We've been together nonstop since Sean died." Dude started pacing in frustration.

"Okay, or . . . ?" Plum let her voice trail off. Not because she was trying to prompt the answer, but because it seemed impossible; the image of Brittlyn asphyxiating was too vivid. Too real.

"She wasn't dead," Marlowe whispered.

Plum nodded. "And that could mean one of two things. Either she was supposed to die and somehow didn't, or she faked her poisoning."

"And if she did that, then *she's* the killer!" Jalen said. "What better way to hide than to die first?"

"Or to pretend to," Sofia said, her brown eyes wide. "Whoa, that's creepy."

Plum suddenly felt like she was being watched. Was it possible?

Was Brittlyn the killer?

10

"Whoa. The dead girl is the killer." Jude pulled his hand back from the butler's pantry door.

"I mean, she might not be the killer," Plum argued. "Just, she could be."

"*You Never Asked Me*!" Marlowe grabbed and squeezed Plum's hand.

"I would, but, I mean, do you know something?" Dude asked, perplexed.

"No, it's an old movie! Continent Pictures, 1946, starring Ester Winslow and Gerald Sterling. In it, a man fakes his own death so he can have his vengeance on his estranged wife and her lover, who conspired to kill him in the first place."

"But why?" Jude asked.

"For the insurance money. You know, it was after *Double Indemnity*, and everyone was riding that femme-fatale-out-for-insurance wave." Marlowe shrugged, one hand on her hip.

She looked like a femme fatale herself, Plum thought. Even

if her usually perfect clothes were a bit rumpled.

"No, I mean, but why would Brittlyn be the killer?" Dude asked, sounding somewhat wounded at the thought that anyone would have a premeditated reason to want to kill him.

Plum wanted to gently take him by the arms, look earnestly into his eyes, and ask him, if they all made it off this island, did he perhaps want to rethink his entire social media strategy? Did he really want to be the *Killing it* dude if he was going to be so consistently hurt when people didn't like him?

"Revenge," Marlowe said. "I mean, she clearly had a chip on her shoulder."

"That doesn't make her a killer," Sofia argued, repositioning Henrietta on her hip.

"Well, she clearly didn't like Sean," Marlowe said.

"Who are we talking about again?" Peach asked, pushing through the doorway from the atrium.

"The first murder victim, Brittlyn, is missing," Dude tried to sum up.

"Listen, none of this matters right now," Plum said. Suddenly the way ahead was totally clear.

Dude popped back into the room from the swinging door that linked with the conservatory.

Plum hadn't noticed he'd left. That was unsettling.

"Sean's still there. Still dead," Dude reported.

"Hey, we should still stick together," Plum scolded Dude.

"Oh, sure." Dude looked abashed. "You're right. Sorry."

"Now what?" Jalen pulled out a chair and sat heavily. "Do we just search again? Look for wherever she's hidden or hiding?"

"No one moved her! We've been together nonstop since last night!" Dude argued.

"That we know of," Plum said. "You just went into the conservatory, and I didn't notice you'd left. How hard would it have been for any one of us to slip away for a few moments?"

"You think one of us just tiptoed in here." Dude's voice took on an edge. "Moved a *body* just easy-peasy like it was nothing, and what? Threw it off the cliff? Put it in a cabinet?"

"I don't *know*," Plum protested. "I'm just saying it's possible, so we should still stick to the plan, stay in groups."

"Yeah," Marlowe agreed. "I mean, if we stay in groups, even if Brittlyn is lurking somewhere, waiting to kill us or attack, then there'll always be two others who can fight her off."

"Okay, let's move Sean, at least." Jude looked determined.

"I honestly don't think I can take it if he starts to smell," Jalen said.

"Ugh, me either," Sofia agreed.

"Sure," Dude said, nodding. "If we're going to stick to the plan, then we should stick to that part of the plan, too." He made ironic little quote marks with his fingers. "'Move the bodies,'" he said.

"Well"—Jalen smirked—"the body we have."

"Why is this funny to you?" Sofia asked, but a telltale smile hovered around her own mouth.

"Stress?" Plum suggested, feeling a giggle fit bubble up within her own chest.

"You kids are sick," Peach proclaimed without looking up from her phone.

11

"This way, then." Jalen jerked a thumb toward the conservatory, where Sean's body waited.

"Wait," Dude said. "It doesn't seem right not to tell those three on watch what's going on."

"Yeah, we should send someone out," Marlowe piped up. "Wouldn't you want to know as soon as everyone else did?"

"I guess," Jude agreed, nodding. "And, like, what if Brittlyn is the killer, and she just walked out to the tent, or, like, she stumbled out there, like she was hurt, but she was *pretending,* and the others, they don't suspect her at all, and Brittlyn is able to stab them or whatever . . ."

"Jesus, kid, you've got quite an imagination," Jalen said.

"No, that's totally what happens in *Murder by Degrees,*" Marlowe agreed eagerly, her blue-green eyes wide.

"Another one with a cliff house, right?" Jude asked.

"Let me guess, your grandma, right?" Marlowe smiled. "Man, she's got excellent taste in movies."

Jude smiled happily. Then, all at once, but visibly, like a collapsing ice floe, Jude's face shifted from happy to sad. "I hope I get to see her again," he said, his voice tight with a knot of emotion.

"Dude." Dude's tone was bracing. "Dude, you're totally going to. We're all going to."

"You want to see my grandma?" Jude asked happily, swiping his fingers under his eyes.

"No, I mean we're all going to see our own grand . . ." Dude trailed off at Jude's confused, hopeful expression. "Sure, sure," Dude said. He squeezed Jude's shoulder. "We're all going to see your grandma. Why not?"

Jude smiled again, his face so happy it was as if he emitted light.

"This day's not getting any cooler," Jalen prodded.

Plum turned to her best friends and her sister. "We'll go tell the watch duty what happened."

"We'll come out and tell you after we take care of this," Dude said. He turned and walked to the door to the conservatory. "Let's see if there's a blanket or something we can move the body onto." Dude's voice diminished as he pushed through the door.

"See you soon!" Jude followed Jalen out of the dining room.

"That feels like bad luck to say," Sofia murmured.

12

The girls walked out through the front door of the villa onto the rough path toward the cliff edge. Peach led the way, several paces out in front. She was messing with her phone, apparently still trying to find a signal.

The sun was in the west, lowering in the sky.

Marlowe sighed and stretched her arms over her head. "This feels nice," she said. "We should aim for watch time at this time, really. It's the nicest part of the day."

Sofia snorted.

"What?" Plum asked.

"Nothing, just I really hope angling for the best watch time doesn't have to become part of our lives now."

"Ugh, seriously," Marlowe agreed.

They walked slowly toward the beehive-style FEMA tent set near the new bonfire.

There was a sudden squawking. Henrietta was flapping, struggling and scratching in Sofia's arms.

"Oh my *God*, calm down!" Sofia yelped.

"Here!" Plum lifted her shirttail and placed it over the bird's head. Henrietta calmed instantly.

"What was that all about?" Marlowe asked, returning the few steps she'd retreated.

"I think she saw that?" Sofia pointed to a curled piece of dried palm frond on the path. "It looks like a worm." Sofia shrugged.

"She's hungry again, I bet," Plum suggested.

"Yeah, I just gave her some beans," Sofia said. "Let me tell you, it is not easy having a dependent."

"We need to get you a stroller or something," Plum said.

"Maybe like some kind of carrier," Marlowe agreed.

"I love this bird and everything—" Sofia began as they started walking again.

Plum held her breath. Next to her, Marlowe paused on the path.

It felt like Sofia was on the verge of a major confession, admitting that she wished she hadn't taken on the burden of Henrietta.

"—but yeah, that would really help," Sofia finished, sighing.

Marlowe glanced at Plum. They'd both thought the same thing.

Marlowe put a hand on Sofia's shoulder. "Can I call you Farmer Torres?"

"Oh my God, I swear," Sofia warned, but she was smiling.

The smile didn't last.

"I take care of everything. Everyone. Too much, especially with

Krystal at college now," Sofia said. She dragged her feet on the path, almost as if she was feeling self-conscious. "And . . . don't judge me, okay?" Sofia's voice was small. "For flirting with Warix before . . . I love Louis! But he isn't here and I just . . . I liked . . ."

"It's okay." Marlowe hurried to reassure their petite friend.

"I liked the way Warix looked at me. It's been a while since I felt . . . I don't know. Young?" She didn't look up. "It's just sometimes it feels like my whole life is right there, like I'm on a train, and my life is following the tracks. And the tracks aren't *bad*. They lead to good things! It's just . . . sometimes . . . I want to . . . go somewhere else. I guess."

Marlowe moved to Sofia's side. She wrapped an arm around the smaller girl's waist. "Hey, it's okay," Marlowe said. "I understand. We get it."

Plum squeezed Sofia's hand. "Yeah! That's normal! That's like me! I just wanted an adventure, and that's why we, um, ended up in this mess."

"I know," Sofia said. She closed her eyes. "I'm sorry, too. It's just . . . it doesn't particularly help anything."

"Hey, wait." Marlowe stepped forward, frowning. "Are you mad at Plum now? After asking us not to judge you?"

Sofia took a step back and shifted so the chicken was between her and Marlowe. "Don't start, Lowe," she snapped, shifting into their private nickname. "It's bad enough that you already second everything she says. I don't need you guilting me about being *upset* that we let her talk us *into everything*."

"Don't fight, you guys." Plum's heart felt like it was filled with wet sand. Her friends were fighting because of her.

"Hold on one minute!" Marlowe turned to Sofia. "It's not Plum's fault. We agreed to it. We're weak for—"

"Oh my God, did you just call me weak?"

"Don't start with me."

"I swear, if you weren't so lovesick about—"

"Stop, y'all," Plum finally broke in.

"Don't you *dare* talk about my heart!" Marlowe shot back at Sofia. She looked absolutely furious, which was a rare occurrence. Her eyes narrow, her teeth bared.

Plum glanced at Sofia. She was squared up, firmly in Marlowe's face.

It was unusual for Marlowe and Sofia to truly fight, but when they did, it was like this: all at once, like how smoke can cause a flash-over fire in an instant.

"Then YOU STOP TELLING ME ABOUT IT AND DO SOMETHING ALREADY."

"Y'all, please." Plum felt like she might start to cry. "What are you even fighting about right now? Honestly."

"Jesus!" Sofia yelled. "I don't know who's more ridiculous!"

"You're the one holding a chicken," Marlowe sniped.

"You're the one scared of a chicken."

"Y'all!" Plum yelled. Marlowe and Sofia turned to look at her. On the path ahead, Peach turned back, surprised at the commotion.

In front of them, Cici, Shelley, and Warix stood next to the FEMA tent, watching the fight. Plum had barely realized they'd finally reached the other group.

"Are they always like this?" Peach asked Cici with an arched eyebrow. "I thought they were friends."

"Don't you know? She's *your* sister. Or is that only good online when it's Siblings Day?" Cici sniped, clearly shocking Peach, who had obviously expected a warm, eager-to-please reaction from the lesser celebrity.

"Excuse *you?*" Peach fumed.

"OH MY GOD, DON'T YOU HAVE A JOB TO DO?" Marlowe yelled to Cici and Peach, gesturing wildly at the expanse of horizon beyond the cliff's edge. "Like watching for rescue?"

Cici put her hands on her hips and turned in an exaggerated fashion, swinging her dark ponytail out wide.

Warix shook his head at them.

Shelley looked sad. "Oh," she breathed. "I thought nothing would come between you three."

"STOW IT, STAR CHILD!" Sofia yelled.

"YEAH!" Plum yelled back. "Families FIGHT."

"Yeah! They do!" Marlowe joined in the yelling, then blinked in surprise.

Sofia let out a little huff of laughter.

Marlowe looked like she wasn't sure if she should keep yelling or smile back at Sofia. The smile won out. Her cascading laugh followed.

"What were you even fighting about?" Plum asked, starting to smile in relief. "I mean, I thought I knew at first, then it got confusing."

"Don't worry about it," Marlowe said.

"Aw! Babe in the woods," Sofia cooed, turning and grabbing Plum's hand. "I love you, girl."

Plum realized she wasn't getting an explanation. She tried to be mad about it for a minute, but the happy scatter of light in her heart from both her friends' smiles took over instead.

"I love you, too," Plum hiccupped.

"Wait, what's happening?" Warix asked Shelley.

"That's right, get it over with," Cici sassed, waving the back of her pink-tipped fingers at them, not taking her eyes off the ocean.

"You're exasperating, and I love you, too," Marlowe said. "Both of you."

"Me too," Sofia said. "Sorry I said anything about your heart. I love your heart."

"It's okay, we're all under stress." Plum swiped her fingers under her eyelashes. "I love you guys so much."

"Does anyone want to tell me why you're here?" Warix thrust his palms forward in exasperation.

Sofia sniffed. Marlowe handed over her linen pocket square. Sofia took it and dabbed at her nose and her eyes. "Yeah," she said to Warix. "Brittlyn's body is missing."

13

It took less explaining than Plum expected. Perhaps that was given their unusual circumstances. Maybe they were all burned out on shock and horror.

"We wanted to let you know so you wouldn't be surprised or fooled by her if she appeared suddenly," Plum concluded.

"The good news is Sean's still dead." Sofia winced. "And I did *not* mean that the way it sounded."

"Where are the others?" Warix asked.

Marlowe explained about them deciding to still move Sean's body, and that they still needed to stick together. "Nothing's changed," she concluded. "We're still trapped here. There's still someone—"

"Or some*ones*," Cici interjected.

Marlowe nodded. "Or someones trapping us here, and we need to stay safe and try to get off this damn island."

"Got it," Warix said.

His eyes narrowed as he looked over the three friends' heads, staring back at the villa.

"Quick question, does the new plan involve setting the villa on fire?"

Plum whirled around. Thick white smoke was pouring out of a small window several yards away from the doors to the conservatory.

"Where is that?" Marlowe yelled as they started running toward it.

"It must be the kitchen!" Sofia yelled back.

Henrietta was letting out a fusillade of squawks as she bounced in Sofia's arms. Even Peach and Cici were keeping up as they raced back the path to the villa.

"Where's the closest door?" Shelley yelled.

"There's two," Warix called back. He skidded to a stop at the stone-paved walkway that led past the conservatory and down toward the window and the corner of the villa. "It's around the same direction both ways," he continued. He jabbed a finger at the conservatory. "Two of you go in there, open the butler's pantry, and make sure they can get out that way."

"We got it!" Cici yelled. She was already joining hands with Shelley. The two girls ran back to the French doors.

"I'll go with them!" Peach called, running in mincing steps after the two other girls.

"Around the corner is the kitchen-garden area. There's a door." Warix started running in that direction.

Plum slowed just a bit, eyeing the smoke billowing forth from the small window.

“What?” Marlowe asked, slowing slightly to match Plum. They followed Warix, leaving the pluming window behind.

“It doesn’t smell like a fire,” Plum explained.

They rounded the corner. The small kitchen garden was just an array of weed-choked pots filled with rocks, sandy soil, and not much else.

Warix pounded on the door.

“This way!” he yelled to whoever might be trapped, unable to see through the smoke inside.

“It’s locked?” Marlowe asked in dismay.

Plum turned and picked up a small statue of a cherub. “Move!” she yelled.

Warix darted to one side. Plum heaved the cherub through the window in the door. In her mind’s eye, the stone winged cherub looked back at her, grateful to be gifted with flight, even just once.

The window smashed. Glass shattered inward.

Warix pulled his sleeve over his fist and knocked out the remaining shards of glass, then reached in and opened the door from the inside. They could hear furious coughing.

When the door opened, a large cloud of white smoke fumed up and out. Jude stumbled into the doorway.

“I got you.” Warix looped Jude’s arm over his shoulders, helping him out and onto the garden grounds.

“Where are the others?” Marlowe asked.

“What happened?” Warix asked.

Jude tried to talk but couldn't stop coughing.

"Just yes-or-no questions!" Plum said.

"Is it a fire?" Warix asked.

Jude shook his head.

"Did the others get out?" Marlowe asked.

Jude shook his head.

Plum and Warix spun on their heels and headed back to the kitchen door. The smoke had dissipated almost completely. They moved through the kitchen door into a sort of mudroom.

"Dude!" Warix yelled.

The chemical-sweet scent of the smoke still hung in the air.

They edged past the hallway and into the kitchen itself. The large stainless steel door to the walk-in refrigerator hung open, meeting the freestanding butcher block island and acting as a sort of temporary wall.

On the exterior wall of the villa to her left, Plum saw the baker's rack piled with copper-bottomed pots and pans, and above it the high, narrow window, which was partially open, allowing some of the smoke to pour outside and alert them. Plum tried to reach the window to open it wider. Even though she was tall, she still had to climb on the bottom shelf of the rack. Pots and pans shivered, rattling with her slightest move.

The window was open as wide as it could go. Plum turned and knocked a saucepan off the shelf. It landed on the tiled floor with an impressively loud clatter. Plum gasped at the noise.

What if the killer was still in the kitchen and knew exactly where she was now?

Plum scrambled off the rack. From the window above, she heard shouts. She saw first Peach's platform espadrilles, then Cici's platform sandals and Shelley's Birkenstocks, the two girls half supporting, half dragging a man, his black sneakers stumbling between them.

"We have Dude!" Cici's scream carried into the kitchen.

"We have Jude!" Sofia called back.

"Does anyone see Jalen?" Plum yelled.

"No!" Warix yelled back. "Maybe he went through the villa!"

Plum nodded. She followed Warix back outside.

Peach led the way with Cici and Shelley following her and dragging Dude around the corner, stumbling down the slope into the kitchen garden. They dropped more than lowered Dude onto the scrub grass near Jude. Then again, Dude was twice Cici's size, and practically twice Shelley's size as well. Dude lay on the grass, panting and coughing as hard as Jude had.

"Dude!" Jude croaked. The boy leaned over and wrapped an arm around the older man's shoulder.

Dude tried to reply but was seized with further coughing.

"What happened?" Shelley asked.

"We broke into the door." Warix gestured behind them.

"Jude said they were still inside," Plum continued. "Did Jalen come your way? Through the villa?"

"We were already out here, maybe?" Shelley suggested.

"Oh my God," Peach interrupted, eyes wide. She was bouncing a little on her toes, full of adrenaline. "That was *sick*. Smoke everywhere, we went in, you know, to help, and we couldn't see, but then this big guy was just there, and they grabbed him and we got out!" Her tone was triumphant.

Peach swiped at her phone, then held it out, putting up a peace sign as she captured a selfie with the two smoke-inhalation victims lying on the stubbled grass behind her.

Dude redoubled his coughing as he flapped a hand at the kitchen door. "Jalen didn't get out."

14

There was a pervasive feeling of dread. The house was quiet. The smoke had cleared. And they were all here.

But there was no Jalen.

Everything was eerily silent.

"What happened?" Plum breathed the question. As if knowing what had happened would somehow change what they would inevitably find when they walked inside.

Jude shook his head. His pompadour was limp from smoke and sweat. It flapped rather than bounced, in a flattened wing. "We got Sean," he said. "It wasn't easy, but we managed to . . . um . . . extricate him from the globe." He shuddered. "We wrapped him in a blanket and carried him into the kitchen. We got to the fridge and opened the door. And that's when a smoke bomb or whatever it was went off."

Dude nodded. He coughed, stopping long enough to say "dropped Sean," and then started coughing again.

"Yeah, we dropped him, I climbed over the butcher block,

and Dude was there, and we couldn't see anything," Jude said.

"I opened window." Dude coughed.

"I bumped into you," Jude said, apologetically. "Sorry."

"Wasn't me." Dude shook his head.

Cici's perfectly lined eyes went wide. "There was another person there!"

"Unless it was Jalen?" Plum suggested.

"No, he shoved past us trying to get *into* the fridge," Jude explained. "When the smoke bomb went off. He closed the door and wouldn't open it again."

"I guess, that's . . . pretty smart?" Cici said. "If you think the killer is coming after you and you don't know what to do?"

Peach nodded emphatically. "Cold but smart."

Plum shrugged. "He does a murder podcast."

Peach made a face, a flash of an expression of disgust that she quickly smoothed over. "Anyway," Peach said. "I'm sure he's fine now."

"That's right!" Shelley exclaimed. "He should be safe, but he's stuck in there. Serves him right, maybe, for locking you guys out. But we can go get him . . ." She trailed off, glancing between Warix's grim expression and Plum's shaking head. "What?" Shelley breathed at last.

"The fridge can be opened from the inside," Warix answered. "Jalen should be standing here with us right now. If . . ." He didn't finish the statement.

He didn't have to.

"Maybe someone messed with the door!" Shelley offered.

"Yeah!" Peach agreed. "The same person you bumped into, Jude. They set off the bomb and locked the door from the outside."

"No." Plum shook her head. She was growing to hate the feeling of delivering dire news, the feeling when everyone turned their eyes to her. "When we were just in there," Plum explained, "the fridge door was open. Just hanging wide open."

As one, they turned to stare at the kitchen of the grand villa.

"Guess we better go find out what happened to Jalen," Dude rasped.

15

Jalen was lying curled on his side in the center of the large walk-in fridge. A knife handle, stabbing through a piece of paper, protruded from his chest.

He'd not been safely hiding in the refrigerator. He'd been dead all this time.

Plum wanted to cry or scream. They hadn't been able to avoid the killer at all, even with all their careful plans.

"That's, um, is that . . . that's paper," Peach stammered.

"A poem, yes," Warix answered, his voice equally thin.

"That's a lot of blood," Shelley said. The astrological poet looked more wan than usual.

"Deep breath," Sofia coached. Henrietta clucked sympathetically. Or at least it sounded sympathetic to Plum.

Their group stood unmoving in the open door of the fridge. Arctic air blew out.

The pool of blood spreading down the podcaster's shirt was impressive.

"Who's gonna . . . ?" Dude began.

"Oh, for Pete's sake." Plum moved into the fridge and knelt. She put a hand on the paper, trying to decide if it was safe to rip it off the knife.

"What's it say?" Cici asked.

Jalen liked bloody ground.

Well, now it's all around.

His podcast was yucky,

it's true he was sucky.

Still, that's not why I killed him.

I did it for the mocking that fulfilled him.

Now you can't run or hide.

It's time the next one died.

Shelley snorted, then glanced around. "Sorry." She waved a hand. "It's not funny. Not funny at all." She tittered again. "It rhymes though! All the way through!"

"Yeah, our killer's getting better," Jude agreed. "At poems," he amended.

"It was *Brittlyn*," Cici spat. "She's still missing. Maybe she was the one you ran into."

"I don't think so . . ." Jude began.

"Why not?" Cici asked.

"The person felt . . . bigger than that. I thought it was Dude." Jude said.

"But it wasn't me," Dude interjected. His dark eyebrows pressed upward toward his spiked hair.

"It might not have been a man at all, you just thought that because that's what you expected," Cici urged.

"Maybe." Jude didn't seem convinced. "Pretty sure he was big though."

"None of this matters." Dude waved his hands in frustration. "What I mean is, it matters but not much. It doesn't change anything. Right now, no one's at the watch tent, no one's at the fire, no one's doing their jobs and—"

There was a sudden moan, eerie and gasping.

Peach shrieked. It reverberated off the metal walls of the refrigerator. Peach grabbed at Cici and pulled the beauty expert in front of her.

Jalen suddenly sat up. He rubbed the back of his head, gazing at them blearily. He blinked, winced, and looked down at the knife protruding from his chest. "I've been stabbed!" he stated. "Someone get a picture for the podcast notes."

16

Jalen seemed fine. Well, mostly fine. Apart from the knife sticking out of him.

And apart from all the blood.

"Oh my God." Shelley knelt next to the podcaster. Her hands flapped around him, like she wanted to help, was going to touch his shoulder, or the knife, then had a second thought about if that was wise. Her hands looked like fluttering moths.

"Did you get the picture?" Jalen asked Jude, who'd immediately pulled out his phone to complete the podcaster's request.

"Yeah," Jude said. "Let me just get one more. Shelley, move, please. Jalen, say . . . uh . . . 'killer!' "

"Killer!" Jalen said, smiling, with the knife still sticking out of him. "Now do a serious one."

Jude moved around the walk-in refrigerator and snapped a few pictures, one where Jalen looked solemnly into the camera, another where Jalen let his eyes roll back slightly, his face a mask of pain.

"Dude," Dude breathed. "Doesn't that hurt?" He gestured at the knife handle.

Jalen nodded. "Hell yeah, but not as much as you'd think." He started to shiver.

"You're in shock!" Peach exclaimed. "That's one of the signs!"

"I'm also in a fridge," Jalen said.

"Yeah, let's get him out of here." Warix leaned over, offering a hand to the podcaster.

"Hold up," Jalen said. Then, without warning, he reached his hand up and yanked the knife out of his chest.

"Gah!" Peach screamed.

"Oh, shit." Warix almost whooped in delight.

Marlowe grabbed a kitchen towel off the butcher block and rushed into the fridge. "That was so reckless!" Marlowe fussed, pressing the towel into Jalen's chest. "You're not supposed to just yank knives out—what if it was on an artery or something?" She cautiously lifted the towel. No spurts of blood.

Jalen looked at the knife in his hand. The blade was surprisingly slender and curved upward.

"I didn't know that," he said. "About not taking it out, I mean." He winced and worked his chest lightly.

"I found the first aid kit!" Jude yelped from the kitchen behind them.

They helped Jalen out of the fridge and tied the towel to his chest with an ACE bandage.

Dude used some more dishtowels to make a loose sling that

held Jalen's arm and shoulder immobile by looping his wrist up by his neck.

Plum pointed at Sean's blanket-wrapped body, lying where it had been dropped on the kitchen floor. "We should still put him in the fridge, right?"

She was proud of how steady her voice was.

Dude nodded and gestured to Jude and Warix.

When the body was in the fridge, they closed the door.

Warix turned to Jalen.

"Who stabbed you?" Warix didn't seem able to take his eyes off the slender curving knife still in Jalen's hand.

"I don't know," Jalen said ruefully. "There was smoke everywhere. I thought I'd get in the fridge when the smoke bomb went off."

"Yeah, thanks so much for *that,*" Dude said sarcastically.

"Listen, we know there's a killer—hell, one of us is the killer—so yeah, I'm not sorry for trying to save my own life," Jalen said.

Dude shrugged but still looked annoyed.

"We were supposed to stay together," Jude said.

"How, when I couldn't see anything? And when a trap went off? I thought there could be another explosion!"

"Okay, so you got in the fridge and closed the door. Then what happened?" Plum asked.

"I held the door closed," Jalen said. "I heard Dude pounding on it, pulling on it, but I held it closed. Then it was like

Dude left, 'cause it was quiet for a moment or two. Then someone really strong yanked it open and shoved me, hard." He shook his head and glanced down at his sling. "I started to fall and twisted to one side, and it was right then that I got stabbed. Then I fell. I don't remember hitting my head, but I must have." Jalen gingerly touched the side of his head. "I don't remember anything else till I looked up and you were all standing there holding that page. Is it another poem?"

Plum nodded and handed him the poem.

Jalen read it silently.

Peach gestured at the knife. "That boning knife and your slip probably combined to save your life."

Jalen laughed. "A knife saved my life?" He shook his head. "That's a good episode title for later."

Peach pointed to the butcher block. An array of knives sat in a knife block on top of it. "The killer probably meant to grab something like this." She pulled out a vicious, wide butcher knife with a wicked edge. Peach touched the tip daintily. She then replaced it in the knife block. "See? And this is where the boning knife goes." She touched an empty slit beside the butcher knife.

Jalen looked at the knife in his hand.

"Boning knife?" Jude asked.

"Yeah," Peach said. "It's for deboning meats. It's curved so you can cut easily alongside the bone."

Plum felt herself staring at Peach in surprise.

Peach shrugged. "I was bored on a yacht, so the chef

explained about all the knives." She fluffed her hair. "Anyway, it means when it went into Jalen, it didn't go in straight but curved up. And that probably saved his life, because it didn't go into his lung or his heart."

Jalen winced at the knife. "Thanks, little boning knife. I guess." He gestured into the kitchen. "Can someone get me a towel or a baggie or something? I wanna keep it."

Warix handed the podcaster a dishtowel.

"The killer clearly thought you were going to die," Plum said. She pointed at the note in Jalen's hand.

She didn't say it, but the thought jumped into her mind: Jalen had been the puppet destined to die. The rest of them were the puppets dancing, jerked on unseen strings.

"Dude, you got to see your own murder poem," Dude said.

"Yeah, that's wild." Jalen glanced down at the page in his hand.

"No, it's good," Plum said. She felt a spark of hope in her chest.

All eyes turned to her, waiting for the explanation.

"It means we have a clue."

17

They returned to the ballroom—it was safer away from the knives, and they'd already checked it for traps. Shoes and clothes spilled out of different bags set in various corners, along with charging cords and toiletries.

"Okay, so what's the clue?" Dude asked as he lowered himself to the floor.

The others settled on the floor as well, in a loose circle. Jalen sank down gingerly with Shelley's help and leaned against a wall.

"The note," Plum said. "We have a motive."

Warix frowned. "Didn't we have that before?" he asked. "When the previous poem said something about settling scores, right? So it's revenge?"

Plum nodded. "Yes, but we didn't know revenge for *what*."

Shelley's eyes widened. "That's right, we just thought it was because the killer didn't like influencers."

Cici leaned over to Peach. "We went around the room,

saying why we thought the killer had a grudge against us specifically, since we are all clearly being targeted."

Peach's eyes grew wide, and her mouth formed an exaggerated O. "You mean it's not an accident that you guys are here?" she asked. She looked around the group for confirmation. "I just thought you were, like, party crashers. You mean you actually got invitations?"

Plum sighed. "Not exactly the time to start comparing clout scores, Peach."

Peach huffed and smoothed her minidress. "I'm just saying I'm surprised I got invited and you guys also got invited. I didn't mean anything by it."

"Yes, you got invited. Maybe think about what that means," Shelley scolded, twining her long red hair into a coil.

"I get invited to lots of things," Peach sniffed.

"Oh my God, it means you're a target, too, okay?" Shelley wound the coil into a bun.

Peach's mouth opened as if she wanted to argue. Then it snapped shut.

"If we could just get to the point," Dude grumbled.

"Right, what's the motive?" Jalen asked wearily.

"The motive is revenge for mocking," Plum said.

"That's ridiculous!" Dude let a huff of disbelief. "I mean! That's what happens online! Hell, that's what happens on *playgrounds*! This guy should grow a damn backbone, suck it up, and move on!"

Marlowe jabbed a finger at Dude. "Sure, sure, that's what *normal* people would do. The killer isn't normal. How many times do we have to say it?"

Dude blew out a breath. He swiped his sunglasses off his head and started twirling them rapidly.

"You're just nervous because if mockery is the reason, you're definitely the next one to die," Warix said, laughing.

"Listen, let's not argue. Let's work with what we have," Plum interjected before Dude could start another fight. "The advantage we have, which the killer didn't count on, is that Jalen's alive."

Cici gasped. "That's right! Jalen can tell us who he mocked! We can figure out which one of us is the killer!"

"Um, the thing is," Jalen stammered.

"I'm not the killer, so, like, maybe I should be the judge," Peach said.

"Excuse me, what?" Warix turned with a gobsmacked expression on his face.

"We're not the killer, either." Plum gestured to herself and her friends. "Like we pointed out before, since we weren't really targets."

"So you *say*." Dude threw his hands up in the air in exasperation. "But there's no way to prove it, even if, yes, it does seem less likely. You could still be the killer, or killers, working in cahoots."

"What about Brittlyn?" Jude asked. "Didn't we decide she's

the killer? And she's hiding somewhere on the island?"

"No way was she the one who stabbed me," Jalen said. "She's not strong enough."

"Great, now we can add sexism to the mix." Cici crossed her arms. "Just because you think a woman isn't strong enough doesn't mean she can't be! I can totally picture Brittlyn stabbing you with no problem."

"It's not sexism, I just—whoever opened that door was—" Jalen stammered.

"Listen, it's not me, okay? You know how you can know? Because I literally just got here." Peach's hands bobbed with each word, emphasizing her point.

"So you say. You could have been hiding in that shed. Just being the devil's advocate," Dude argued, holding his hands up.

"But we searched everywhere?" Plum asked him.

Dude shrugged. "It could be like hide-and-seek. You know, if the killer moved from hiding place to hiding place, we could search and still not find them."

"Oh my God, you *saw* Andre's helicopter!" Peach argued.

"Listen, this is all getting us off track," Plum interjected. "And we don't need a judge, Peach, but thanks for offering."

Peach made a face at Dude, then dipped her shoulder at Plum in a *you're welcome* bob.

Plum took a deep breath. "What we should be talking about is Jalen. And who he relentlessly mocked. Because that's how we can maybe figure out who the killer is."

Jalen winced and looked down at his feet. "Remember what I told you? About my show before *Bloody Grounds*?"

"What was it?" Peach asked. "Have I heard of it?"

Jalen kept his gaze on the floor. "I don't know. It was called *Epic Fail*. It mocked everyone. I wasn't going out *harassing* anyone, but if there was a viral video or whatever, I'd crack jokes, play it, play it in slo-mo, you know."

Plum felt the bubble of hope sinking in her chest. "There's no way to narrow it down?" she asked, desperately trying to keep it afloat.

Jalen shook his head.

"That was nice while that lasted," Warix said, his voice dripping with bitterness.

"What was?" Jude asked.

"Thinking we had the upper hand."

18

"Well, that was pretty pointless," Dude said. "If it's about mocking someone and the mocked person getting their revenge . . . I mean. Between just the two of us"—Dude gestured between himself and Jalen, then pointed at Warix—"and you too, probably, I mean . . . who *haven't* we pissed off?" He heaved a sigh. "I need to quit it. I need a new line of work."

Shelley squeezed his shoulder. "That's good. That's growth."

"How about you, Shelley?" Jude asked suddenly. "Who did you mock?"

Shelley shook her head in bewilderment. "No one! I mean, like, no one ever!"

"Me too," Cici said with a sigh. "I mean, me either. Or neither."

"Oh, like you're both too nice?" Warix sniped. "Whatever, I've heard girls talk before."

"No, it's just we're not about that online," Cici snapped. "Unlike you."

"Yeah . . . but . . . you can't be sure," Dude said slowly. He scrubbed at his bleached spikes in frustration. "You're online. You use GIFs and stuff. Memes. What if . . . what if it was something like that?"

"A GIF? Someone's going to kill me because I used the wrong *GIF?!*" Shelley's voice climbed in both tone and register.

"I'm just saying." Dude held out his hand. "Jalen said he did an internet clip show. Viral stuff."

"Yeah." Jude's eyebrows lifted in sudden understanding. "Viral stuff is everywhere."

"That's why they call it viral, hon," Peach said to him, condescendingly, Plum thought, but Jude beamed like he was suddenly and for the first time the teacher's pet.

"I guess that's possible," Cici said, nodding. "It's possible I used some GIFs or clips. It's all about jazzing up the makeup videos, you know."

"Who *doesn't* communicate with GIFs?" Shelley asked exasperatedly.

"How about you?" Dude asked, turning to Jude.

"Oh yeah, I mean, yeah. I've been on a few shows, you know, with the Holsy twins and Aaron Forster. They can get a bit rough, you know, not mean-mean but a little mean? Girls like it when they think there's a rivalry or something. So yeah, maybe."

"Can you think of one clip in particular? Or one time you felt bad about?" Dude asked.

Jude shook his head, dropping his eyes. "Not really. I mean, if we had the internet, I could look it up, but I don't remember anything off the top of my head."

Plum turned to her sister. "How about you, Peach?"

Peach flashed dramatically wide eyes and tented her fingers on her collarbones. "Me? I'm not *mean*."

Plum had to agree. The hurt she felt from Peach was more about neglect rather than active malice.

Didn't mean that the hurt was any less.

"It's not about being mean," Cici said. "It's about just using a viral clip or something without thinking about it."

"I think about everything I post, thank you very much." Peach sat up straighter. "You don't get a million followers without *curating your brand*."

"Forget it!" Cici snapped, tossing her ponytail over her shoulder.

"I have *stalkers*, okay? Like, I'm at *that* level!"

"I think it's fair to say we all have stalkers," Warix drawled. "Well, we all share one, at least." He snorted.

"Yes, fine," Peach retorted. "But I have more than one. There's a billionaire who's OB-SESSED with me! He sends me flowers every day, he lets me use his car service, and if I'm going to a public event, he will be there the moment I post about it. He's kinda cute, actually."

"Oh my God, it's like Fifty Shades. Make it stop," Sofia pleaded.

"Yeah, yeah, you told us about Andre already," Shelley said in exhaustion. "With the helicopter."

"Oh, honey, oh no, Andre's not a billionaire," Peach said brightly.

Plum tipped her head. Was he just a regular guy, like a helicopter pilot?

"He's a millionaire," Peach explained, looking around the group.

"This is hell," Warix said. "Did we all die in the kitchen? 'Cause this is definitely hell."

19

After that, it seemed the best thing to do was return to their previous plan.

Stick in their groups: one on watch at the cliff, with a new signal fire ready to be lit. Another group resting, and a third to search the island again, looking for Brittlyn.

Peach had somehow managed to be in the resting group two times in a row. Maybe it was the power of fame, but none of the others seemed to mind.

"How about we volunteer for watch?" Plum murmured. "I could use a break from this house."

"Yeah, and Henrietta could stretch her legs," Sofia agreed.

The girls grabbed a few generic sodas and a sleeve of crackers, and headed out to the FEMA tent at the top of the cliff.

The sun was setting, a spectacular blaze of glittering diamonds cast across the ocean in a broad swath.

"I'm so scared," Marlowe said conversationally as she stared out at the water.

Plum turned to her best friend. A fine net of wrinkles, unfamiliar on Marlowe's usually smooth face, stitched across her brow and stamped into the corners of her eyes.

"Me too," Sofia agreed.

They were sitting in the shelter of the FEMA tent, effectively blocking the entrance with their bodies, while Henrietta happily pecked among the weeds and grasses that they'd uprooted and thrown into the tent.

"This is so horrible. It almost doesn't feel real," Plum muttered. "I'm sorry, I know it is. I just can't accept it."

"We just got lucky, huh?" Sofia agreed sarcastically. "The one time I do something rebellious."

"No, I got greedy," Plum said. Something burned in her heart, a dose of hot pinpricks in her cheeks, nausea and regret and . . . shame.

"It doesn't help to go into all this," Marlowe said firmly. "We can't go back and change the past. We're here now. We have to figure out how to get out."

"Do you really think we'll be killed?" Sofia asked. "Since we weren't the real target?"

"I don't think the killer will care," Plum said softly. "Whoever they are, they've been planning this thing for a long time. They're not going to stop just because we showed up."

"Adopt, adapt, and improve, eh?" Marlowe said, her voice sad and wry. It was a quote from an old British comedy sketch about a bungling burglar who realized he was holding up the wrong shop.

Plum sighed. "Yeah, exactly." Even though she was looking out over the ocean and currently safe with her two best friends and their chicken, it was difficult not to feel a fatalistic pull. Difficult not to feel a twinge of hopelessness.

What else could they do? They were already doing everything they could think of.

Jude, Dude, and a bitterly complaining Warix were searching the villa and its grounds again, looking for the person Jude had bumped into in the thick smoke. Or for Brittlyn. Or both.

Peach, Shelley, Cici, and Jalen were resting in the ballroom, trying to get some sleep so they'd be ready for a later watch shift.

And they were out here. On watch. Facing Saint Vitus, praying for a miracle.

"Do you think they'll find her?" Sofia asked, their minds running parallel as always, because no one had to ask who she meant.

Marlowe shook her head. "The more important question is, why would the killer move her body?"

Plum glanced away from the flame-edged horizon, looking away from the spectacular beauty of a Caribbean sunset to take in her best friend's equally spectacular profile.

"Wait, what?" Plum asked. "How can you sound so sure that Brittlyn isn't the killer after all?"

Marlowe glanced at Plum, a slight smile on the edges of her mouth. "I'm not, not really, but she *looked* dead, right?"

Sofia nodded. "Completely. Ow!" She twisted and shoved Henrietta back. "That's a *mole*, you silly bird," Sofia snapped. Henrietta torqued her head, pointing first one eye, then the other, at the tempting it-must-be-a-bug-seeming mole on Sofia's shoulder.

"Here." Plum handed her friend her tuxedo jacket.

"I'm not sure at all, but also, if this was a classic movie, it's something the killer would do, right?" Marlowe continued once Sofia's shoulder was covered.

"Move a body? Why?" Plum couldn't imagine it. Sure, killing people made sense, she guessed, to a deranged killer, but *why* in the world would they take an already dead body and play hide-and-seek with it?

"To get us to think exactly what we were thinking," Marlowe said. "That Brittlyn was the killer. That no one else is truly the suspect."

Sofia's eyes went round. "Oh," she breathed. "Oh, that's clever. And disturbing."

They all paused to take it in for a second.

"I mean, it's as disturbing as everything else," Sofia amended. "It makes sense, in a sick sort of way. To divert suspicion."

Marlowe stared back out at the sun, almost disappeared now. "Watch for the flash," she urged them, as if there weren't a whole other conversation going on about a rampant murderer.

As if they were just having a normal island sunset on their spring break adventure.

As if they weren't trapped on an island with dwindling supplies, no method of communication with the outside world, and one dead body. Well, two, probably, somewhere.

As if they might not be next.

The sun disappeared, and the turquoise flash arced out in a gorgeous blink-and-you'll-miss-it shine.

"Beautiful," Sofia murmured.

Marlowe sighed happily. Then she shook her head again. "If they find anything, it'll be Brittlyn's body. But I don't think they'll find even that. Our killer has other plans."

The Second Night of Pyre Festival

The Island of Little Esau

Three Will Die

1

The fading reds and pinks of the sunset were disappearing, edged by gray and the blackness of falling night.

Sofia switched on their lantern-style flashlight. She set it to the side of the tent, giving them just enough light to see by and still allowing their eyes to grow somewhat accustomed to the dark.

"Good girl," Sofia said in such an approving tone that Plum felt a rush of pride in whatever she'd just done or said to gain such an affirming remark.

Sofia was looking in the tent behind them, at Henrietta.

The chicken had settled on a bed of grasses, her feet covered by her feathers, head tilted toward the underside of one wing, as if seeking permission.

"Go ahead and sleep," Sofia murmured to the bird. "I'll wake you up if anything happens, I promise."

Henrietta gave a murmuring cluck and tucked her beak under her wing.

"Awwww," Marlowe breathed.

"She's growing on you, huh?" Sofia said with no small amount of smug self-satisfaction.

"No," Marlowe retorted, but with a loving smile. "I was saying 'aw' at you, you dope."

Sofia snorted and jostled into Marlowe's shoulder. "Aw right back, chickenhearted one."

Watching her friends, Plum felt a surge of love for them, an actual surge in her veins like a superpower. She loved them so much. She would do anything to protect them.

"That bird's lucky you took her under *your* wing," Marlowe said. She turned merry eyes to Plum. "Get it? Under her wing? See what I did there?"

Sofia groaned.

Plum laughed.

Marlowe looked pleased.

Plum felt a different surge of emotion, a sparking kind of love, the kind that wanted to catch fire, wanted so desperately to catch fire.

Fire.

"Something doesn't make sense," Plum murmured.

Marlowe sighed. "None of this makes sense." She sounded sad to be dragged back to the present moment.

"No, I mean, something's not right." Plum shook her head. "I can't shake the feeling that I'm missing something. Something obvious."

Sofia shrugged. "Well, if you missed it, we all missed it."

Plum turned to her two friends. She leaned across Marlowe so she could see Sofia as easily. She tried not to get distracted by the soft skin of Marlowe's arm touching hers. Plum couldn't help it—she turned, helplessly, and looked in Marlowe's blue-green eyes.

Marlowe looked back. It was almost as if Marlowe was holding her breath, too.

"What?" Sofia asked.

Plum gave herself a tiny mental shake and made herself look away from Marlowe. "The killer," Plum said. "I feel like I'm missing a clue. Or something. If I could just make it make sense."

Marlowe sat up straighter. "Let's talk about what we know."

Sofia nodded eagerly. "We don't have a whiteboard or anything, but if we were on one of those detective shows my dad likes, we'd have all this on some kind of big display in front of us. With, like, red yarn and stuff."

"Good!" Plum nodded.

So they began mapping it out. Everything that had happened. The times they'd arrived, the buffet, no water, the reveal that there was no real festival. The name of the festival itself a dire warning—a pyre to burn a corpse.

Sofia shuddered at that. "Ugh," she said. "I feel so stupid we didn't have more pause at that."

"It sounded edgy. Cool." Marlowe smiled with self-deprecating humor. "I fell for it, too. Like Burning Man. That sounds bad, too, and it's a cool thing, right?"

"Pyre Festival." Plum shook her head. "Set the night on fire." She hoped the motto wasn't literal.

2

They talked through the events as the moon came out. The dinner, the first death: Brittlyn. Dude finally stepping forward, risking his life on the failed but still noble attempt at CPR.

Thinking it was an accident. Then the poem.

"Just because Shelley writes bad poetry doesn't make her the killer," Marlowe noted.

"True," Sofia said. "But also, Shelley just seems too . . . I don't know. Floaty? To be a killer?"

"Yes, but that could be an act. Just like Jude," Plum argued.

Marlowe shook her head. "I don't know. Is anyone *that* good of an actor?"

"I mean, award-winning actors are?" Sofia suggested with a laugh.

They sketched out the rest of it, up to where they were now. Peach's arrival. Brittlyn's body going missing. The attack on Jalen and the smoke bomb in the kitchen.

Peach, Shelley, and Cici had gone to the inside door, and Plum and her friends had gone with Warix to the lower garden door. Jude stumbled out their door; Dude fell out the other with the girls.

"Jalen was unconscious in the fridge with a knife in him," Marlowe said, eyes focused on the middle distance, as if she were looking at the scene in her memory.

"Unless he did it to himself, to divert our suspicion." Sofia shuddered.

"Yes." Marlowe frowned.

"Just up and stabbed his own chest with a boning knife," Sofia supplied.

"Oof. Okay, now I feel like throwing up," Marlowe groaned.

"Sorry," Sofia said. "It's just that if it wasn't Jalen, it means our killer is *strong*. I don't think it could be Cici, for example."

"Maybe it depends on how sharp the knife was?" Plum suggested.

"Uuuuugh," Marlowe groaned again.

"Let's keep moving," Plum urged, glancing at her pale friend.

"So then Jalen's unconscious inside the walk-in fridge." Sofia gestured at the ground in front of her.

"Right, and the fridge door was open when we went in," Plum said, remembering the scene.

"Yeah, but both Jude and Dude said that Jalen went *into* the fridge when the smoke bomb went off and wouldn't let them in," Sofia said.

"Meanwhile, they *both* said they bumped into someone," Marlowe said.

Plum shook her head. "No way. I don't believe it."

"What, they're both lying?" Marlowe asked. "Or they're working together?"

"No." Plum shook her head again. "Only one of them is lying." She blew out a breath, trying to release the tension in her chest. "There's no room in that kitchen for a fourth person to hide—it's not modern, not this big open space. Remember, it was crowded, and no closets.

"Jude, Jalen, and Dude carried the body through the butler's pantry, and so the 'other' person couldn't hide in there. And the door to the garden was closed, just like the windows. And once the smoke bomb went off—if the killer or this mythical other person had come from the outside, they would have let out a plume of smoke from the back door—we would have seen that," Plum said.

"The only smoke was coming from that one window," Sofia agreed.

The window.

Plum rocked back suddenly.

"What?" It was Marlowe's turn to lean across her friend, staring into her eyes.

"Oh." Plum breathed, blinking. "Oh no."

"What?" Sofia yelped. "Tell us!"

Plum felt like her heart was trying to beat out of her chest, trying to escape with the surge of adrenaline in her veins.

"I know who the killer is."

3

"Who?" Sofia urged.

"The person who's lying." Plum reached out and grasped her friends' hands in hers, squeezing urgently. "The window. Remember? Dude said that when the smoke bomb went off, he and Jude separated. Dude said he went straight to the window to open it."

Her friends waited.

"So many things are wrong with that story, I don't know where to begin!" Plum said. "Firstly, why go to the window? Why not the door?"

"Because he was looking for the door, but he found the window first," Sofia explained, taking the devil's advocate position.

"Right, except the window is high on that wall. He'd have to climb on the rack like I did to reach it."

"So he made a bad choice about climbing to that window instead of getting to a door." Marlowe shrugged. "Doesn't make him a liar."

"But don't you see? It *does*," Plum urged. "He never went to the window! I think the window was already open—that window, specifically—to let the smoke out. And he lied about opening it to cover himself."

Marlowe still looked doubtful. "Why do it at all?" she rebutted. "The smoke, I mean. Why let it out of the kitchen at all?"

"To summon us," Sofia said.

"Right!" Plum agreed. "He's a planner. He planned *all of this* in advance. And the window was to bring all of us rushing in to add confusion. It gave him both time to go *back* to the refrigerator, open it, and try to kill Jalen! And with all of us there, it deflected suspicion from him, because the killer could have been any of us."

"I mean, that is all *possible*," Marlowe said. "What shows that Dude's a liar?"

Plum took a deep breath. She needed to make sure she was clear, that her reasoning was explained well. Their lives depended on it. "Because if he was desperately trying to get out, found the rack, realized he could climb it to the window, then—"

Sofia gasped, clapping her hand over her mouth.

Plum nodded. "Then he would have knocked over the pans, like I did."

"Oh my God," Marlowe said.

"No pans were on the floor when we went in there. Nothing looked disturbed at the window until *I* knocked the pans over."

Sofia nodded vigorously. "If he wasn't able to see, he would've knocked one over. If he'd tried to climb the rack to open a window, he'd have knocked more onto the floor."

"So the window was already open," Marlowe said.

"Yes! And the person Jude bumped into . . ." Plum said, leading her friend.

"Was Dude going to get the knife!" Marlowe nearly shouted. Her grip on Plum's hand was tight.

"Thank God he grabbed the wrong handle!" Plum squeezed Marlowe's hand in return.

Sofia cursed in Spanish. Then she sprang to her feet and swept the sleeping Henrietta up in her arms. "We have to go warn the others," she said.

4

Jude was standing to one side of the shed, actually a derelict caretaker's cottage. The teen scrubbed at his sticky, semi-floppy mop of hair.

"Jude!" Plum called when they dashed up.

"Hey." Jude frowned at them. "Aren't you supposed to be on watch?"

"Where's Dude?" Marlowe asked, lowering her voice.

"And Warix?" Sofia added. She swiftly bent down, placing Henrietta at their feet. The chicken pecked at the ground, moving slowly away from the cottage and their group.

The girls formed a protective semicircle around Jude.

"They're inside." Jude tilted his head toward the cottage. "Searching. Well, Dude's searching. Warix wanted to get away from the bugs."

"You're supposed to stick together!" Marlowe fussed.

"I know, but it's gross in there, and I like the stars," Jude began, then his voice trailed off as he finally seemed to register their urgent faces. "Brittlyn's the killer, so it's safe, right?"

"Dude's the killer," Plum told him.

Jude frowned and gave her an indulgent little smile. "No way," he said. "Dude's all right. He's cool."

"No! He's just *pretending*," Sofia urged. "Didn't your parents or your grandmother ever warn you about certain people?"

"Dude's the killer. He lied about the window." Plum explained about the shelf and the pots on it, about the height of the window. How Dude had lied about all of it.

"He didn't even *go* to the window, because it was already open!" Marlowe said.

"He stayed behind to open the fridge and stab Jalen!" Plum said.

"No way," Jude breathed. Then his eyes went wide with horror. "Warix is in there with him!"

"Get out!" The sudden, muffled shout came from inside the cottage.

Dude fell across the doorway. His eyes landed on the girls and Jude.

Plum grasped Sofia's and Marlowe's arms, pulling them away from Dude.

"Get back!" Dude waved one arm in a wide sweep. "This whole place is rigged with explosives!"

"Warix is in there!" Jude shrieked. He lunged toward the open door of the cottage.

"Oh, shi—" Dude cursed. "I'll get him, damn it. You stay

back!" He took a breath so deep it squared his shoulders, then lunged into the darkness of the cottage.

"That's brave!" Jude waved a hand at the cottage. "He's going to save Warix!"

Plum shook her head. "Don't trust him," she urged. "It's a trap."

Jude whirled on her, screaming, "HE TOLD US TO STAY BACK, HOW IS THAT A TRA—"

A hot wind and a percussive bang blasted outward from the cottage. An invisible and simultaneous sweep of force knocked the foursome back, throwing them onto the dried and prickly grass of the villa lawn.

5

Plum coughed. Her back hurt, her ribs ached, and she couldn't see very well. There was a bright film covering everything—like the aftershock of a camera flash in the dark.

The acrid tang of smoke filled her nostrils.

"Help," she rasped. "Help."

Had she said anything? She couldn't hear, not even the muted warble of her voice reverberating in her own head. The ringing in her ears drowned out all other noise.

Plum sat up. Her bones ached, her back felt scraped raw.

She twisted her hand and touched behind her. Her hand didn't feel any wetness, finding instead a dirt-crusted T-shirt.

Okay, so she wasn't bleeding.

"What happened?" she asked aloud. Or at least, she thought she asked it out loud.

"Marlowe! Sofia!"

Her hands flailed out. She blinked furiously. Her hand found an ankle next to her.

Cool hands reached down and gripped her own.

It was Marlowe. Plum would know her touch, the soft cool of her hands, the wafting of her scent, even under the smoke, better than anything.

Plum squeezed the hands tight, blinking tears of relief out of her eyes. The tears were helping her vision. At least, it seemed that shapes were resolving more clearly.

Plum extricated one hand from Marlowe's tight grip and reached out to her other side.

A hand touched her right shoulder.

Plum yelped.

This time, she heard it, as well as the responding yelp and then the rapid cadence of Sofia's speech.

Both her friends were okay.

Plum sobbed.

Sofia patted her shoulder.

Sounds washed in and out, but that didn't matter.

Both her friends were safe. But what about the others?

6

The cottage was in utter ruin. A plume of smoke was still rising, but there were only small fires burning fitfully where a few pieces of wood had scattered from the explosion.

The front of the cottage was completely destroyed. Just a pile of stone and masonry with a roof collapsed on top. It looked vaguely like a child had knocked down the front and sides.

The chimney still stood tall, somehow, along with the back wall of the cottage.

"Warix! Dude!" Jude's ragged voice pieced the fading ringing in Plum's ears.

Jude stumbled forward, waving his arms at the steadily thinning smoke. "Dude!" he yelled again.

"We should help him look," Sofia said.

"No one could have survived that." Marlowe shook her head in dismay.

But they all stood, helping each other up, wincing at various scrapes and twinges.

Jude was walking along the rubble pile, yelling sporadically as he edged forward.

They followed, peering into the piles of rock for any sign of life. Or for any sign of anything other than rock and timber.

They turned the corner and edged along the fallen rubble toward the still-standing rear wall of the house. There was an unmistakable Converse high-top, printed with a bright galaxy swirl, sitting on the scrubby lawn a few feet away from the ruin.

"Warix!" Jude gasped. He rushed forward and picked up the shoe, clutching it like it was Cinderella's slipper.

Jude looked puzzled. He glanced down.

His face instantly transformed, almost cramping with revulsion. He flung the shoe away.

It landed about three yards from the girls, tipping onto its side, revealing a bloody, meaty mass and a fat shard of gleaming white bone inside.

Sofia let out a shriek. Marlowe gasped and clutched Plum's arm.

Plum felt a wave of nausea.

Warix's foot.

It was still in his shoe.

On the path ahead of them, Jude bent over, throwing up into the grass.

7

It only got worse after that.

They found more remains. A leg poking out from under a collapsed wall. Indisputably Warix's, wearing the glossy, satiny track pants and the other galaxy shoe.

Farther around the back of the cottage, they found more—a broad swath of blood, spreading out from beneath the largest pile of rubble. Plum shivered. How close were they to ending up just like Warix? How could the gamer just be killed like that? And . . . where was Dude?

The night had advanced, steadily and mercifully robbing color from their eyes.

Marlowe's face was smudged with tears and dirt. Sofia had a graze on her shoulder, a slight trickle of blood showing through her torn pink tank top.

Plum ripped a piece from the hem of her oversized white T-shirt and dabbed at her friend's shoulder.

From the flickering glare of the few remaining rubble fires,

Plum could distinctly see more . . . tissue. Gore-smeared, indistinguishable as human.

And a ruined pair of mirrored aviator sunglasses.

Bile rose in her throat again.

"Dude," Marlowe said.

They shuffled forward together in a shell-shocked daze.

"Dude," Jude agreed mournfully.

"Look." Sofia was pointing to an overturned wheelbarrow.

A piece of paper fluttered from its back.

They stumbled to it. Plum took it and read.

It's over for Warix now.

Isn't that sad?

No, not really,

it isn't that bad.

One minute here, now he's died in the night.

But influencers all want to blow up, am I right?

"That's not nice," Jude murmured flatly.

"Our killer's not nice," Plum agreed.

"Didn't we agree to call them '*the* killer'?" Marlowe murmured.

"Where's Dude's poem?" Sofia looked around. "There should be another one, right?"

"I don't think the killer meant to kill both of them," Plum said slowly. "Remember how Dude ran back in? He should have been outside . . ."

"Just like with Brittlyn," Marlowe said, and Plum didn't have to ask to know what she meant.

She was thinking about how Dude hadn't hesitated to perform mouth-to-mouth while the rest of them were worrying about poison.

"He was . . . brave," Sofia said.

Plum felt a rush of guilt and self-reprimand. Here she'd thought Dude might be the killer, all because his story hadn't made sense. She was wrong. He'd risked his life again for one of them—and this time he didn't make it out alive.

They turned back around, facing the smoldering ruin.

There was nothing else to be done.

They were in no state to dig through the thousands of pounds of rubble, to do what? Locate mangled, crushed, severed bodies? To do what with them then?

Carry them to a walk-in fridge?

There was a sudden, loud cluck. Sofia let out a little gasp.

"Oh, thank goodness!" Sofia bent, reaching into the base of a bush. She pulled out the shell-shocked chicken.

Henrietta immediately tucked her beak under Sofia's forearm.

Plum slowly turned their group away from the ruined cottage, back toward the villa. They started shuffling up the path.

They had to find Cici, Shelley, Peach, and Jalen.

They had to tell them what happened.

Come to think of it . . . shouldn't they be outside by now? Shouldn't they have come running at the noise?

A deepening feeling of unease settled on Plum's shoulders, almost like a constricting cloak, tightening around her ribs, across her shoulders, behind her neck.

Without talking, they stumbled forward faster.

8

The villa's atrium was eerily silent and dark.

Henrietta muttered a worried cluck.

No one else made a sound.

They shuffled forward in lockstep toward the interior hallway that opened into the ballroom.

The door groaned open, almost comically loud. Like a bad sound effect in a cheesy horror movie, revealing the tableau inside.

Peach, Cici, and Jalen stood huddled tightly together directly in front of them, a mirror of how Plum, Sofia, Marlowe, and Jude clung to each other. Peach, Cici, and Jalen swiveled their heads to the doorway. Their faces wore the same shell-shocked look Plum assumed hers did. A short-circuited expression strung between surprise, horror, and exhaustion.

Cici's eyes were round, her mouth open slightly in shock.

Peach extricated one of her hands from Cici's grip long enough to point at something that Plum couldn't see from the doorway.

The cluster of four new arrivals to the scene shuffled into the room, turning almost as one unit, like meerkats scenting danger.

Shelley was lying flat on her back, her arms and legs spread out like a starfish's. Her body was near the wall by the stereo system that Warix had uncovered earlier.

Her phone and a charging cord lay on the ground. The wall, where the cord was plugged in, had a large black scorch mark tracing up from the socket.

The ungrounded, ancient socket.

"She . . . she . . ." Cici stammered.

Jalen shook his head forcefully. He winced as the gesture disturbed his bandaged chest.

Through her shock, Peach seemed to register that Warix and Dude were missing. Her eyes traveled to the empty door behind her sister and her friends, then back to their group, then back to the empty door, as if waiting for the two men to appear.

Plum shook her head. "There was an explosion."

Peach nodded dazedly.

"Oh, we thought that was the transformer," Cici said. Her sculpted eyebrows were pressed together in a frown of shock and sorrow. Tear tracks were etched in her makeup.

There was no note waiting near the body. Still, no one suspected that Shelley's death had been an accident.

Their killer had trained them too well for that.

9

They found the poem eventually. Of course they did. It was placed exactly where the killer knew they would go.

On the inside of the fuse-box door, on the first floor, east wing of the house.

Peach had found it, taking it down to read,

Her poems and astrology were crap,

but mockery is why she got zapped.

"Wow, that's succinct. And tasteless," Peach said. She dropped the note to the floor and flipped the ancient levers, and the steady hum of power returned to the dark villa.

"I mean, writing a poem after murdering someone isn't what I'd call classy," Cici murmured. Even though she sounded vaguely like she was joking, her lower lip trembled.

"At least that one was short. And rhymed," Jalen said.

The lights flickered on.

They all shuffled back into the ballroom. The dark of night pressed against the glass windows and doors.

The lights within made the glass a reflection, showing the inhabitants their wide eyes, , their hands grasping each other as they waited, and waited, for the killer to make the next move.

Shelley was dead. Warix and Dude were dead. Sean. And maybe Brittlyn.

It was too much. Plum felt her brain shy back from thinking about any of it, recoil from the memories of the aftermath of the explosion, the grisly body parts, gore, blood.

Best not to think about it.

Poor Shelley. Poor Warix. Poor Dude.

She couldn't take her emotions any deeper. It was like a gauze bandage were carefully cocooning her emotions. She was terrified. But it was at a remove somehow. As if held only in her intellect and not in her body.

The others must have felt something similar. Shocked and exhausted eyes peered out of mostly slack faces.

Plum's eyes circled the remaining attendees of Pyre Festival. Jude, Jalen, Cici, Peach, Marlowe, Sofia, and herself.

That was it. Seven people.

Jude was the first to crack.

"Something's moving!" he gasped, pointing out the double doors.

Plum whirled around. All she could see was her own reflection.

Jude looked terrified. His smudged muscle shirt, soot-streaked face, and tear tracks, his greasy hair flat in his face. "No, I *saw* it!" he shouted. He moved sideways, a sudden lunge, as if trying to catch the lurker with the sudden feint.

"Dude, we can't see anything out there." Cici's voice was tight with nerves.

"DUDE would BELIEVE ME!" Jude yelled. Then he sobbed and brought the back of his hand up to swipe at his face. "We're sitting ducks."

On the floor, Henrietta clucked in agreement and helpfully began pecking at Jude's shoelaces.

"Well, I'm not going to stay a sitting duck!" Jude ranted, yanking his foot back. He edged to the doorway that led into the hall.

"Wait!" Plum urged. "We have to stick together!"

"Yeah, 'cause that keeps *not* working," Jude snapped. "This whole place could be rigged already." Jude put his hand on the door, turning back to look at them. "If it is, then it doesn't matter if we're careful. It doesn't matter if we stick together. And if one of you is the killer, I'd rather not make it easy for you."

He turned and headed into the hall.

Sofia scooped up Henrietta and followed him. "Wait, Jude," she called.

The rest of the group slowly trailed Jude into the atrium. "You guys can do what you want." Jude started climbing the stairs. "But I'm barricading myself in my room and getting some sleep."

He stopped at the top landing and turned a sad smile down at them, like a member of that singing family in that movie, sorry to say good night. "And if the killer planned for me to do that, then I guess they get me." Jude turned and walked into the hallway beyond.

A few moments later, they heard him slam and lock one of the bedroom doors. Then the heavy scrape of a piece of furniture being dragged across the floor.

Then silence.

Jalen sighed deeply. "He's right, in a way." Jalen stepped away from the group, following Jude's path to the stairwell. "I don't know if it's the shock, or the exhaustion, but I'm going to do what he's doing." Jalen jabbed a finger in the direction of Jude's room. He turned and smiled tiredly at them. "Good night." The pleasantry was profoundly at odds with the rest of their reality.

Jalen climbed the steps and disappeared down the hall. They heard his door close and the scrape of furniture being moved.

"I'm not going back into that room," Peach said. A shudder shook her.

"The body's still there," Cici agreed.

"And who knows what other trap," Plum added.

Cici grabbed Peach's hands. The shorter girl tilted her

ponytail toward the stairs. "At least up there we can sleep in a bed," she said.

Peach nodded.

"Hey," Plum called after her sister. "Maybe you want to go with us? You know?" She gestured to herself and her friends. Shouldn't Peach stick with her? They were family, after all.

Peach gave an apologetic wince. "Oh, thank you, but you snore."

Plum felt her mouth hanging open. Sometimes she snored, like anyone. But not habitually, except for when she was in third grade and kept getting strep so bad she had to get her tonsils out. Was Peach remembering that?

Peach turned to Cici. "You don't snore, do you?"

Cici shook her head. She gave Plum an apologetic shrug and followed Peach up the stairs.

Before she disappeared into the hallway at the top of the curving stairwell, Peach looked back at Plum. Her expression was . . . Was it sad? A pretend regret at leaving her for a stranger she barely knew?

Plum heaved a sigh and tried not to feel hurt.

A door closed. The familiar noises of lock and barricade followed.

Plum turned to her two best friends. "Well, my sister has decided to bunk down with someone she just met, so that's not at all hurtful." She blew out a breath. "Not that it matters, relatively speaking."

Sofia and Marlowe stepped in close, giving Plum the hugs she didn't know she needed.

"What do you want to do?" Plum asked them.

Marlowe pointed at the stairwell.

"Go lock ourselves in," Sofia said.

"Right. If we can't all be together in the same room, at least we can all be in the same part of the villa," Plum said.

The three friends climbed the stairs and locked themselves in their room. They shoved the heavy chest in front of the door.

Marlowe started knocking on the walls at regular intervals. "Looking for secret doors or passages," she explained at Sofia's quizzical look.

Plum nodded and went to the windows. They were still painted shut, like the French doors onto the Juliet balcony.

Sofia carried Henrietta into the bathroom, closing the door on the hen in the shower. "I'm sorry, I just need a break." She looked both guilty and defiant.

Plum climbed into the saggy-centered bed. She lay down with a sigh.

Marlowe climbed in on one side of her, and Sofia on the other.

"Here, wait," Sofia said. "Hand me your phones. We should keep them charged in case anything happens and we can actually use them."

Plum and Marlowe thrust their phones out for Sofia. Sofia winced for a moment before plugging them in—maybe remembering what had happened to Shelley. But nothing happened. Then Sofia crawled back on the bed, on Plum's other side.

Before her eyes were even closed, Plum felt a floating sense of fatigue setting in. "I'm sorry, you guys," she murmured.

"Don't start that," Marlowe murmured back.

At the same time, Sofia answered, "Yeah, you are." But there was only fondness in her tone.

They fell asleep.

The Final Day of Pyre Festival

Melt Your Face Off

1

The morning light streaming in through the windows woke Plum.

That, and an insistent chiming.

"What's going on?" Marlowe grumbled. She sat up, her head adorably mussed, Plum thought, as her friend scrubbed her eyes.

"Shh, still sleeping," Sofia complained.

"Whose phone is going off?" Plum asked. She scooted on her butt to the edge of the bed—as she was still in the middle.

"It's mine," Sofia and Marlowe answered at the same time.

Plum was now awake enough to recognize that the chime was coming from her phone as well. "Mine too." She got up and went to the small writing desk where Sofia had left their phones. She unplugged her phone, flipped it over, and tossed Marlowe's and Sofia's phones to them on the bed.

With a sinking feeling, Plum saw her screen.

"Pyre Signs," Marlowe said.

On all their screens, bright red flames blazed around a body-shaped bier. *Like uninstalling the app will be enough to disable the malware.* Warix's mocking voice replayed in Plum's head.

"What's it doing?" Sofia asked, her forehead furrowed. "Why now?"

"I guess we'll find out." Marlowe sounded calm. Coolheaded. Not at all as if fear was jangling in every nerve. But still, she hitched closer to Sofia on the bed. She was scared, too. No matter how she sounded.

Plum crossed back to the bed and scooted in next to her friends.

They stared at their phones, waiting for whatever message the killer wanted to send.

The screen went black. Then, letter by letter, bloody red words started appearing across their screens.

No more fun and games.

Each one of you will die.

Peach Winter: For your conspicuous consumption. For your vacuous display of wealth. For giving everyone FOMO and making yourself seem "just like everyone else (except better)"—and for how you mocked me.

You will die today.

Cici Bello: For your upholding of impossible beauty standards. For your quiet, inherent body-shaming of anyone who isn't a Western ideal of attractive—and for mocking me.

You will die today.

Jude Romeo: For pandering to online celebrities. For desperately trying to be someone you're not. For your insipid insistence that anyone can be special—and for mocking me.

You will die today.

Jalen Jones: For your opportunistic, ghoulish, and exploitative behavior toward tragedy. For your trite minimization of others' suffering—and for mocking me.

You will die today. (But, hey, take comfort in the thought that maybe they'll make a podcast about you someday.)

Plum Winter, Marlowe Blake, and Sofia Torres: Because you're here, and therefore no better than the rest of them. Because you wanted to be important, while only narrowly defining what that means. Because you covet stupid things. Because I have no doubt you mocked me—and everything I stand for—in the past.

You will die today.

All of you. You will all die today.

You will die screaming.

Their phone screens went blank simultaneously.

"What do we do?" Sofia breathed.

At the same instant, a furious yell sounded from the room next door. Plum started at the familiar exasperated sound of her sister cursing.

In the hallway on the other side of the heavy door, there was frantic banging. "I never mocked you!" Jude's voice was muffled as he shouted from somewhere down the hall. "Whoever you are! I wouldn't do that!"

Jalen's shout chimed in from farther away. "YEAH!" he yelled. "And if I DID mock you, then I'm sorry! Maybe just write a think piece about it? About toxic internet culture? I bet that would feel good, huh?"

"They're losing it," Sofia said. "The killer isn't someone you can reason with, obviously."

"What do we do?" Plum asked.

"The doors are all locked," Marlowe said as the three friends jumped off the bed.

"Who did we mock?" Sofia asked. "Who's the killer? Everyone got accused—all of us—so which one of us is the killer?"

"Help me with this," Marlowe asked. Together, Plum and Marlowe scraped as much as slid the heavy chest away from the door. Marlowe unlocked the bolt, but the door wouldn't open. The girls tugged, pulled, and pushed at the door as hard as they could. It wouldn't move.

Plum's heart sank. No matter how much they'd wanted to keep the killer out, it seemed they were now stuck in their rooms.

Outside their door, down the hall, someone else joined in the banging as the remaining guests of Pyre Festival must have been realizing the same thing they were: they were all locked in.

Distantly, Plum heard Jude shouting some more.

There was a tremendous bang from their bathroom. Henrietta squawked in terror.

"Plum!" Peach's voice sounded surprisingly near.

Plum darted to the bathroom. She pounded her fist on the wall. "Peach, I'm here!" she called.

"Take a step back, okay? I'm coming to get you." Peach sounded *furious*. And determined.

A flower of memory bloomed in Plum's mind, summoned by that exact tone of her sister's voice. Plum had been five or six years old, at the neighborhood pool. And her amazing, fierce teenage sister was yelling at the bully who had held Plum underwater. Her protector. At one time in her life, it had been true.

"Okay!" Plum called back to her sister, not doubting for one second that Peach would get to her.

Although . . . how?

Sofia picked up Henrietta, holding the hen in a tight grip as they stepped back into the bathroom doorway.

There was a series of light taps from the opposite side of the wall. Then a loud bang. Then a flurry of bangs. The smooth expanse of wall suddenly cracked; then at eye level, and with a shower of dust, a hole appeared.

Plum glimpsed something elongated and square in the hole before it disappeared. It appeared again, knocking more pieces of the wall loose with every forceful strike.

Marlowe's voice was at Plum's shoulder. "Is that a shoe?"

Plum nodded.

The shoe broke a huge chunk of the wall off. Plum caught a glimpse of her sister's hand, grasping the bulky platform sandal by the heel strap.

Then her sister's face appeared in the hole.

"Almost there," Peach said. "Once you find the studs, the drywall comes down easy."

Now that Peach pointed it out, Plum could see the twin pieces of wood on either side of the hole her sister had created.

Peach turned around and started donkey-kicking the wall with her foot, and soon the two holes joined, creating a narrow gap. Peach and Cici squeezed through.

Plum had enough time to notice that Peach was wearing only one platform sandal, because of course the other was in her hand, as her sister lurched across the bathroom and seized her in a hug.

"Okay," Peach said, still squeezing Plum tight. "We're going to get out of this. We're going to figure it out."

"That was impressive," Marlowe told Peach as Plum hugged her sister back.

Peach finally let go and moved to the bed. She flopped down and put the sandal she'd used as a hammer back on. Cici looked a little stunned as she leaned against the wall.

"Well, sometimes a little practical knowledge goes a long way," Peach said.

Plum made a mental note to ask her sister how she knew how to demolish a wall, and that it had been drywall in the first place, whatever that was.

Peach stood back up, crossed to Plum, and grabbed her upper arms. "We have to get you out of here," she said. Her glance took in Sofia and Marlowe. "All of you. You shouldn't even be here."

Plum sighed. "Believe me, I regret coming, okay? But don't scold me, because how could we know it was going to be like *this*?"

Peach shook her head. "I mean you shouldn't be a target! I'm not mad at you for wanting an adventure. There's nothing wrong with that. But you're just kids! More than that." She squeezed Plum again. "You're my kid sister."

"No one deserves any of this," Sofia said firmly. "No matter what that stupid app says."

Henrietta clucked.

Cici nodded so vigorously her ponytail bounced.

"I thought if we split up," Peach began, "if I stayed away from you. If you went with your friends, and I went with another influencer instead of you, I thought you'd be safe."

Plum felt her breath freeze in her lungs.

Peach *had* wanted to protect her. Going with Cici hadn't been about shunning Plum. Or about not liking her, not finding her interesting, or liking a fellow influencer better. Peach had known that as one of the most successful influencers in the country, much less at the "festival," she was a huge target. Peach hoped there was a chance the killer would pass by Plum and her friends. If she just stayed away.

And at the moment the app had said they would all die, Peach had busted down an actual wall trying to get to her baby sister.

Plum's heart expanded in her chest. "I love you, too," she said.

Peach looked confused for an instant.

Plum gestured to the hole in the bathroom wall.

Peach smiled. "Doofus," she said.

"I know you are, but what am I?" Plum replied.

There was a smattering of banging coming from the hallway beyond their door.

"What do we do?" Sofia asked. "Everyone's locked in. The killer locked us all in!"

The banging continued unabated in the hallway.

"We just busted down a wall, and we're still trapped," Cici groaned.

2

"If we were sitting ducks before, what does that make us *now*?" Marlowe asked, a pressured but still cutting edge to her words.

"Cooked geese," Plum replied.

"No!" Sofia kicked the door, then hopped back, cradling her toe. "Ow!" She glared at the door. "I refuse to be outsmarted!" She glanced around wildly. "We have to find weapons."

She gently set Henrietta on the floor. The hen started a slow examination of the room.

"We have to escape," Marlowe said.

They turned to look where she was looking.

The painted-shut French doors.

The Juliet balcony.

"Good idea," Peach said. "We should split up, though. There won't be much time. You three find a way out to the balcony, and Cici and I will see if there's any more shoddy renovations in this room."

"What?" Cici seemed as confused as Plum felt.

"We were only able to break through the bathroom because it had been poorly subdivided," Peach explained. "It's shoddy . . . obvious work."

Marlowe was already tugging on the balcony doors. "We'll have to break the glass."

"That will draw attention," Plum said. "We need to make our plan before we do it."

Peach gave Plum another quick hug. "Cici and I will look to see if there's more drywall. Maybe the back of the closet wall is another renovation. If so, we can get to Jude, or Jalen, or whoever is next door."

"Jalen," Sofia said. "He's next door."

"We can team up. Be ready for the killer when they come," Cici said. She planted her hands on her hips, looking fierce. With her ponytail up high like that and her makeup perfect, she could almost be a comic book superhero, Plum thought.

"Or," Cici continued, "we could at least keep on the move and mess them up that way."

"And we might find another way out," Peach said.

"When we break out from the balcony, I'll find something to get the doors open," Plum said. "A fire ax, or crowbar, or a chair, even."

"We'll make a lot of noise," Peach said, building on Plum's ideas. "To cover for you."

Peach hugged Plum once again, quick and tight. Then she

peeled off her shoe and lurched over to the opposite wall. She started knocking methodically with a knuckle.

Plum turned to her friends. "After we break the glass, you have to lower me down quickly," she said urgently. "You have to do it while everyone's making noise and the killer is reveling in how clever they are."

"If that's what they're doing," Marlowe interjected.

"Well, it's either that or getting ready to come pick us off one by one," Sofia said, not at all comfortingly.

"Either way, I have to go. Now's our chance," Plum said.

"How is this supposed to be a good idea? I thought you said we should stick together," Marlowe argued.

"We can't all go through the window. The drop is too far. But if you lower me, I can go get the ax and break down the doors."

"I agree, we need to do something," Marlowe said, "I just don't think that it's you that should go."

"Don't start, Marlowe. We don't have time!" Plum snapped.

"I'm the lightest. I should be the one lowered," Sofia said.

"But I'm the tallest," Plum argued. "I'm taller than you, Sofia, by a lot, and I'm lighter than you, Marlowe, don't look mad, you're perfect just the way you are, I just mean—"

"You think I'm perfect?"

Plum stammered at the shining look in her friend's eyes. "Yeah . . . yeah . . . of course."

"We don't have time for this now," Sofia snapped.

"I'll have the shortest drop," Plum reasoned, coming back to the moment. Putting the vision of Marlowe looking at her like *that* out of her mind. There would be time to unpack whatever that was later. When she got them all through this. "If I climb over the railing, then crouch and grab your hands pushed through the bars, you can lower me. It won't be that far a drop at all." Plum tried to feel as confident as she sounded.

Sofia was shaking her head. "I still think you should lower me."

"No," Marlowe said reluctantly. "Plum's right. Extra inches could make all the difference here, and we don't need you breaking your ankle. Or worse."

"I don't like it," Sofia repeated. "What if the killer's out there waiting for you?"

Plum shrugged. "I'll run. I'll figure out something. At the very least I'll get the killer away from you guys, from the villa. You can try following me, Sofia. As a backup plan."

"I should be lowered first," Sofia insisted.

"How are you going to run on a broken ankle?" Marlowe asked.

Sofia hit Marlowe's shoulder. "I don't *have* a broken ankle!"

"We're wasting time." Plum crossed the room and looked out the windows. "Help me, and I'll get us all out of this."

"I don't like it," Sofia said again.

Marlowe picked up a moldering old book from a shelf. "On three?" She hefted the book, aiming at the largest glass pane.

Plum nodded.

The shattering of glass joined the incessant knocking and banging from the other captives.

Plum knocked the remaining glass out with another book. She kicked out the wooden cross pieces of the French door.

Without looking back, she stepped out and climbed over the narrow railing.

3

It was a bad idea to start with.

Plum could see that now that it was too late.

Above her, Marlowe grunted with effort.

The ground was still so far away.

Plum closed her eyes. "On three," she whispered up to her friends, who were lying flat and holding her arms. "One," Plum started. "Two . . ."

Plum's hands slid out of their grip. She felt herself drop.

She told herself it wasn't as far as it had looked. Her eyes were six feet higher from the ground than her feet, for starters.

She landed hard, but her knees were bent, so she absorbed it, rolling sideways and forward.

"Yesss!" Above her, Sofia was whisper-cheering and clapping quietly.

Plum stood in a crouch, glancing around her.

No one was around.

No movement.

Plum glanced up and sent a broad smile of triumph and a thumbs-up to her friends.

GO! Marlowe mouthed, hugging herself in her nervousness.

Plum nodded and moved next to the wall of the house. She glanced into the ballroom, shielding her face against the brightness outside in order to see in. There was no movement.

Plum darted across the window and waited at the next window. She peeked inside again.

Nothing.

She rushed down the exterior wall of the villa this way, pausing, peering, running, until she was at the corner.

She peered around the corner along the shorter edge of wall that made up the end of this wing.

No one.

It was going exactly according to plan.

Plum took a deep breath and rounded the corner. She darted into the open space. There wasn't even a scrubby bush or a piece of patio furniture to hide behind—it was just a long path winding around to the more interesting sides of the house.

Plum rushed toward the opposite side, hoping to make it to the main door into the atrium, hopefully still standing open to the morning ocean breeze.

A man stepped around the edge of the house.

Plum rocked back on her heels, skidding so abruptly she pinwheeled her legs.

Dude stood in front of her, carrying two jugs of gasoline. He gave her a bright, murderous smile.

Plum's brain felt slowed—no, it felt like the world was suddenly moving in slow motion as her disbelief caught up with her adrenaline.

Dude was alive?

The feeling of confusion was chased by sudden certainty.

Dude was *the killer.*

"Oh, hello there," he chirped. "You got out of your room!" He put the gas cans down. "I was getting ready to finish up. You know. *Pyre Festival! Melt your face off*!" He laughed at his bad joke.

One hand went to his back. He drew out a wicked-looking hunting knife.

"I guess I'll have to take care of you here," he said regretfully.

4

The knife was mesmerizing.

Dude smiled at her. "Pretty, isn't it?" He feinted a lunge forward.

Plum jerked away so hard she stumbled and fell back on her butt.

Dude just laughed.

"How . . ." Plum panted, climbing quickly to her feet. She had to keep him talking—she had to find out what had happened. "You went in the cottage . . ."

Dude tapped the tip of the knife against his chin, as if he was amused. "This old house has a secret passageway. A tunnel that leads from the butler's pantry to the cottage."

Plum remembered Marlowe knocking on the panels in their bedroom last night. Right instinct, wrong place.

Plum didn't have to ask for more details, she could already picture it. An underground passage that opened *inside* the cottage. Maybe Warix had already been dead when Dude had come outside, warning them of the explosives.

Dude was nodding, as if he could see the trail of her thoughts. "I heard you talking," he said. "I had just knocked out that idiot Warix, and I was coming for that other idiot, Jude. *You* told him it was me." He pointed the knife tip at Plum. "Well done, by the way. Really A-plus thinking. I had to move fast, so I ran out, said I'd found explosives, and ran back inside to 'save' Warix."

Goose bumps rose on Plum's skin at the calmness with which he said it.

"I went into the secret passage and blew the place up."

As if summoned by his words, Plum could almost feel a hot rush of air, the glare of the explosion. The remains of the cottage and the remains of the two people who had been inside.

"*Brittlyn* was the other body in the cottage," Plum said. "The blood . . . the . . . pieces . . ." She gulped back a knot of nausea. "No wonder we couldn't find her in the villa. You moved her body to the passageway, then to the cottage."

It would have been easy: Dude waiting for the right moment of confusion, perhaps even while the rest of them discovered Sean was impaled. It would have been the work of a moment for Dude to drag Brittlyn the short distance from the dining room to the butler's pantry and the secret passageway inside.

Dude nodded excitedly, as if glad to have someone to share his homicidal brilliance with. "Then later, I moved her down to the cottage for the fireworks, so to speak. *I* was the one

Jude bumped into in the kitchen. I stabbed Jalen in the fridge. Wrong knife, but ah, well. I don't need to paint you a picture."

He swirled the knife in the air as if it were a paintbrush.

Plum had only one question left. If she was going to die, she wanted to know.

5

"Why?" Plum asked. She edged backward. Of course, he was following her, but if she could get around the corner of the house, maybe . . . just maybe.

"It's a long story, princess," Dude said.

"Give me the *SparkNotes*, then," Plum replied.

Dude stopped advancing. "Let's see if this rings any bells." His posture changed suddenly. He drew himself up to full height and extended an imperious hand. "Do not TEST ME, seeker!" His voice was accented, vaguely British, but his voice was also high. "None may approach!" His voice cracked.

He sounded eerily exactly like the preteen boy in that video . . .

"TASTE my WROTH!" Dude mimicked. Then he made a *cssssh!* sound and mimed drawing a sword, then another. *"Wheeeeew, wheeew!"* He made whistling noises as he whirled the imaginary swords.

He stopped suddenly, then raised an eyebrow at Plum. "Any of that familiar?"

Plum's retreat had led her almost to the edge of the house.

"It's . . ." Plum glanced behind her, checking the distance to the corner. "Wizard kid?"

The video still cropped up even now. It had gone viral when she was just in elementary school, before she even had her own phone. This young teen playacting in a forest, pretending to be a wizard knight from his favorite series of movies. It was everywhere on the internet.

It was hilarious, but it was also the kind of funny that always made Plum feel slightly poisoned. Shameful, somehow.

Because even though he'd clearly filmed himself, there was no way the sweat-stained, acne-faced teen had ever intended his video to go online. Much less to go viral.

"Wizard kid," Plum said again.

Dude nodded and waited, with his eyebrows still elevated, like a teacher waiting for the rest of the answer.

"*You're* wizard kid?" Plum couldn't believe it. She felt as if she'd fallen down some rabbit hole into an alternate dimension.

"Bingo!" Dude crowed, actually seeming happy.

He looked nothing like himself. Or rather, he looked nothing like that awkward teen.

Plum guessed aging might do that to someone. He was so tall, for one thing, and filled out, as an adult man. But also he'd changed everything about himself: no longer a fanboy but a mocking cool guy with spiky bleached hair and a perpetual ironic smile. Expensive sunglasses, hip clothes.

And a wicked hunting knife.

6

"I don't understand," Plum said.

The corner was almost beside her, the open space at the front of the villa stretching away in her peripheral vison.

"Well, your sister would," Dude said, his tone suddenly as sharp as the blade in his hand.

"What?" Plum stumbled on a rock, caught herself with her hand on the wall. "What did Peach ever do to you?"

She turned the corner, leading Dude under the windows as she retreated.

"What did *all* of them *do*?" His eyes flashed with anger. "They kept it ALIVE. They kept USING IT, PROFITING OFF ANOTHER'S MISFORTUNE, after it would have died a natural death. But no, first the podcaster . . ."

Jalen.

"He skewered it on his damn show, then it took off again, then the ENDLESS repetitions." Dude waved his hands in a swooping circle, swinging the knife with complete disregard for its sharp edge.

He was furious.

Plum felt a shiver march over her skin. "You still shouldn't *kill people*!" she shouted, hoping the noise would draw the other survivors to their windows.

"They all MOCKED ME and built whatever PATHETIC PLATFORMS THEY HAVE on the BACK of MY PAIN!" He was bellowing like an enraged bull now, taut tendons standing out on his neck.

There was a crash and a scattering of glass as something large and white plummeted to the ground in front of them. Plum ducked and darted to one side. Dude followed.

Jude came out on the Juliet balcony of his room, directly above them.

The white porcelain lid to a toilet's water tank lay in two pieces on the ground where it had landed.

"You're alive!" Jude called, pointing at Dude and for an instant seeming transcendently happy. Then a clouded expression passed over his face.

"Wait—you're the killer, Dude." Jude shook his head.

Dude glared up at the teen. "You're a hypocrite. You tell all your followers about being positive, being kind, but when those straw-headed idiots had you on their livestream and started mocking me, what did you do? How kind were *you*?"

Jude looked abashed.

"Okay, so he'll say he's sorry. You don't KILL PEOPLE over that!" Plum yelled.

"Yeah, I'm sorry, Dude." On the balcony, Jude ruffled his hair. It was, unfortunately, a practiced move. As if Jude had rehearsed a sidelong puppy dog look in the mirror many times before.

"It's too late!" Dude yelled. Spittle flecked his upper lip. "I've already become the bully, the villain of the piece. I'm what you wannabe LOSERS made me!"

There was no talking to him, no reasoning.

Plum shook her head. "No . . . this is all you."

"No one even knows my real name," Dude said. "No one cares about Sammy Ponder. Once you're all dead, no one will ever know who did it. I'll escape into my nonentity, and all this"—he waved his knife around in a circle—"will be a huge mystery. I'm untraceable. Invisible."

He smiled wickedly.

"And then I'll do it again. Maybe I'll throw an awards show, see which influencers I can lure. Wire the room to blow. I'll just keep going."

"You can't get them all," Plum said. "Everyone who ever saw the video. Everyone who mocked it or laughed at it or shared it."

He gave that excited smile again. "Maybe not. But then again, look at how well *Pyre Festival* turned out! Everyone on this island maligned me personally—and now they're dead . . . or about to be."

Plum raised her voice, shouting back. “People make mistakes! You have to move on!”

“Easy to say when your whole life hasn’t been defined by a personal embarrassment and endless mockery!”

“You’re choosing to define your whole life by that moment! You!” Plum yelled. “No one else!”

“No.” Dude’s eyes tightened, the terrifying smile returned. “I’m choosing to define myself by something else now.”

He lunged, moving forward with such abruptness that Plum was almost taken by surprise.

“Run, Plum!” Jude yelled encouragement.

Plum spun and sprinted away, across the path.

The killer chased her.

7

Plum sprinted under the windows of Mabuz Villa.

Though she couldn't spare the breath, she knew she had to scream a warning, just in case the locked-in inhabitants above hadn't already heard them.

Just in case Jude didn't quite get it.

"It's DUDE! He's going to burn the house down!" Plum shrieked. Actually physically feeling the cry shorten her steps, even as adrenaline pumped her legs harder.

Did they hear? Did they see? Plum couldn't spare the moment to look.

"Stop chasing her!" a familiar voice shrieked.

Plum darted a glance up.

Peach must have made good on her promise to break into the next room, because she stood at the farthest window, with Jalen beside her.

A platform sandal whizzed over Plum's head.

Dude made a nearly cartoonish "oof" as the sandal knocked

into his chest. "Wait your turn!" he shouted to Peach.

"Help me down!" Peach urged Jalen as she climbed over the balcony.

Plum had gained only a few yards on Dude. But maybe that was all she needed to keep him from going back in and burning the house down . . . before her friends could get out.

There was a flurry of movement at one of the other windows, but Plum couldn't spare a moment to glance up. She hoped it was Marlowe and Sofia.

There was a scattering of loose pebbles under her feet as the stone walkway turned into a dirt path. Plum skidded, losing precious seconds as she regained her balance.

"Run, little girl. Run!" Dude's voice was behind her, mocking encouragement. His voice was getting closer. "Where are you going to go?"

Something grazed at Plum's shoulder. A finger, his hand—perhaps he was that close.

Then the pain came, and Plum stumbled sideways, surprised as she lost focus on the path.

It was a lucky stumble. It might have saved her life.

The knife whistled through the air where she'd been. Plum hit the ground hard and rolled sideways, taking out Dude's legs at the ankle. She barely felt the impact as he fell next to her. Her shoulder, that was another matter, stinging and wet with what she had to assume was blood.

She didn't have time to wonder how badly he'd cut her. She

popped up onto her feet and took off. Her shoulder shrieked with the pain, spots bloomed in her eyes.

Okay, so it was quite a deep cut, then. Plum tucked her left arm up tight and kept running.

Behind her, Dude shouted a laugh as he jumped up and began pursuit again.

Two goats looked up from the shrub they were methodically destroying as Plum ran past.

Dude was right. There was nowhere to go.

Worse, when she'd fallen, and when she'd gotten up, she'd allowed him to claim the ground between her and this side of the villa.

Which left nowhere to hide.

Just the last expanse of dirt pathway, then the sandy gravel and scrub grass beyond, leading all the way to the cliff.

Plum glanced behind her.

Dude was resting.

He'd seen it, too: nowhere to run. No weapon she could pick up.

Plum's heart thundered like a rabbit's, her instinct urging her to run, run, keep running.

Dude was advancing slowly, resting as he approached.

Plum feinted to the left, then darted to the right.

Dude wasn't as fast as she was, but he didn't have to be. He still reached her path in time to cut her off.

Literally.

He kept advancing, slashing the air as if he liked it so much he couldn't stop himself.

Plum screamed a scream of pure frustration and terror.

Dude laughed and screamed back, advancing on her.

Plum Winter never expected it to end this way. "It" being both her life and Pyre Festival.

The festival was supposed to end with a celebrity-packed booze cruise.

As for her life's end, Plum didn't like to think about it, but when she did, she always imagined being a really old lady who died peacefully in her sleep.

But here she was, at the end of it all, and there were absolutely no boats, booze, or beds.

Instead, Plum had to decide which of two extremely unattractive deaths she would rather have.

Maybe she could save some people. Her people: Marlowe, Sofia, and Peach.

In front of her, Dude slashed the vicious knife in terrifying arcs. He was edging closer and closer.

This was where all her schemes had led her.

With no one to witness her last—some would say only—act of courage.

No one other than the killer . . . and the goats.

As if on cue, the black-and-white billy goat munching on the bush to Plum's right let out an annoyed-sounding bleat.

It sounded like a heckler in a comedy club, like the goat was yelling "Meh!"

No doubt the billy goat was annoyed at the humans trampling his favorite grazing patch.

"Yeah, buddy," Plum breathed, taking a tiny step back, feeling the wind from the cliff edge grabbing at her hair, snatching it up. "You and me both," Plum muttered.

There was nowhere else to go. She had to do something.

Maybe she could take the killer with her.

Plum took a deep breath and screamed.

Dude smiled, rushing at her with the knife outstretched.

So. This was how it was all going to end.

Plum Winter desperately hoped there would be a heaven for clueless kids who just wanted to have a good time.

8

Dude flipped the knife around showily.

"Like that's so original!" Plum snipped, angry at him for enjoying it, angry at herself for being trapped.

Dude shrugged.

Plum was furious. She was going to go out with a fight, no matter what he thought was going to happen. The words jumped into her mouth before she thought.

"Woooo!" she screamed at the top of her lungs. "*Killing it, dude!*" she mocked him. "Look at you! Coming at an innocent girl! WOOO, really STICKING IT TO THE INFLUENCERS!"

A cloud passed over Dude's face. Then he shook his head. "Don't act like you're any better," he said dismissively. "It's over for you, no matter who you are."

Plum screamed again, aiming her cry at the house behind them.

Dude laughed. "None of them are going to hear you, kid." He pouted in a fake expression of sorrow.

No one from the house, maybe.

But behind Dude, the black-and-white billy goat was watching them with a gimlet, creepy eye.

Plum screamed again, as high and shrill as she could make it. She hoped it sounded defiant and not bloodcurdling.

"You're not too bright, are you?" Dude mocked. "No. One. Can. Hear. You."

He slashed the knife over the air. Then he tensed his head, rolling his neck and shoulders like a fighter warming up.

He rolled his shoulders once more, then gave a few more swipes at the air with the knife.

Plum edged another step back.

The wind at her back snatched at her hair, almost like the wind itself was warning her: *NOT ONE MORE STEP.*

"Easy!" Dude called out, his face a sudden mask of concern. "Wouldn't want you to fall!" He grabbed a hand at her, as if he would truly yank her back from the brink of death. "Wouldn't be as fun that way," he said. A cruel smile twisted his mouth.

Plum took a tremendous breath. She tensed herself on the balls of her feet. If she had to, she'd put her shoulder into him. She'd duck the whistling arc of the knife. She'd fight.

Plum let out the highest, loudest, most defiant shriek of all. It felt like a war cry. Like she was a Viking shield-maid or a warrior princess with an ax. Not a high school senior with a cut shoulder and no weapon.

Well, she had one weapon.

Plum finished screaming when her breath ran out. She panted.

Dude cocked an eyebrow at her. "Done?" he asked.

Plum's head felt light. She took a deep breath. Behind Dude, she couldn't see the billy goat anymore.

She opened her mouth to scream again. Dude ran at her, knife outstretched.

Plum's scream merged with another.

Time slowed down, and in that moment between one breath and the next, and as the knife arced toward her, Plum had all the time in the world to notice several things at once.

Dude looked surprised.

He lunged at her, finally, flying at her in a tackle.

But the large goat was running in the same direction as Dude. And in a moment the goat was right under him, its impressive curled horns boosting Dude's legs into the air.

Plum dropped and rolled to the side, away from both the edge of the cliff and Dude.

Propelled by the goat, Dude flailed in the air, and then landed on one shoulder at the cliff's edge, the knife skittering out of his hands and over the sheer drop.

But Dude's momentum didn't stop. He kept falling, pulled by the weight of his own legs dangling into the open air. His scrabbling hands couldn't stop his fall off the cliff.

His scream as he fell was hideous. Mercifully, it didn't last long.

Plum lay on her stomach.

Shock swirled in her head, the jangled nerves of her body twitching, urging her to run, to move, to fight, unable to process that the killer with the knife was gone, had met his own end, that she'd done it.

She'd saved herself.

She'd saved everyone else.

The billy goat turned its furious yellow eyes to her. Two white-stockinged forelegs stomped the ground.

"MEH!" the goat screamed at her.

Okay. So she probably hadn't saved herself. At least she'd saved everyone else.

How hard would it hurt if the goat headbutted her now? A lot. Plum bet it would hurt a lot.

She squeezed her eyes closed and nested her arms over her head. It would be worth it. A headbutted-to-death death. It was all worth it if she'd saved her friends.

Kissing noises carried over the moaning wind at the cliff's edge.

A high, sweet, and somewhat annoyingly singsong yet altogether precious and familiar voice called out gently. "Here, goaty. Here, goaty-woat. Who's a lovely little goaty?"

Plum sobbed in relief as the billy goat turned like a child hearing an enchanted piper dressed in harlequin colors.

Plum's eyes followed the goat's movement. Sofia was limping forward, supported by a clearly terrified yet determined

Marlowe. A drooping bundle of scrawny clover tempted the billy goat.

Sofia let go of Marlowe, hobbled one more step on her own. Then Sofia sat on the ground, wincing at her foot. But she held out the offering to the goat.

The goat's ears lifted.

He trotted forward and nuzzled at the greens like they were the finest of delicacies.

Her friends had saved her right back.

9

After the goat was mollified, Plum and her friends embraced each other tightly.

"I'm so glad you're okay," Sofia said, swiping her fingertips under her eyes.

"Me too," Plum agreed.

Marlowe couldn't speak. Every time she tried to, she started bawling.

It was a lot, Plum thought. Of course, they'd all been through an ordeal. But it was a bit strange how Marlowe was looking at her, with shining eyes, eyes that looked like whole speeches, like she was trying to communicate something, like she couldn't look enough.

It was confusing.

"How'd you get out, anyway?" Plum asked as they made slow progress back to the villa.

"Marlowe lowered me." Sofia winced, hopping every third step and hobbling after the others.

"Oh no," Plum breathed. "Your poor ankle."

"You both jinxed me," Sofia sniffed. "I never would have gotten hurt if Marlowe hadn't gone on about it. I overthought my landing."

Plum shook her head in sympathy. "I was worried you'd break it," Marlowe said.

Sofia sniffed. "Shows how much you know," she said with a self-satisfied smirk. "It's just a bad sprain."

"That's good, at least," Plum said.

"Anyway, I went back inside, let Marlowe out, we unlocked Jude's room, told him to get the others, and then we ran out to save you," Sofia said.

"I was so scared that you—that he . . ." Marlowe began, then tears welled up in her eyes again.

"Oh, don't start," Plum scolded.

"I can't help it," Marlowe cried. "He was coming at you and you just—you were so brave and I thought I'd never see you again and—" Marlowe couldn't finish the thought.

Plum stopped on the path. "Hey, hey, it's okay, Lowe." She put a knuckle under Marlowe's chin, trying to do a hokey buck-up-little-camper gesture.

Then Marlowe's remarkable blue-green eyes met hers.

And she was so lovely.

And her eyelashes were wet.

And her breath, Plum could almost swear she could feel it on her wrist.

Marlowe suddenly leaned forward, pressing her mouth against Plum's. Her lips were soft and plush and tasted like the berry-scented lip gloss she used.

Plum had time to notice all this.

She had time to notice that Marlowe's eyes closed, her eyelids so pink, like the inside of a seashell.

She had time to feel the press of Marlowe's body. The twining of her friend's arms around the small of her back.

She had time to feel happiness burst in her veins like fireworks, the kind that rain down a shower of sparks, bright and clean and so beautiful.

Marlowe leaned back.

It had only been the barest of moments.

The briefest of kisses.

Marlowe opened her eyes.

The look in her eyes. Plum had seen a faint glimmer of it when Marlowe would look at Lars. That was love.

Plum knew it.

"I . . ." Plum began. "I don't understand."

Marlowe smiled, that gorgeous swerve of her lips. "Don't you get it, Plummy?" She rolled her eyes in embarrassment and performed silliness. "I fancy you."

She'd said it in an accent, rounded and ridiculous. Vaguely joking. But her eyes were serious.

"It's okay." Marlowe waved a dismissive hand. "You don't have to—"

Plum pushed both her hands into Marlowe's hair, holding her head steady as she brought her mouth in close to Marlowe's again.

"I get it," Plum said, smiling so wide it ached her face.

"Oh, thank God," Sofia chirped. "It's about time."

Marlowe smiled back at her, their breath mingled. Plum felt her heart shoot off disco-ball flecks of light.

Sofia hobbled a few steps away. "Don't mind me. I'll just be over here with my ankle." Her tone was amused more than scolding.

Plum brought her lips to Marlowe's again.

This time it wasn't a short kiss at all.

10

They'd slowly made their way back to Mabuz Villa.

Plum's heart had been warmed to hear the cheers as she and Marlowe helped Sofia up the path.

And she was shocked to see her sister's tear-streaked face first.

Peach rushed up to Plum and caught her in a tight hug, unintentionally hurting her shoulder

"Oh my God, Plum!" Peach wailed. "I thought he was going to get you! When I looked out the window and saw you running and him chasing you with a knife! I just—" Peach started sobbing, clutching at Plum, pulling her closer, then pushing back to check with her own eyes that Plum was okay, then clutching her closer again.

Plum felt a confused rush of gratitude and love at the display. "I'm good," Plum said. "Except my shoulder . . ."

"I'm sorry!" Peach wailed again, squeezing Plum tight again. "About your back! And not being in touch more. I should call more . . ."

"Yeah, but I mean, you're busy," Plum stammered. She glanced around her sister and met Cici's eyes.

Cici mouthed, *You're welcome,* and flipped her ponytail over her shoulder in a self-satisfied way.

"It's okay," Plum said. "We should talk and stuff."

"Yes!" Peach agreed. She squeezed Plum into another tight hug.

Plum let out a gasp of pain.

"Oh my God, you're hurt!" Peach cried. She abruptly let go of Plum and rushed around her. "Your poor back!"

"It's okay," Plum said. She couldn't explain it, because even though her shoulder did hurt, she felt fine. Better than fine.

She squeezed Marlowe's hand. "I feel great," she said.

"That's the endorphins talking. Sit down. I have a linen jacket in my suitcase—we'll make you a bandage." Peach tugged her sister toward the ballroom doors.

"You did it!" Jude rushed up and squeezed Plum's arm tightly, a delighted smile stretched across his face. "I'm so glad you're not dead!"

"Me too!" Plum agreed, laughing.

"I'm so glad it wasn't *you*," Sofia said, hugging Jude.

"I never suspected you, for the record," Jalen told Jude. "You don't have the face of a killer." Jalen looked pleased at his own words. He held up his phone. "He didn't have the face of a serial killer," he intoned. "But then, what does a serial killer look like?"

"Not me, at least!" Jude called, angling his mouth toward Jalen's phone.

Plum started laughing, and then Sofia did. It was like a trickle that started a waterfall. Soon they were all hugging, laughing, and talking.

Inside, Peach sat Plum down and ripped a bandage and strips to tie it with from her linen coat. Marlowe squeezed Plum's hand and tipped her chin toward the atrium. Marlowe and Sofia quietly stood, heading upstairs to get Henrietta. Cici, Jalen, and Jude nodded at Plum and slipped out the door.

Plum was alone with her sister.

For the first time in . . . forever.

Peach seemed to recognize it at the same moment. She swiped her fingertips underneath her eyelashes. "I'm glad you're okay," Peach said.

"Me too. Glad you're okay, I mean," Plum replied. "Thanks for throwing your shoe. And for busting down the wall like that."

"You're welcome." Peach gave a little sniff and swiped under her eyelashes again.

"Useful thing to know," Plum joked, feeling her own eyes well up inexplicably. "You can use a shoe to break through drywall."

"You never know what's going to come in handy," Peach agreed. She nodded sagely, then turned, staring into Plum's eyes intently. "Plum, I'm so sorry. That you feel . . . left out. That I made you feel bad. Like I didn't care."

"It's okay. I know you're busy," Plum interrupted.

"It's not okay!" Peach replied. "I did exclude you! But I didn't think you cared."

"What? No!"

"I mean . . . that didn't come out the way I wanted. I meant that I didn't realize you missed me." Peach gave Plum a decidedly watery smile. It was the kind of smile that seemed happy, and brave, and remorseful all at once.

"Of course I missed you!" Plum felt like she was looking at one of those weird pencil drawings where you think you're looking at birds, but then it turns into sets of grasping hands.

Had Peach never realized how much Plum cared about her? Or how much she simply missed her big sister?

"I missed you all the time," Plum said.

Peach laid her hand gently on Plum's arm. "I know that *now*."

Peach blew out a slight breath. "It's just . . . I'm ten years older than you. And look at you! You're practically grown, and you're so cool. You're your own person, you've got your own world, and friends. And—"

"I still need you." Plum put her hand over Peach's, resting on her arm. "I love you. And I missed you."

"I missed you, too." Peach's lower lip trembled and pushed out. "I never meant to make you feel abandoned!" she cried.

Plum had to swipe under her own eyes now. "It's okay," she said. "Just . . . promise not to do it again."

"I promise!" Peach traced her finger over her heart. "Cross

my heart and hope to . . . okay, to not actually die, but to live longer so I can do better."

Peach leaned forward, gingerly hugging Plum around the bandage.

"I'm so glad I came," Peach said, starting to wail again a bit. "Because it brought us closer as sisters. And now that we're closer, as sisters, we'll be better, closer." Peach's voice got wobbly, each word drawing out longer with her tears. "I'm so glad I came to the murder festival!" she sobbed.

Plum had to laugh. She couldn't help it.

11

When they'd finished talking, Peach and Plum made their way back outside to join the others basking in the midmorning sunlight, enjoying the freedom of *not* having a demented killer at their backs.

Henrietta contentedly pecked at the ground, moving slowly around their group.

Plum explained Dude's entire plan. About the tunnel, using Brittlyn's body to make it look like he'd died in the cottage. About how his finale was to burn them all in the villa inside their locked rooms.

Jude lay stretched on the lawn. Henrietta cocked an eye at the teen's hair within her reach.

"Well, thank God it's over." Jude sighed happily. He swatted lightly at the chicken.

"We still have to get off this island," Cici said.

"I'm not worried," Plum said. "Dude had a plan. He planned to get off here, and there's no other way off this island. I bet you anything tomorrow a boat will come. Or something."

"And if not, we can start eating the goats," Jalen offered.

"No way, that goat saved my life," Plum said.

"Well, maybe wherever he is now, Dude's happy," Jude suggested.

"What do you mean?" Cici asked.

Jude sat up. Little bits of grass stuck to his hair. "Just that he was doing all those poetic deaths, you know?" He turned bright eyes around the group.

"What's poetic about a billy goat butting him in the butt?" Peach asked, then tittered at the words.

They all started giggling.

Jude still managed to get his words out. "Just . . . you know . . . billy goats."

Plum started coughing on her own spit, she was laughing so hard.

Marlowe squeezed her hand. "I don't get it." Marlowe wasn't the only one smiling, ready to laugh at whatever was transporting Plum, Jude, Peach, and Cici.

"You know . . . 'cause he was a *troll*." Plum wheezed the last word. If it was wrong to laugh, safe in the sun, at the way an evil murderer had died, well.

Sue her.

Cici stopped laughing and put a hand up to shield her eyes. She was staring out at the ocean.

"Do you see—" Peach began, squinting in the same direction.

"A boat!" Marlowe shouted, jumping to her feet and pointing.

"Hot damn, we're saved!" Jude yelped.

Sofia scooped up Henrietta. Marlowe helped Plum up. They assisted each other down the cliff path as the small boat grew larger as it got closer. On the pebble beach, they stood near the remains of the burned dock.

It wasn't just a boat.

It was a yacht.

Party music was clearly audible as the boat arrived in the small bay. People crowded the decks, dancing, waving, and cheering. There was a blast of sound as the yacht honked at them.

"Is that . . . ?" Cici murmured.

". . . the booze cruise?" Sofia finished the thought.

"No way," Jude breathed. "With everything else fake, why would that be real? It doesn't make any sense."

"Um." Peach's voice was light.

They all turned to her. Peach was blushing, playing with the tips of her hair.

"Oh." Marlowe started to laugh.

Plum still didn't get it.

"It's her billionaire," Marlowe explained.

Cici snorted. "Fifty Shades guy? How'd he know to come here?"

Peach preened with barely suppressed delight. "Remember?

I posted on Instagram and TikTok about the fest from the helicopter! I guess it went through after all!"

On the boat, a well-dressed man waited by the railing as his crew maneuvered as close as possible. There was a flurry of activity, an anchor lowering, a smaller boat being prepared.

The man was younger than Plum expected, perhaps in his thirties, good-looking with a bright smile. "Peach, I found you!" he called out.

Peach did a curtsy dip. "I'm *so* glad!" she called back. "What are you going to do about it?"

The man dived off the boat without a moment's hesitation. The partiers on the yacht cheered as he swam and then splashed ashore.

"Oh my God, it's like a movie." Cici breathed appreciatively.

The man swiped water out of his face. He walked up the rocky beach to where they stood.

"Edward, this is my baby sister, Plum," Peach said.

"Nice to meet you." Edward smiled at her.

"Same. Um, so, do you have a radio on that boat?" Plum asked. "We've got to get the authorities out here."

"Hold up, Plum, give him a minute," Peach interrupted.

"Peach Winter, you're exhausting," Edward said, but he was smiling.

Peach threw her hat aside, took three long strides, and wrapped Edward in a passionate embrace.

After a moment of surprise, Edward returned it.

The partiers cheered as the yacht horn blasted.

"This is too much." Marlowe laughed. But she squeezed Plum's hand, stroking her thumb along the back of it.

A delicious shiver curled in Plum's belly. "Yeah, you guys," Plum teased her sister when she stopped kissing Edward. "Get a room."

And Plum was surprised, in that moment, to feel . . . complete. No sense of longing or of missing out. Just a profound gratitude to be alive, with her best friends, with Marlowe now her girlfriend—she still couldn't believe that part.

For once, Plum Winter didn't want to be anyone else, didn't want to be anywhere else. The gnawing feeling was gone, the anxiety that she wasn't enough, that life was passing her by, the yearning hunger to run away. To get away from herself by becoming someone else.

All that was an illusion, anyway. Fame, the internet, the careful presentation of a seemingly beautiful life. Her sister was just a person, like other people. The other influencers all had the same problems, the same emotions, the same longings.

Just like everyone. Just like anyone.

The first boatload of partiers arrived, splashing out of the dinghy and rushing ashore.

"Oh, Peach, you look divine! Is that blood on your dress?" a woman with a vaguely familiar face asked.

Plum realized she recognized her as another influencer who often partied with Peach.

"Yes, it's all the rage," Peach stated blandly.

"Oh, I can't wait to hear all about it. Where's the villa? Who are these people?" the woman asked.

Jude stepped forward, his hand out. "I'm Jude. Jude Turner."

"Turner?" Cici asked.

Jude shrugged. "It's my real last name."

"Nice to meet you," the woman said perfunctorily.

A wide smile crossed Cici's face. "I'm Cici Bello." She was talking to their small group, not the new arrivals. "That is my real name, and I do love makeup."

"It looks good on you," Plum said.

"Beauty culture can be toxic, though." Cici put her hands on her hips, a pose that reminded Plum of a superhero lecturing the kids they'd just saved from the runaway train. "I'll be more careful about that part."

"I'm Marlowe," Marlowe said, reintroducing herself to their group. "And this is my girlfriend, Plum. She finally knows how I feel."

Peach gave a cheer. Edward whistled.

"I'm Plum, and these are my closest friends for life, Marlowe and Sofia." Plum felt a goofy smile spread across her face. "They forgive me and understand me when I don't even understand myself."

Sofia swatted Plum's arm. "Oh my gosh, stop. I'm gonna cry." She was smiling though as she turned back to Jude, completing their circle.

"I'm Sofia, and I shouldn't even be here right now. I'm so grounded. But that's okay." She laughed and leaned into Plum's arm. "My older sister will be there for me, just like yours."

Plum glanced at Peach.

Peach gave a confident nod. They would face Plum's mom and their dad together.

That disco ball started spinning in Plum's heart again.

"Do you think Krystal will be mad there's no swag bags?" Marlowe asked Sofia with a smile.

"She'll be happy we made it out alive," Plum promised.

"Well, it's not like I'm coming home empty-handed." Sofia gently bounced the hen on her hip. She turned to their group, completing their new introductions. "This is Henrietta, my rescue chicken. I'm going to spoil the hell out of her from now on."

"I want to see that!" Cici said. "You better make her an Instagram."

"Henrietta looks more like a TikTok star to me," Jude suggested.

"What are they talking about?" the woman influencer asked Peach. "Do they have heatstroke?"

"You've arrived at a murder festival," Peach explained. "But it's over now."

The woman looked crestfallen. "No Diplo?"

Plum suppressed a laugh. "No, you missed him. You missed everything."

"Damn it!" the woman cursed.

Plum started laughing. Sofia and Marlowe joined in, the three of them leaning against one another helplessly.

"We really should call the police," Peach told Edward.

"Wait, that's real blood? What happened here?" Edward asked, his eyes wide in shock.

"Yeah," Peach said. "We kind of all had to escape a killer."

Jalen shook his head at the others, laughing and hugging. He held up his phone under his mouth. "The strain was too much to bear," he said in his profound podcast voice. "The other influencers at Pyre Festival have taken refuge in hysterics."

Plum snatched the phone out of Jalen's hand. "That word has a sexist history," she narrated into the mic. "I object. We're not influencers, either. For the record."

Jalen sighed. "Fine, fine, give it back."

Plum returned his phone.

"This has been *Bloody Grounds*. I'm your host, Jalen Jones. And this was Pyre Festival."

A raucous whoop sounded behind them.

A trio of young people, a girl and two guys, splashed ashore from the dinghy.

"Woooo!" one of the guys cheered. "Pyre Festival!"

The girl pumped her arm in the air. "Set the night on fire!" she cheered.

Plum slung an arm around her girlfriend, Marlowe, and her best friend, Sofia. "Have fun, kids," she told the trio. "We can't wait to get home."

Acknowledgments

Special thanks to my editor, Kelsey Murphy—I'm so fortunate to be working with you. I appreciate your wit and wisdom, especially during 2020. My thanks also to the team at Philomel, specifically Jill Santopolo for her watchful eye and Cheryl Eissing for her enthusiasm. Extended thanks are due to the publicity team at Penguin Young Readers: 2020 tried to test y'all, and it failed. Brava!

Adriana M. Martínez Figueroa, I deeply appreciate your insights and expertise. Any remaining errors are my own.

To my agent, Jodi Reamer, I continue to appreciate your prowess and guidance.

For my family, thank you for everything.

Special acknowledgement is due to Kara Bietz and Vicky Alvear Shecter. Kara, thank you for your amazing sense of humor and near daily check-ins. Vicky, thank you for your big, beautiful heart and for falling down story rabbit holes with me.

This book wouldn't exist if my dad hadn't fed my love of mysteries. Every week when I was in seventh grade, he would take me to the used book store or the library to get a new Agatha Christie novel. I know he would have loved to see how those excursions resulted in my own mystery book. Thank you, Dad.

Lastly, to my readers, my profound thanks.